The Baronet Who Thwarted Me

BEDLAM ACADEMY BOOK 1

AMY MCNULTY

Crimson Fox
PUBLISHING

For Mom:
Thank you for encouraging me to be a reader.
I miss you.

Chapter One

Our world didn't stand a chance if Dinah Sinclair got what she wanted.

But that shouldn't have mattered to me. I'd be dead by then.

"Georgiana, don't." Nora took hold of my elbow, practically yanking me back to her side. Most at this institution may have pegged me for a wallflower—timid, soft, invisible—but Honora Fletcher actually *was* those things in every way. But in circumstances like these, she could summon a strength I'd find hard to best.

"You'll be expelled," she added, a tense line narrowing her cloudy-gray eyes. A lock of fine, straw-colored hair fell out of her mob cap, draping over her face.

I surrendered.

She wasn't wrong.

And being expelled meant consequences—for me and for my family.

Whether that family deserved the courtesy of my concern for their welfare or not.

Dinah's laugh was shrill, almost comically unreal as she watched Thomas and William carry their latest victim to the top of the hill behind Bedlam Academy. Below them was an expanse of grass, ending in rocks that buffeted the ocean's shores. An ocean currently raging with waves that almost drowned out any hope of hearing what Dinah and her group were up to.

Almost.

"Please!" the student said. I'd only seen him around the hallways a few times, so I didn't remember his name. But he looked younger than Dinah and her minions and Nora and me. We were all seniors. Eighteen or nineteen years of age for the women, twenty or twenty-one for the men.

Certainly far too old for these types of games.

This young man—boy, even—barely fit in the suit that was one of Bedlam Academy's uniforms. His livery—the crisp, blue jacket, with long coattails and ten large, silver buttons, over white breeches and white stockings—marked him as a servant candidate.

As did Nora's cotton-blue dress with white apron and the white mob cap threaded through with a blue-ribbon trim.

Nora squeezed my hand, and I realized my feet had drifted off the path that was supposed to offer us a tranquil walk between classes, to the grasses in the direction of the tormentors.

Unity let out a little shriek, her tanned complexion growing wan as Dinah's pink, delicate, little nose scrunched, her ice-white brows scrunching. "Toss him!" she shouted.

Both as tall and broad as boulders and as intelligent as them too, William and Thomas exchanged a look before swinging the boy back.

"*Georgiana*," Nora hissed behind me. I'd been drawn to the spectacle again. I handed her my textbook without a backward glance and walked toward the gentry candidates, the elite of the elite at Bedlam Academy, and was about to tell them off.

That wouldn't go well for me.

But it might save that boy from tumbling down rough terrain into even rougher land below.

As I was halfway to them, a force rushed past me, straight for William and Thomas.

"Stop acting like idiots!" spoke the deep voice. Aylmer Linden removed his black top hat as his breaths grew shallow, his sprint across the yard in gentlemen's finery no doubt adding to the exertion he'd experienced. "No gentleman would be so foolish."

I froze, as did William and Thomas. Their grip on the boy grew slack, and he managed to squirm away, darting a few steps out to grab a book fallen in the grasses, then rushing past his tormentors, his face beet red as he passed me without even glancing my way.

"Aylmer," said Dinah smoothly, wiping her palms against her pale-yellow dress that didn't particularly flatter her fair complexion.

But Dinah Sinclair wouldn't have traded it for another color for all the world. The short-sleeved dress, cinched under her breasts and flowing in a curtain of long, loose skirt below, marked her as a lady candidate. The same dress flattered Unity's darker complexion far better beside her, her curly, brown hair tumbling out of a bun and in a cluster over one shoulder, almost in mirror to Dinah's lock of ice-white blonde hair dangling out of a bun and over the other shoulder beside her.

Whatever Dinah said to Aylmer, looping her arm through his and directing him back to the Academy behind me, it didn't seem to alleviate the wrinkled brow on Aylmer's face. His dark-brown eyes didn't light up, his thin lips didn't worm their way into a smile like I'd seen on virtually any other young man with Dinah Sinclair on his arm. He settled his hat back on the top of his head and let Dinah lead him back toward the building behind me. Unity, Thomas, and William shuffled their feet and lined up behind them, Thomas taking Unity's arm to escort her.

"—just a bit of fun and games." Dinah's voice caught on the wind as the group neared me. "Now you and I, it's clear we're going to be chosen. The very first—the most important—candidates. So I *wish* you would stop expecting the worst of me. You and I, we ought to be friends." Dinah's face darkened. "Your life may very well depend on it."

Her eyes flicked to mine, and I realized I hadn't moved since Aylmer had put an end to the spectacle.

"Everyone's lives do," Dinah added, staring straight at me as she spoke.

Aylmer and Dinah, arm in arm, stood in front of me now, and if I were a servant candidate, it would have been expected of me to look away, to not dare meet their eyes.

But I wasn't.

The dress I wore wasn't like Nora's or Dinah and Unity's. It had longer sleeves, and a thicker heft to it. The color was emerald green with false pearls beaded along the cuffs of my sleeves, the square hemline exposing my creamy décolletage. I wore a silver necklace, too, a bracelet that matched it, and a silver ring—all gifts from a family that had cast me out to save their own hides. Gifts I could not remove outside of my room here at the Academy. Gifts that marked me as a sacrifice.

Fancy jewelry that would one day adorn some Academy Board member's wrist, finger, neck, perhaps passed down to a daughter one day. A daughter just like Dinah.

Dinah wore no jewelry now, though if she made it through to the other world—as everyone in Bedlam Academy seemed certain was an inevitability—finer jewels than the ones I wore might be expected of her to display her social status. Here, the jewelry marked one for imminent demise.

"Well, what do we have here?" Dinah's gaze flicked up and down my body, landing on these silver adornments of death one after the other. I turned over my shoulder to search for Nora, to excuse myself back to my friend, but she was gone. The tormented boy, too.

Both clearly had too much sense to wait around and gain Dinah Sinclair's attention. Sense I usually shared—but that I was sorely lacking at the moment.

"Can we *help you*, pawn?" Dinah *tsked*. "They let you types keep your hair rather short, don't they? You could never style it into a bun like that."

My gaze flicked almost guiltily to Aylmer as my fingers ran over a lock of my wavy, chestnut-brown hair. It didn't quite reach my shoulders. It was thick, and I'd grown tired of growing it out and pinning it back in the mornings.

My hair didn't matter as much as everyone else's. I wasn't supposed to actually make the journey to the other world, even if I went through the motions and learned everything one needed to know to blend in successfully there.

"I suppose it doesn't matter, though," continued Dinah. "What *your* hair looks like after the Sacrament. Since you'll be..." She fluffed her free hand in the air, leaving the rest unsaid.

Dead.

"Dinah, just leave her alone. We have class to get to." Aylmer swallowed as his eyes flicked my way, then to the ground.

For most people, it was better not to know the sacrifice. It was why I could blend in so easily. Usually.

Nora was the exception. We'd grown up together, next-door neighbors in the quaint and modest townhouses assigned to our families in the Lower Zone.

Lower-Zone children marked for Bedlam had two possible fates: training to be a possible servant in the other world or offering themselves as the sacrifice for the Sacrament.

It took place every year. I wasn't the only pawn walking the halls of Bedlam Academy.

But it was my turn this year.

My turn to power the portal that would send select graduates of Bedlam Academy into the other world.

"Oh, Aylmer, you are such a stick in the mud." Dinah tittered, her laugh sure to turn heads in any ballroom in which she might find herself in the near future—and not in a way that would do her any favors as a marriage prospect.

If it weren't for Nora and any other innocent in this place who had a future that I didn't have a hope of seeing, I wouldn't have cared in the least.

Dinah and Aylmer brushed past me, Dinah's pack of followers hot on her tail. Only Unity spared me a glance as they passed, her eyes quickly darting away when I met her gaze—as if what I had was contagious.

I clasped my hands together and waited, looking out across the grass and to the ocean far beyond. Waited until I was sure they'd gone inside, that I was all alone.

The wind whipped across my cheeks, the shorter strands of my hair masking my eyes. The salty tang on the air invigorated my senses, filling my lungs with the promise of something more. Something beyond this place.

A promise that would never be fulfilled. Not for me.

My feet moved through the grass, my legs kicking aside the long, billowy skirt of my dress that would never blend in with the fashions worn in the other world, just like my shorter hair. I would never see it. I would have to take my professors' word that it even existed, a place with simpler technology, no knowledge of magic, and a Society with elaborate rules of honor and propriety almost more suffocating than our own.

Most people here never saw it, but they all at least had a *chance* to escape our world for that one.

I looked over the hill, at the rocks far below that may have bashed that poor boy's head in if William and Thomas had sent him tumbling down the hillside.

Would they have suffered any consequences? Would Dinah have batted her eyelashes and insisted to the headmaster it had all been an accident, like every other incident where a student had been bullied, bruised, and otherwise injured?

Would murder have been a step too far for Bedlam Academy's rising-star pupil?

Perhaps not. She wasn't wrong. Everyone's lives

depended on her success—if she was indeed chosen for the Sacrament.

Everyone's lives but my own.

My own that I could take right now.

Tumbling down this hill, as those brutes had intended for the gangly servant candidate.

My foot shifted forward an inch. Another inch.

My arms spread out to either side of me, the wind whipping up and rustling my skirt.

Just one more step, and I'd see how badly injured that boy might have been if not for Aylmer stopping them.

One more step, and my death might be my own.

"Georgiana!" Nora's voice called over the winds, louder even than the crash of waves below. "Georgiana, what are you doing?"

I blinked, took a step back.

There was a chance tumbling down that hill would do nothing but injure me. Surely, even Dinah hadn't *assumed* her victim would fall to his death.

I couldn't risk it. Grievous injury that would only add to my suffering, that wouldn't put an end to this.

"Georgiana!"

I ran backward, meeting Nora halfway. "We're late?" I asked, moving back toward the Academy building.

She frowned but turned around, stepping in beside me. "Almost. What were you doing back there? I saw Dinah and her gaggle head back inside, and you didn't show and I—" She swallowed.

"They didn't hurt me," I assured her. "I didn't even step in to get them to stop what they were doing. Aylmer did."

Nora's cheeks turned crimson, particularly noticeable beneath the spattering of freckles that crossed over the bridge of her nose. "I always did think he was better than the rest of them."

"I don't even think he belongs with 'the rest of them.'" The expansive Academy grew more imposing the closer we moved toward it. Dark-red bricks stacked meticulously perfectly together, one on top of the other, soared up, up above us for three stories that ended in pointed roofs covered in black shingles. And the bell tower, the highest point of all. The bell tower only opened its doors once a year, and only the graduates and professors were invited inside it. "Aylmer is cordial to everyone." *Except me, of course.*

"That he is." Nora sighed dreamily. From the stack in her arms, she handed me back my book, which she must have taken inside with her when she'd retreated out of sight.

"Even if you're selected to go to the other world, you won't remember him," I pointed out. That was why it was so important the Academy choose the best persons for the job. Because they wouldn't even remember they were *on a job* for our world once they crossed over. It all had to happen on instinct, more or less.

But the fact that we were still standing here meant no one had failed in the task before, even so. The few who ever returned were corroborators to that fact.

"I know," Nora said softly, shuffling her feet across the stone tile of the walkway we'd just returned to. "And even if I *did* remember him, I'd ruin any chances he had of a good reputation if I turned his head my way. Since I'd be a servant, and him a gentleman."

"Well, that world seems even more patriarchal than our own," I muttered. "Seems like he could easily have a fling with a servant and then turn around and marry a gentleman's daughter. It's the *women* who are ruined if they ever attempt such a thing."

"True, true." She bit her lip as we crossed through the large, open wooden doorway that led inside. "And I might find myself a husband, too. Someone of the servant class. I could get married and have a family and everything." She nodded, as if encouraging herself. "That's not so bad a fate, even if I have to work my entire life."

"With one whole day a month off," I added.

"Yeah..." She sighed. "But it's not like two days off a week is much fun here, either. There's nothing to do but study. At least there, I'll be able to turn my mind off and lose myself in some physical labor. I'm lucky, you know? I don't want the world's fate resting on my shoulders."

I couldn't agree more. At least *that* was one benefit of being the pawn. There wasn't much to it. Just die for the magic of the portal to have the energy to open. Frightening, maybe, but effortless.

I nudged her upper arm with my own as we ascended the large, stone staircase that led to the second floor of classrooms. "I'm happy for you," I said. "And you'd make a great servant. You *have* to be chosen. Then you can have your servant husband and kids and your days off together and your fresh air and hard work."

"And maybe an occasional affair with a gentleman." She snickered. "Since it wouldn't hurt his reputation."

I rolled my eyes. "You'll be so happy with your muscled, strapping servant husband, you *won't want* to mess about with those layabouts."

She wrinkled her nose. "Professor Wraxall did warn us that gentlemen can get a bit addicted to drink and gambling if they don't find something else to do."

"Like hunting," I said. "Or just shooting birds flushed out by gamekeepers. How incredibly entertaining."

She giggled. The dripping sarcasm in my words could have formed puddles.

Maybe Aylmer clung to a notion that gentlemen were more righteous people than they actually were. Maybe that was why he was the leading gentleman candidate.

"And ladies have needlepoint and art and music," Nora said. "And languages and dances!" She did a little twirl as we approached our classroom.

"Men have dances, too. And books. Gentlemen *and* ladies are allowed to read books."

"Unless you're a lady with a father who disapproves of those things. Because a lady is just the property of her father —until she's the property of her husband." Nora frowned and we stopped just outside of the classroom. She was practically repeating Professor Morton's words now. She was the one who instructed all those who might cross the world as ladies—and the ladies' servants—in those particular matters that men would not need to bother with. "I *am* glad I won't be one of them," she said. "There's a bit more leeway with those sorts of things for servants."

"Not entirely," I pointed out. "You'd be an oddity as a lower servant who read, if you even found the time for such a thing. And you could still be shamed if caught messing around with anyone before you're married."

"Then I better find my strapping, muscled head groom as soon as I get there." She took my hand and led me into the classroom.

"A head groom?" I asked wryly. "Have you already decided on his occupation?"

She winked. "I like animals. My head groom husband will let me sneak a ride or two on a gentlelady's horse."

"Oh, he will, will he?"

We both broke into giggles—cut short when we walked into the classroom and all eyes turned on us.

Neither of us was particularly fond of all eyes being turned in our direction.

Nora dropped my hand and we both hunched over, heading up the shallow steps for the back of the classroom.

The stares broke away, other members of the class turning back to those seated beside them.

Though I noticed... Aylmer's eyes were still locked on us. Fortunately, Dinah and her group were nowhere to be found, though I expected them to parade inside the classroom at any moment.

But they didn't beat Professor Wraxall inside.

The older man shuffled inside, slamming the stack of books and papers he carried with him onto the lectern. A puff of air from the action sent a lock of his wispy, gray hair flapping. The man had a portly figure he kept hidden under slimming, scarlet robes, like he kept the shiny, rose palette of his scalp hidden under his black, tasseled scholar's cap.

He sighed, his breath loud enough to silence any lingering conversations. Nora tensed beside me, her back growing rigid in her wooden chair.

"Class, this is your last lecture." Professor Wraxall spoke as if almost bored, and he looked not out at us, but at his thick, round glasses, which he removed from his face in order to buff with the edge of his overly wide sleeve. Murmurs spread throughout the classroom, the voices too hushed for me to make out any words. "I know it's several weeks earlier than expected, but as of tonight, you shall all be graduates." He looked up at us as he slipped his glasses back on.

My breath caught in my throat.

"One final review," he said, his tenor voice echoing out around us thanks to the rounded room's acoustics. "And then the pawn will need to report to the headmaster's office." His eyes locked on me.

The entire classroom shifted, all turning to stare over their shoulders and look at me.

"The Sacrament is tonight," he clarified, as if we couldn't figure out what he meant by us all becoming graduates weeks ahead of schedule.

Which meant... Tonight was the night I died.

Chapter Two

I shot to my feet.

I was supposed to have a few more weeks.

What was the point of class—of *anything*—if the Sacrament was tonight?

"Miss Radcliff, please sit down," Professor Wraxall stated, not even bothering to look over his shoulder at me as he picked up a marker and began writing on the dry erase board. "It's tradition that the graduating class have one final review." He stopped writing in order to lock eyes with me across the vast space of the room. "Even the pawn is not excused before it's done."

"Georgiana," Nora whispered, tugging on my billowy sleeve. Her eyes watered as they met mine. I looked around —at all the faces, the indifference on so many of them, the curiosity on others. Aylmer's head turned down almost as soon as my gaze traveled over him, the Adam's apple at his throat bobbing and the muscles in his jaw tightening.

"Georgiana," Nora whispered again.

My knees buckled beneath me, and I sat down in my seat again, numb, just as Dinah and her retinue walked into the classroom.

"Tardy," said Professor Wraxall, pushing the glasses up his nose.

Dinah flung her single loose lock of hair over her shoulder, her lips in a tight line as Unity, Thomas, and William fanned out around her and slipped into the vacant seats left in the front row.

"We have a pass, Professor." She flourished a folded letter in her hand complete with wax seal. "*Some of us* had to be consulted about a change in plans."

"Yes, yes, we're all aware now." Professor Wraxall yanked the letter from her grip and threw it on his lectern without opening it. "Have a seat."

Clearly ruffled for a moment, Dinah tossed her shoulders back and stuck her nose in the air before settling in an open chair beside Unity. She looked over her shoulder and directed her dazzling teeth in Aylmer's direction. He focused on the board in the front of the room.

Dinah's father was on the Academy Board. He must have wanted to give her advanced warning about the change in plans, perhaps bid her a private goodbye. Her friends, too, had parents on the Board. No wonder they'd all been taken aside. Aylmer's family was also from the Higher Zone, but none of them enjoyed a seat on the Academy's Board.

Nora reached across her desk and took my hand in hers. Her palm was as sweaty as mine was.

At least Dinah's late arrival had diverted the classroom's attention, and most everyone settled in to focus on Professor Wraxall's last lecture to our class.

"Now, in review," he started, picking up the marker again and walking back and forth in front of the board. "What is the Sacrament?" He pointed at those very words written in red. Red on white, reminding me of the blood involved in the sacrifice.

I swallowed. Not literally. It wouldn't be bloody. No one ever spoke of the pawn exhibiting wounds of any kind.

I'd witnessed it myself. The pawn just... collapsed. Lifeless.

Dinah's hand shot in the air, but Professor Wraxall ignored her.

"The Sacrament"—he underlined the word on the board—"is the annual ritual that keeps our planet from collapse." He capped the marker and walked to his lectern, dropping the marker atop the letter and his books in order to grab both sides of the furniture. "Our world is, in effect, unbalanced. Too much damage done to its natural systems for it to repair itself, for this planet to be hospitable to human life, if left to its own devices."

He slammed his hands against the edge of the lectern, startling Nora enough to drop her hold on me. "The Sacrament—sending our finest, our brightest to the other world—allows for an infusion of magic back into this world. It allows our world to keep existing."

Dinah had sat straighter in her seat, her back stiff and her lips clamped together in evident amusement, ever since Professor Wraxall had mentioned "our finest." I wasn't so entirely lost in the rapid thud of my heart to forego the usual surge of annoyance I felt at Bedlam Academy's leading lady candidate.

"While there, our leading lady candidate inhabits the life of a woman of the gentry, our leading gentleman the same for a man of the gentry." Professor Wraxall uncapped his marker and went back to the board, drawing up a social hierarchy chart I'd seen a dozen times before. "It will be as if they've always lived there, the residents of that world none the wiser as to our own students' sudden appearance in their lives."

None of that mattered to me.

"Each graduating year has a particular goal, a job they set out to complete, brought back by *the one who returns*." Professor Wraxall spoke that title reverently. It was a title that had applied to him one year.

"That student is the only one who reports on the graduating year's success. And as they pass through the portal brought about by another Sacrifice, they learn the goal for the following year's class."

I played with the ring on my finger, turning it, not entirely unaware that the professor had quickly tossed out the idea of "another Sacrifice" as if it were no more than a mere trifle. Somewhere on the other side of things, another pawn died. More often than not, a person who belonged to that other world, who would have had no idea their death would power open a portal to this one. But sometimes, it had been the death of another student crossed over instead.

My eyes glanced at Nora, wondering if she was in any danger on the other side as a pawn. Her face was wan, her attention transfixed by the lecture we'd heard so many times before.

At least... if it *was* to be her, she wouldn't know it was coming. Because once she crossed over to that world, she'd forget.

"Of course, the one who returns doesn't remember any of this *until* the portal appears on the other side. Until they cross back over." Professor Wraxall capped the marker again and tapped it to his lips as he kept walking back and forth in front of the board. "There is nothing that can be done on that side to plan for any of this—nothing but relying on instinct, and providence. And thankfully, that has always been enough." He looked back up at us, his eyes sweeping across us all.

"The one who returned from last year's graduating class spoke the words of providence upon her return. And she had a most unusual job for you all."

Dinah and Unity giggled demurely as they exchanged a glance at the front of the classroom. Of course they imagined this to be Dinah's personal objective.

"It is not the gentleman candidate who has to accomplish anything of note this year. No need for election to Parliament, securing a woman of significant dowry as a bride, or traveling the Continent and beyond, as previous gentlemen have been tasked with doing." Professor Wraxall nodded, more to himself than to any of us. "No, this year, it is the lady candidate on whose shoulders our fate rests."

His eyes flew across the classroom, landing on Unity, who shrunk back in her seat as Dinah's jaw dropped.

As if the professor's current focus were the deciding factor in choosing which gentry candidate was awarded which role.

Nora whispered under her breath in almost perfect tandem with the professor's next words. "The lady candidate must marry a viscount's son." Professor Wraxall settled back behind his lectern, sharing the next part with us all. "Uninterested in settling down, the viscount finding our candidate just a tad lacking in wealth and status for his son, the lady must push through and secure both men's favor—and become the viscount's son's bride before the year is done."

Good luck to Dinah—or better yet, Unity, if Dinah's pinched expression and evident sulking were any indication there was a risk of her pliant friend inhabiting the role instead.

They could enjoy a year of courtship and romance, their memories of this world wiped so they didn't quite feel the *weight* of the importance of the task.

Unburdened, they could fall in love. A feeling I would never know, not in this world or any other.

"The rest of you who make it through the portal to the other world will be put into lives that support this task—in some way, great or small." Professor Wraxall walked around to the front of his lectern now, gesturing one arm behind him at the social hierarchy chart. "And those who walk through the portal, only to remain here in this world, glancing right through to the other side, you'll be provided with opportunities to serve this Academy and your planet in various ways. You might become a professor's assistant if your grades are particularly impressive." His gaze lingered on Dinah, and I wondered if he was stopping himself short of mentioning a parent on the Academy's Board wouldn't hurt when it came to determining such a position, either. Dinah wouldn't be satisfied with second-best, though. She couldn't even be a professor if she didn't ever go to the other world. Only the ones who returned became that. Like Professor Wraxall had, decades and decades before.

"But we'll find you something regardless. All graduates from Bedlam Academy are afforded enviable lives." His gaze flicked to me, as if remembering I was in the room for the first time in ages. "Or their families are."

That was all. The extent of my acknowledgement in this story.

Or at least, it should have been all.

Dinah, in a sour mood, wouldn't let it be. She turned over her shoulder and raised her hand.

At first, I thought Professor Wraxall might continue to ignore her, but her hand shook harder, her back gone straighter.

"Yes, Miss Sinclair?" he asked with a furrowed brow.

Dinah looked from me to the professor and back. "I wonder if you might review the role of the Sacrifice," she said. "In this noble venture of ours."

A harried breath escaped the professor's lips. "The graduating class's pawn plays a crucial role," he said, oblivious or just not caring about the fact that my blood ran cold, darkness edging in at the corners of my eyes. "Without their sacrifice, the portal will not open." He fixed his glasses up the bridge of his nose and stared at me, a hint of a soul creeping onto his expression in the form of a small, sympathetic smile. "A family that sacrifices their child for the Academy's Sacrament is a heroic one."

Not if *they're* not the ones giving up their lives, they aren't.

I fumbled with the bracelet at my wrist, remembering the day my dad told me what he'd signed me up for.

"Hey, there, Georgie. Come here, will ya?" Dad was home early from working at the factory. His breath smelled stronger than usual, that sort of moldy-bread smell lingering in the air even some distance away after he spoke. He took his cap off his

head for a moment and scratched the back of his black-and-silver hair, which was cropped tightly around the sides and back of his head. His scalp shone red today, his pale complexion mottled with either drink or anger. Or both.

I was ten. I'd have been expected in the grade school allowed for general Lower-Zone children, but Mom had bade me to stay home to weed the garden and make breakfast and dinner because she'd had a headache. She always had headaches. She'd promised to come out to make supper, but I knew better. Nothing could lure her from her dark, cramped room.

I shuffled closer, wiping the sweat from my brow in the sun, the skin of my arm coming back streaked in dirt that I'd probably just smeared across my face.

"That's it, girlie." Dad beckoned me. "Dad's got a surprise for you."

For a brief moment, there was a drumming in my chest, a lightness in my step. Then I remembered that my dad had never given anything to me, and my stomach dropped, drowning in the heavier stench.

He didn't seem to notice, dropping to a knee and putting a hand on my back. It was a light touch, as if he wasn't quite sure how to interact with me.

He probably wasn't.

"You like that neighbor girl, don'tcha? That little Leonora?"

"Honora," I said, my voice soft and cracking due to misuse.

"That's the one." Dad punched my shoulder lightly. I flinched. He'd never punched me before—not really—but I'd seen him do it to Mom loads of times. To the wall one time, too, except that it had cracked his knuckles and made them bleed for days afterward.

He'd learned his lesson just that once.

"Well, she's going to Bedlam Academy tomorrow, did you know that?" he asked. He grinned, two of his teeth blackened from lack of care, the rest a yellowing, crooked mess.

I nodded. My best and only friend was leaving me tomor-

row. Off for an adventure at the greatest school anyone could ever attend: Bedlam Academy, which trained its students for life in another world.

Life far away from this place.

"Bet you didn't think we'd be able to send you, did you? Your ma and me." Dad smiled wider, a glint of light crossing his eyes. "But we did. We always meant to. Your ma didn't want to have kids, you see, and I'm the one who convinced her to pop you out."

He gave my shoulder a squeeze, as if we were old friends. As if I owed him one.

"You're going to be your graduating year's pawn, my love." It was the first time he'd mentioned "love" anywhere around me. "It's a great honor. And you was born for that role. Our family's great sacrifice."

My breath caught in my throat, and I wobbled on unsteady feet.

Dad clutched me harder, more to force me to stand than to prevent my fall. His grip began to hurt.

I stood steady.

"That's it, girl. Chin up." He ran a filthy finger under my chin, forcing my head upward. "You go have fun with your little friend—for eight whole years. You'll love it. And your ma and I, we'll live proudly knowing you'll bring us great riches when all's said and done." He leaned forward, his breath hot on my cheek as he aimed for—and missed—my ear. "You're our ticket out of this place, kid. It's all you're good for, ain't it?"

Blinking back tears, I snapped back to the moment. That was so long ago, but the memory burned a gaping hole inside me.

If they were all I'd known of this world, they could rot along with it, for all I cared. Nora seemed to read something on my face, a tear streaming down her cheek as she stared at me, Professor Wraxall's words an indecipherable echo behind my pounding heart, my wayward thoughts.

But there was Nora. And though her parents hadn't been cruel like mine, they'd all struggled here. She, at least, deserved a new life somewhere else. Somewhere simpler, where her hard work could be rewarded.

And my sacrifice might allow her that.

I took her hand in mine and squeezed.

I just wished I could know if Nora went through.

Whatever the professor was droning on about now, once he'd paused to walk toward the dry erase board and remove the writing on the surface, Aylmer's hand shot into the air.

He was a good student, true, but he didn't tend to talk in class unless called upon.

It drew my attention, and Nora's too. Our hands fell apart.

Professor Wraxall did a double-take over his shoulder once he'd observed Aylmer's hand in the air. "Yes, Mr. Linden?"

"But you still haven't explained why the Sacrament was moved up to tonight, sir," he said. "Has a Sacrament ever been performed ahead of schedule?"

Professor Wraxall waved a hand. "Oh, yes. Yes, indeed. You may be too young to have witnessed such a thing, but yes, before your time, there were a couple of early Sacraments." He pinched his lips. "It comes to the one who returned in a dream, you see. Then they consult with the Board to be sure they're not mistaken, and the Board makes the decision. That must mean Professor Finch awoke from a potent dream this morning. There can be no mistake."

He nodded and stacked his papers on his lectern once more. So it was Professor Finch's fault. I didn't have her for any classes. She'd been a student here only last year, returned to tell us the previous graduating class's purpose had been fulfilled a few months ago. "Professor" was an honorary title for her until she settled into her new life of instructing classes in the ways of that other world.

"My dad said there was something off about the dream, though," said William, unbidden.

Thomas's eyes widened and he elbowed his obtuse friend. "We weren't supposed to say that," he hissed.

William winced, and murmurs started around the classroom.

Dinah laughed loudly, perhaps in an attempt to drown them out.

"They'll have discussed the dream and determined as a group that we're making the best choice. The Sacrament is tonight." Professor Wraxall stared straight out at me. "And there's no more debate to be had about it. Miss Radcliff, you are now excused early to begin your prayers. Meet Professor Harding in the courtyard."

The class went silent, all eyes back on me as I stood once more. Aylmer, at least, had the presence of mind to look ashamed, unable to stare so fixatedly as the rest. Nora's lips trembled, but her stare, I didn't mind.

"I'll see you tonight," I whispered, half-resigned, half clinging on to what little hope I had. Seeing my friend one last time.

"Tonight," she murmured, staring at her desk.

I grabbed my textbook and made my way past the other students to the end of the row, then down toward the exit, feeling the silence weighing heavily, the lingering looks. I stumbled on a shallow step at the bottom of the classroom and Dinah snorted, Thomas and William chuckling.

"All right, all right. We still have some things to go over," Professor Wraxall said, turning his attention to the remaining members of the class.

They had a future to plan for.

I stopped myself from looking back at them once more. I'd see them all again tonight. For now, I'd hold my head high.

Chapter Three

Professor Wraxall's voice became small and tinny as I exited out into the hallway alone, no one anywhere in my path as I made my way to the staircase. I passed other classrooms full of younger students, preparing for objectives down the line, after someone from my class made it to the other world and back and continued the never-ending cycle on which Bedlam Academy had been founded.

The world had been bedlam before the portal to the other world had opened. Before the founders of this Academy had figured out how to harness the magic and make it all work.

Bedlam Academy had been named such as a reminder of what would exist without this institution.

At least I'd be a footnote of some small importance in the grand, non-ending cycle continuing from one decade to the next.

At the bottom of the steps, I hesitated, looking to the end of the hallway that led out to the dorms for my year. I didn't know if I'd be allowed time to go back to my dorm before the Sacrament—if there was any need for me to gather what few belongings I had stashed there. They'd probably send them to my parents, who would use the fireplace in their new Higher-Zone home to burn the box first thing.

Perhaps there was no need for me to return there.

I walked outside again, toward the courtyard, memories of the bullied student and Aylmer stopping Dinah and her ridiculous group of friends from sullying the Sacrament Day with their wanton cruelty. At least beyond what typical cruelty they engaged in on any given day.

The roaring sounds of the ocean no longer lured me to the edge of the cliff, but they acted as a balm to my wounds, the first thing—and among the only things—to bring me joy in this place.

"Look, Georgiana!" Little Nora bounced down the grass waving at the vast, blue body of water. "The ocean!"

Lower-Zone kids never saw the ocean. Not unless they enrolled in Bedlam Academy.

The first deep breath I took, the salty, fresh air. I'd closed my eyes, and for a moment, at ten years old, I'd known peace. Perhaps for the first time in my memory.

I opened my eyes in the present, heading down the courtyard, scanning for signs of Professor Harding—for anybody. Most were in class, to be sure, but Professor Wraxall had sent me here, so I had reason to believe Professor Harding would be here. He was my special tutor in the ways of prayer, prayer to call forth the portal during Sacrament. He taught me with fire and passion, lecturing constantly about the great need for my sacrifice, and never once treating me as an individual person. I was sure each pawn here got the same treatment from him.

He wasn't at the edge of the cliff. His fiery-red professor robes would have been hard to miss.

But I wasn't alone out here.

I almost didn't see her at first. Crumpled on her knees in the grass, wearing a light-blue scholarly robe denoting her still-just-honorary status, was Professor Finch, her hands clasped together in prayer in front of her as she faced the ocean. Wind rustled her long, coiled black hair across her olive complexion, but she didn't move to swipe it away, her lips moving quickly, murmuring near silently.

I'd never been alone with the woman before. I vaguely remembered her being a student in years previous, but our paths had never crossed, really.

Not until today.

When she was here, in place of my tutor, who was to prepare me for the Sacrament tonight.

The one who'd returned most recently. The one whose dream had prematurely sealed my fate.

"Professor Finch," I said quietly. My voice came out in time with an especially thunderous ocean wave crashing against the rocks below.

But she heard me even so.

"Oh!" Professor Finch fell from her knees to her thighs on the grass, a trembling arm shooting out into the thick blades to keep her upright. "The pawn! Shouldn't you be in the headmaster's office?"

I frowned. I knew my attire made me identifiable as the pawn on sight, but I didn't particularly like being addressed as such.

If my family was to reap the most direct benefits of my sacrifice, and the entire Academy needed my blood to achieve their current goal, the least the staff could do here was remember my name.

"Georgiana," I said. "Georgiana Radcliff." I tossed my textbook to the ground without ceremony and scooped my long skirt under one arm as I moved to sit in the grass beside the young professor only a year or two my elder. "Professor Wraxall sent me to meet with Professor Harding in the courtyard first."

Professor Finch's back stiffened as she gathered her legs and sat on her shins. "He was mistaken," she said curtly, succinctly. Her voice quavered as she gathered some of her robe's material over her knees in both fists. "Professor Harding is waiting for you in the headmaster's office. The pawn always goes to the headmaster's office to prepare."

Professor Wraxall *had* originally told me that was to be my destination after he'd finished his review. I shifted sideways and gazed back at the vast building behind us. Professor Wraxall couldn't have known I'd meet the wrong instructor out here, could he?

I glanced back at Professor Finch, who took a deep breath and closed her eyes, her lips moving just slightly as if in soft prayer.

Professor Wraxall's intent or not, I was here now. With the person whose dream had spurred everything into motion weeks early.

"Professor..." I started.

She didn't respond, only flinch.

"My life ends today," I said bluntly.

That got her to let out a little gasp, and her eyes fluttered open. She couldn't look at me, though, her gaze darting everywhere—over the ocean, the cliffs, my textbook—everywhere but at me.

My heart thundered inside me, the reality I'd had hovering over me for eight years crashing down as my own words became real.

"The least you could do is tell me—" My breaths became shallow and I hugged my legs tightly in front of me, resting my forehead against my knees as the world started to spin. The cold air whapped against my hands, every small bit of exposed skin, snapping me back to reality.

A hand rested on my back, causing me to jump. It patted me softly, cautiously.

I lifted my head up to meet Professor Finch's wide, brown eyes at last.

"I'm sorry," she said, her voice cracking. "I am. I lost..." She looked down and pulled away.

"You were friends with last year's pawn?" I guessed. Here I was, lamenting the fact that that was all I'd be defined as, and I couldn't remember her name. Hypocritical of me, I know. "Bella... Bella—"

"Arabella Weston," she said succinctly. "And I am sorry

for her, but no, I wasn't close to her." She bit the inside of her cheek.

It took me a moment to realize what else might have been bothering her.

"The return trip," I said. "You knew the sacrifice in the other world, the person whose death allowed you to return here."

"A fate I neither sought nor even was aware of, until it happened," she said. A harsh breath escaped her lips. "Who would *choose* to come here?" She sneered as she looked around.

At the ocean. At the grand beauty of this spot, even if others would repeatedly attempt to mar it.

"I imagine anyone whose only other option is oblivion." My fingers traced over the cover of my textbook on the grass beside me, the thick, black cover adorned with silver embellishments at the corner. In the middle was a silver replica of a white plume, five petals, each representing five successful qualities candidates for the other world were said to possess.

Resilience. Determination. Propriety. Gentleness. Character.

As if someone had actually boiled it all down to a formula this institution could hope to replicate in a handful of students each year.

"The dream I had..." Professor Finch spoke up, answering questions I hadn't even been able to pose. "It didn't feel... right."

I'd imagine there'd be *some* guilt associated with sending a pawn to an early death, even if the death was inevitable soon enough. Still, this didn't seem to be that. "How so?"

"Well, I... I don't know what *the* dream is supposed to *feel* like," she admitted. "Every professor here has had it at some point or another, but no one's been able to articulate much beyond the basic structure and the *intensity* of it."

"And your dream was not intense?"

"Oh, no. It *was*. Most certainly." She sent me a sharp look, one that dared me to even try to contradict her.

As if I had any reason to doubt her. "So what was wrong with it?"

She put her hand over mine, which was still tracing the outline of the white plume decoration on my textbook cover.

"You didn't die."

A flutter in my abdomen shot up to my throat. Did I dare to hope?

"Was I supposed to die? Was I supposed to appear in it at all?"

"Yes." Professor Finch pulled her hand away. "Maybe not *you* exactly, down to your very features, but the pawn." She gestured at me, at my dress that marked me as "other" in this place. "From what I gather, we're supposed to see visions of the goal for this year's candidates, almost in reverse. At least, it's in reverse for most." She cocked her head and bit her lip. "That was the best they could articulate it."

"In reverse would mean it ends with my sacrifice."

"Yes," Professor Finch said softly. "But you see... When I found myself there. In that other world." She stared out over the ocean. "I thought it was real at first. That I was really there."

"Dreams are like that," I said. "Even ones far less important."

Professor Finch grabbed a clump of the grass between us and ripped it out by the roots. "I searched for him."

"'For... him'?"

She didn't answer.

My mind filled in the rest. "For the sacrifice? On the other side?"

She nodded, and a single tear traveled down her cheek, her head still pointed forward. "I knew he was dead, and yet I searched for him."

I swallowed. Part of me wanted to offer her gentle platitudes, but I wasn't a part of her life. My words would have little meaning—just like any such words I'd had to "comfort" me about my fate.

A fate this woman might have the key to changing.

Did I want that? To live? At what cost?

If I wasn't sacrificed, could candidates still get through to the other world?

Professor Finch tossed her clump of grass, and the wind caught it, scattering the blades to the far ends of the cliff, bits of dirt trailing alongside them.

"But you saw the goal for the year."

"I did," she said quickly. "I mean... vaguely."

"'Vaguely'?"

"The other professors assured me that is quite normal. I saw a woman getting married to the viscount's son, and the dream worked its way backward, despite me pushing, pushing to stay, to look for..." Her voice went quiet.

"How did you know it was the viscount's son getting married?" I asked after a moment. "You said you saw no one in detail in the dream."

"Everyone at the wedding spoke of it. And I know of the man. The target. The Honourable Richard Gillingham."

"The viscount's son," I confirmed.

She nodded. "His heir and his only child."

"Professor Wraxall didn't name him."

She waved a hand in the air and went back to clutching the robe over her thighs. "The candidates would forget, anyway. It's important they have the *shape* of the goal imprinted into their subconscious. The details just slip through a candidate's grasp regardless." As if to demonstrate, she grabbed another few blades of grass and let them fall back to the ground between her fingers. But the wind picked those up, too, and sent them flying off in different directions, to different places before they withered and rotted without their roots to trap them in the dirt of their birthplace.

"There's no other viscount in the place where we all go," she continued. "There can be no confusion."

"These candidates will go to the same exact world you did?" I asked. "So you knew this viscount's son?"

"I knew *of* him." She shrugged. "I was a servant candidate. My life was filled with too much work to bother with these other details. Though we did like to gossip." A rare smile cracked across her features.

"And what did you learn about The Honourable Richard Gillingham?" I spoke the title almost mockingly. So much for the qualities of "propriety" and "gentleness" that I'd need to be a candidate. Not that *I'd* need them.

"Oh, there was much gossip about him." Her cheeks darkened a shade. "He was quite a rake."

A rake? We'd learned that term. A man—usually of the gentry because who else would have the time or money to waste constantly on such pursuits?—who made a game of flirtation with women.

Flirtation and... more, when he could manage it. A woman of the gentry would never risk any more than delicately structured, public flirtation, though.

At least, she wouldn't if she hoped at all to remain in good standing.

"He had a few of the servants," she said quickly. "Willingly, mind you. He was quite a catch. I was told."

My eyelids fluttered. *He* was the man Dinah or Unity or whoever was chosen as the lady candidate would be after? I felt sorry for them. For a second.

Then again, the likes of Thomas and William were hardly tight-lipped about what they learned in their gentlemen-only classes. *Men* could gain some experience of an intimate nature and not risk too much, depending on the lady in question. It was women of the gentry who would be utterly ruined if they came to a marriage as anything less than a stalwart maid.

It was enough to scare most of the girls here into chastity. Lest they lose the chance to cross over to that other world of hopes and dreams and promises they all worked toward.

Considering my fate, what was my excuse?

There'd never been a man to tempt me.

A picture of Aylmer burst like a firework into my mind.

No. He was handsome and kind enough for a gentry candidate. But I never would have had a chance.

And he didn't seem the type, frankly, to take any girl up on what she was offering.

I couldn't say why. He was just... too much of a gentleman.

"Wow," I said at last, after we descended into an uneasy silence. I didn't know how much longer I had out here before Professor Harding or the headmaster would seek me out. I had the excuse of being sent to the courtyard, sure, but... "He should prove quite a challenge."

"Well, if he's ready to settle—something that seemed quite in doubt when I lived there—a beautiful woman of good fortune should do the job well. I didn't think *love* needed to be a factor, from what I could tell in the dream. Just the marriage."

"I see." And The Honourable Rake would probably continue his pursuits even after the marriage had taken place. Served Dinah right, if that was what fate had in store for her.

"So the lady candidate will be born into fortune?" I asked.

"She has to be," Professor Finch whispered. "Or the Sacrament for this year will be a failure."

"Right." The magic of the ceremony itself would give Bedlam Academy's students what was needed.

"You don't want to know?" she asked after a moment. "How I know you didn't die?"

I leaned forward eagerly, my heart practically thumping out of my throat.

"I saw you there," she said succinctly. "Not *you* exactly—but you. The woman in the dress." She gestured at me. "In the other world itself."

Chapter Four

No pawn in all of Bedlam Academy's history had ever made it to the other world. But Professor Finch had just told me she'd seen me there in her dream of what was to come.

"No one who's returned has reported the pawn being on the other side of the portal," I said. "During the Sacrament, they just... vanish." My voice croaked. "And in their place grows the portal."

Professor Finch nodded. "I know that. But there was just this... feeling I had. Seeing you there—you, vaguely— made me uneasy."

Like seeing a ghost, I supposed.

"And the Board knows all of this?"

She nodded. "They dismissed my *feelings*." She spoke the last word as if it'd been spit back at her in just that same venomous way. "And pointed out that if the pawn isn't sacrificed, there *is no* portal, so obviously, you couldn't be alive on the other side of it."

She hadn't actually kicked me in the gut, but she may as well have.

There was that. Either I died and people crossed over into the other world or I didn't and we all died—eventually.

However long it would take for the consequences of my actions to doom us all. They couldn't skip ahead and try with next year's pawn. It was a once-a-year ceremony.

"But why the rush?" I asked. "Why not wait...?"

"Those who returned usually have the dreams on the right day." She shrugged. "But of course, I didn't. Nothing *about* my experience there seemed to be typical. Why should my experience back here be any different?"

I shifted in place to spread my legs to the side of me and took hold of the textbook, which I clutched to my abdomen as a lifeline of sorts.

"You should go," the professor said softly. "I've told you everything—I've told you too much." She stood, her chest expanding with the deep breath she inhaled. The smallest of smiles crossed her lips as she brushed a lock of curly hair behind her ear. "But perhaps my prayers have been answered. I don't feel so unsettled now that we've spoken."

Arching a brow, I reluctantly got to my feet. That made one of us.

Professor Finch gestured for me to walk in front of her, directing us back toward the Academy.

I took slow steps alongside her. Class hadn't let out yet, so the courtyard continued to be empty.

She cleared her throat. "Your family will be well rewarded for their sacrifice."

I grunted. "You mean *my* sacrifice."

"Yes."

We'd reached the open doorway leading back inside. She cleared her throat again as we stepped into the empty hallways.

"Do you have... *Did* you make any friends here?"

Spoken of in the past tense already.

"No," I said truthfully. Professor Finch swallowed visibly as we headed toward the headmaster's office on the first floor. "But my best friend—Honora—we've known each other since before Bedlam."

She smiled sweetly, the expression clearly forced. "And she's a candidate?"

"A servant candidate."

We stopped in front of the headmaster's office, its large, dark doors towering far over our heads.

"I was very happy as a servant in that world," she said softly. "It was a tough life, but it was an honest one. And I..." She looked away.

She didn't need to say more. She'd cared deeply about someone in that life, that was clear. Someone whose death had sent her spiraling back to a life best unremembered.

"Do it for her," she said, patting my shoulder. She couldn't take my hand because I still clutched my textbook to my chest. "Give her a better life. As hard as it might be, it could be a happy one."

Happiness was hard to come by here, that was true.

At least if you were from the Lower Zone.

She dropped her hand and took hold of the handle, opening the door.

Behind the desk was the headmaster, a skeletal, wrinkled milk-white woman always wearing a powdered white wig with curls worked into a pile high atop her head.

"There you are," she said, her lips worming their way into a devious sort of smile. "Thought I'd have to call for a sweep of the campus to find you."

I stiffened, embracing the textbook even tighter.

"You're late for your prayers," snapped Professor Harding. He stood beside the desk, his gray hair cropped close above a weathered complexion.

"There's still time for that," said the headmaster. "But first, I have a surprise for you." She stood up from behind her desk and gestured beside her. Two figures I hadn't noticed behind the towering Professor Harding shuffled into view. "Your parents have come to say their farewells."

My parents. The selfish, spiteful family that had sent me to this place.

Though the headmaster's office was large, there were

bookshelves packed with volumes of our world's history and all sorts of artifacts and knickknacks—Bedlam Academy seized any and all things the ones who returned brought with them back from the other world—so it felt rather suffocating. More so because there were three professors in here with me, along with two extras.

The extras being my parents.

"Georgie!" said Dad after an awkward moment of silence. He clapped his craggy hands together and extended his arms out, as if for a hug.

I didn't move.

My mom shifted from one foot to the other behind him, her eyes drawn to the floor.

They both looked freshened up, their faces not covered in dirt, their hair—or what remained of it, in Dad's case—slicked back against their scalps. They wore their finest outfits, the same ones I'd last seen them in eight years ago to see me off, though there were a few more patches now, the beige and brown colors of the outfits even more muted.

"Your parents have come all this way," said Headmaster Banfield, a tight smile forcing its way onto her lips. "The pawn typically uses this opportunity to say goodbye."

Then they'd been far more selfless pawns than I was. Was it possible some volunteered to better the lives of their families? Perhaps. I knew I couldn't be the only one tossed aside against her will, though.

Though I may have been the only one born for the express purpose of being sacrificed to Bedlam Academy's annual ritual.

Dad's arms fell, the stern line of his brow causing me to flinch despite myself. I hugged my textbook closer.

And spoke at last. "I said my farewells. Eight years ago." I focused on Professor Harding. "Shall we go over the final prayers?"

Until that moment, I hadn't felt ready. Here, in this cramped space, with the people who'd given me life staring at me, I was more ready than I'd ever been.

"You really ought to—" started the headmaster.

"Georgiana." Mom's voice came out as practically a squeak. Despite myself, I glanced to the side to take a look at her.

She'd stepped forward just slightly, wringing her hands together. Those long, spindly fingers. I always remembered those fingers at work—when she hadn't been lying down with one of her headaches. "I'm sorry," she said softly.

That drew my full attention.

Dad elbowed her in the side and she flinched, her eyes squeezing tightly, her reaction far more than the contact called for. Of course, I knew why, though. I doubted even the promise of a Higher-Zone life once I was sacrificed had been enough to stay his hand the eight years it had taken me to get through Bedlam Academy's curriculum before I would finally be made *useful* to all those concerned.

"No need to apologize, love," he said, the endearment meaningless from his lips. "We sacrificed what we did for the good of the world, yeah?" He looked to each of the robed professors in turn, as if waiting for the "officials" to weigh in and prove him right.

"Yes, yes, of course," said Professor Harding, giving Dad exactly what he wanted, though Professor Harding himself couldn't possibly seem less interested. Dad's chest puffed up, though, and he wrapped an arm around Mom's shoulders. She flinched at that, too.

"It is still a lot to ask," said Professor Finch softly. I'd almost forgotten she was here with us. "For those who lose their lives for it." She bit her lip, and if I wasn't mistaken, her eyes were brimming with tears. "Excuse me," she said. "I'll see you all at the Sacrament." She swept out of the room.

Of course the emotional outburst was for her own experience, not for me in particular. She didn't know me. If there were anything but dry eyes tonight, I'd be astonished.

Well, excepting Nora's, of course. And my own, if I couldn't go to the abyss with my head held high.

"We do ask a lot." The headmaster sighed, perhaps a tad

too dramatically, as she came around her desk. She leaned back against it, clutching her hands in front of her waist. Her smile didn't reach her eyes as she looked at me. "But we appreciate it. And we will do all we can to let you leave this world free of burdens." She gestured at my parents. "That's why we take such good care of the families the pawns leave behind."

"And I promise we'll be happy, Georgie. I'll take good care of your ma."

Dad's eyes seemed to glow with an inner light as he squeezed Mom to his side again.

Mom just looked downward, her wan, long face not unlike mine—though weighted down, as if the years that had changed most of her dark-brown hair to gray had also pulled at the very flesh.

"You'll die a great beauty," Dad said, and coming from him, not the loving father figure I knew those like Nora had been blessed with, I was left with a foul taste on my tongue at the "compliment." "Nearly dropped my jaw when I saw you all grown up. Spitting image of your ma when I met her. Only your beauty, it won't get worn down with time." He laughed.

I was struck with a sudden idea.

I had nothing to lose at this point.

I turned to the headmaster. "If it's my burdens you hope to ease, might it be possible for me to explain what those actually would be?"

Dad's smile fell, and Mom's eyes snapped up.

"What do you mean, Georgie?" Dad asked.

I focused on Headmaster Banfield only. "I wish for the rewards of my sacrifice to be given to another Lower-Zone family."

The room went quiet. Until Dad exploded.

"Now hold on a minute. She can't ask that, can she?" He sneered in my direction. "You ungrateful little brat! You wouldn't *exist* if it weren't for me!"

The headmaster studied my parents a moment, then

looked back to me. "Such a thing has never been asked before."

Dad stopped talking, an audible breath escaping his lips. "That's what I thought."

"But that doesn't mean I can't discuss it with the Board," said the headmaster, walking back around her desk and staring down at it as she shuffled through some papers. "What did you have in mind?"

Dad let out a shout, and Professor Harding arched a brow, slipping around me and out into the hallway.

I clutched my textbook tighter against my chest. "The Fletchers. Honora Fletcher's family."

They needed a better life far more than anyone—and they had other kids to think of. And even so, they never would have suggested Nora aim to be the pawn, the sacrifice.

"Oh, Fred Fletcher's family, huh?" Dad tossed a hand in the air. "Right git that one is. Always so *holy*, thinks he's so much better than the rest of us at the factory, you know? Never should have let you befriend that brat of theirs." He rounded on Mom. "If *you* had gotten off your sorry rear more than once a month, maybe our little girl wouldn't have been running off, forming *attachments* to some no-good family—"

"I'll ask the Board," Headmaster Banfield said sternly, her voice raising an octave. "It's irregular, but I'd say there's a chance. It's not just about the family who sacrifices, but putting the pawn's mind at rest. If you feel the fate of this... Fletcher family... would weigh down your heart more than the fate of your own parents..."

"I do."

I did my best to ignore my dad, catching Mom's eye. For a beat, I felt guilty at the decision I'd made. Mom was, in many ways, more trapped than I was.

"It's *our* sacrifice!" shouted Dad, walking over to the headmaster's office and slamming his palms against it. The headmaster flinched but met his eyes sternly. "She's *my* flesh and blood, not that of some hoity-toity Lower-Zoner who's always imagined himself better than he is—"

"She's not," said Mom, her voice catching on her throat.

Dad went quiet and all eyes turned toward her.

Mom swallowed visibly and clutched the front of her dress, tossing her head back. A tear danced in her eye. "She's not. His blood."

Dad's nostrils flared. "*What* did you say?"

Mom nodded sharply. "She's-She's Fred Fletcher's child," she said, the confession—or lie, I couldn't tell which—tumbling out of her mouth. "So-So that family has as much right to claim the pawn as I do."

"Fred? Fred Bloomin' Fletcher?" Dad closed the distance between the two of them in an instant, and the headmaster quickly maneuvered around the desk. "Are you having a laugh? This better be a bloomin' joke!"

My breath caught in my throat as I stared between my mom and dad—watching my mom for any sign she might be lying. I had never seen Fred Fletcher be anything but loyal to his wife. The idea of Nora and I being sisters filled me with warmth for the briefest of moments, yes, but Mom truly had been lying down alone in her bedroom every time she hadn't been feeling well. I'd checked on her.

I had to believe this was a lie... A lie to help me get what I wanted. Or, perhaps more accurately, to make sure Dad didn't get what *he* wanted.

Even though that meant my mother's own sacrifice of sorts.

"It's-It's the truth," Mom said, each word less certain than the last.

"Can I have her rewarded as well?" I asked the headmaster quickly. "My birth parents both—and my birth dad's family?"

Headmaster Banfield pursed her lips as she looked at me, and then to my mom. "Very well. I'll speak to the Board. You're all dismissed."

Mom's jaw dropped, her hand shaking as she looked to

me, tears spilling from her eyes. "Georgie," she mouthed, but no sound came out. She offered a slight bow of her head.

Dad's weatherworn face grew purple. "Oh, no! Oh, no, no, no—you're not robbing me of my rights here!"

"Mr. Radcliff, I'm afraid you don't have *rights* in this matter," said the headmaster, gesturing to her open door. "It is between the pawn and her *family*."

"I *am* that brat's family!" He rolled down his sleeve and extended his forearm. "Prick me for blood, whatever you gotta do—you'll see! No way this weak-willed, little liar cheated on *me*." He glared at Mom, and she winced, her eyes shutting.

"That won't be necessary." Headmaster Banfield dismissed him with a wave just as Professor Harding returned, this time with two other members of the faculty. The largest members, the two bulky, male professors in charge of Exercises and Hunting. "Proof of relation to the pawn is meaningless if she insists the burdens she'd leave behind to be in another direction. If the Board decides otherwise, you'll be the first to know."

Dad wound up his arm, announcing his next move— one directed straight at me—but he wasn't without witnesses here.

Professors Steele and Ashtown each grabbed a side of the man, practically yanking his arms out of his sockets.

Dad struggled, kicking his legs, his face growing more and more violet. "You'll pay for this, Georgiana Radcliff! That's right—you're a brat *with my name*! You're mine to do what I want with, and I only married this sorry sack of a woman to have you. You're my way to the Higher-Zone, and I—"

"*Mr. Radcliff*," said Headmaster Banfield. "Control yourself. We don't abide a lack of decorum at Bedlam Academy."

"But you'll accept a pawn my wife claims to be a bastard?" He stopped struggling and spat on the floor. "Lack of decorum, my hairy rear end."

"She is not a lady," said the headmaster, folding her hands together. "Her pedigree is of no concern to us."

She had a point. If I'd been in this other world, a lady candidate, it would have been the scandal of the century if I'd been born out of wedlock.

If proven true—or perhaps even just believed to be so—it would have made securing a marriage to a gentleman of higher standing quite impossible. Unless I brought with me a sizable dowry one couldn't resist.

But those were concerns that would never reach me.

"Escort him off-campus, please," said Headmaster Banfield, looking down at the desk.

"You brat!" shouted Dad as he was dragged down the hall. "You lying, traitorous woman and you ungrateful brat! You will pay! The Fletchers will pay! I won't be—"

But his voice died out as he went farther away, and the four of us left in the office stood there awkwardly.

"Mom," I said softly. She bit her lip and looked up at me. I crossed the room and gave her a hug.

It felt odd. More like I was comforting *her* than the other way around. But it still felt like the right thing to do.

"And now that your farewells are taken care of," said the headmaster, with no more concern in her voice than if she were ordering her breakfast, "Professor Harding, perhaps you should begin the prayers with Miss Radcliff."

Chapter Five

"The final day of a pawn's life should be filled with as much serenity and gratitude as possible," Professor Harding droned on.

No mention of the irony of everything that had just happened in the headmaster's office.

"Give thanks to the other world," he said as we approached the bell tower. I hadn't expected to be let in to the place early, but a point among Professor Harding's many lectures the past few minutes was the fact that I was to be the one to first feel a *connection* with the place this year. "Give thanks to this one. Give thanks for the chance to save your world. All of these good things."

If Professor Harding was just going to repeat himself, I decided to tune out the rest of his lecture. This was nothing I hadn't heard before—and he was offering me no new advice that might have applied to me specifically in this situation, like how to *relax* after my dad's outburst. Professor Harding had his script for pawns each year and he was sticking to it.

I chanced a glance at the man's profile, the crook at the bridge of his nose. I wondered what had happened to him in that other world that had made him embrace continuously, year after year, training pawns to end their lives.

Maybe his nose had once been broken. Maybe something in that other world had hardened him.

"Miss Radcliff?" Professor Harding stopped at the top of the stairs and I nearly walked into his back. "Are you paying attention?"

"Of course, Professor." I shook my head to get a lock of hair to stop tickling my nose.

Professor Harding arched a brow but continued droning on.

At last, we reached the top of the stairs, and at the end of a long, narrow hallway—which could surely allow any group approaching to only do so single-file—was a tall, wooden door. It didn't look particularly notable. If I hadn't already been aware of the significance of the room behind it, I might have mistaken it for the entrance to a storage closet.

"The barrier between the worlds must hear your prayer," Professor Harding said as he fished into a pouch at his belt and withdrew a single brass key. He unlocked the room and held the door open, then stared at me as I just stood there.

"Miss Radcliff?" He nodded toward the open door. "I am not mistaken that I explained the significance of you being the first to enter, am I not?"

"No," I said quickly, and I ducked my head—more out of embarrassment than any fear I'd hit the top of the doorway—and stepped inside.

I shivered, the creaking whisper of the wooden walls of this place accompanied by the harsh blow of the oceanside winds. The space inside was vast—far greater than I'd imagined just seeing it from the outside before my first year attending the Sacrament. There wasn't much inside to draw the eye away from the giant, brass bell. It hung from the rafters above over the middle of the room, a circle almost as large as the room engraved into the wooden slats of the floor in the shape of the bell above.

"Stand in the middle. Professor Harding's voice echoed

out into the space, and I spared a glance over my shoulder to see that he'd followed me inside.

Around the room was enough space to hold perhaps two hundred or so, again single-file, against the walls. The graduating class, the professors, the Board—and whatever space could be spared for the underclassmen. The future pawns were always assured a space, as I knew too well. A preview of their own fate in years to come. But other underclassmen made their way to this place each year as well.

And of course, the family of the pawn was allowed inside. Most wept when their child vanished and dissolved into a portal to that other place. Most. But not all.

I wondered if I'd find Mom and Dad or the Fletchers here tonight. And what the Fletchers would think if told this year's pawn had requested that they reap the rewards of my sacrifice.

I wondered if Mr. Fletcher would know to keep quiet about my mom's lie if the Board disagreed with Headmaster Banfield and decreed that a blood tie to the pawn was necessary for a family to reap the rewards.

"The center, Miss Radcliff." Professor Harding grunted, as if tired of speaking to a child unable to grasp his lesson.

I shuffled into the center, under the bell. I'd never stood in this place with the wide room so empty. I'd never stood beneath the bell itself.

I looked up as I neared the middle of the room, at the giant clapper that would swing between the interior of the bell on the hour to herald the passage of time. I wondered how badly it would hurt my ears to be here when it happened—and if it was nearing the hour. The bell would ring to dismiss the classes soon enough.

"Begin your prayers." Professor Harding hadn't moved, but his voice seemed so distant, so quiet out there at the edge of the room, not beneath this bell.

Sighing, I dropped the textbook down to my feet. The loud *clank* of the hefty book on the wooden floor ricocheted around up into the bell. Even Professor Harding flinched across the room.

"Silence, please," he said sternly.

Clasping my hands together, I closed my eyes.

"On your knees," he added.

I knelt. The floor was hard. You'd think they'd be able to get their sacrifice a cushion at least.

There were prayers the professor had practiced with me for years, words that had passed my lips over and over and had never reached my soul. But I mouthed them now, anyway, for lack of anything else to do.

For lack of any method of changing my fate.

I had done something good—if my wishes were indeed going to be respected. I could vanish knowing that at least.

I was on my third repetition of "The Pawn's Lament," as Professor Harding so inaccurately called it, when the bell rang overhead.

I let out a yelp, covering my ears with my hands.

"Don't stop praying!" Professor Harding shouted—or at least I thought that was what he said. It was hard to hear anything over the clang of the bell above.

"I thank the other world for this chance," I said, out loud, as if that were the only way to compete with the sound ringing out above me. "I thank both the worlds for existing, for one allowing the other to feed off its grace—"

The bell grew louder and I screamed.

"Don't stop!" Professor Harding shouted. He covered his own ears, but he walked back and forth, a grimace on his face.

"I thank the—" I stared upward and my voice caught in my throat.

There was something up there in the giant bell above me.

"Why are you stopping?" Professor Harding shouted, his words just barely decipherable over the clang of the bell.

But there was something up there, visible only as the

metal clapper swung from side to side. A bird of some sort. Bright white, its wings fluttering.

"I thank both worlds for existing," I muttered again, my hands clasped in prayer, "for one allowing the other to feed off its grace."

The bird swooped down as the final clang of the clapper rang out, the reverberations shaking into my very soul.

"I thank the Sacrament!" I shouted, a quaver in my voice as the white creature sped right toward me, almost with a vengeance.

I screamed and shielded my head with my arms, crouching closer to the wooden slats below me.

A sharp pain whisked across my finger, my wrist. The flutter, flutter of soft feathers against my skin.

"Enough!"

The flutter continued, harder, a soft *clink*, *clink* and a *thud*, and then the flapping of wings faded away.

I risked a peek. The bird was gone.

Professor Harding drew as near as he dared, close to the circle beneath the bell but not quite into it.

The ring of the bell died off, the last few echoing beats of its songs fading into the now-stagnant air.

"You must take this seriously!" the professor started, his pacing quick and almost erratic. "I should think by now, you would understand the gravity of the position you are in!"

"There was a-a bird," I said softly, lowering my arms, which I'd used to cover my face.

As if this face needed protecting when I was due to vanish in just a few short hours.

"Yes, I saw it. It flew out." He gestured upward, and I craned to see the source of the beam of light above his head, but I couldn't around the vast metal of the bell. "A mere pigeon. No excuse for your poor behavior. Go again."

Letting a deep breath escape my lips, I moved to clasp my hands together, then spotted the cuts. Stripes of red around the ring on my left index finger, the bracelet on my right wrist. Small pearls of blood dotting along the path of taloned feet.

The jewelry I wore as the Sacrament's pawn. I gripped the cold metal of the necklace in my palm. Those pieces and this one. Would it have gone for the necklace next?

"I'm not hearing prayers!" Professor Harding shouted.

Sighing, I clasped my hands together, ignoring the small jolt of pain as my finger rubbed over a cut.

The bird had been white. A pigeon. A dove.

And it had gone straight for my Sacrament jewelry.

Words of prayer passed over my lips, if only to keep Professor Harding at bay. He paced along the circle, his footsteps causing creaks in the boards beneath his feet.

He was right. It was just a bird. Not so strange to think one would make its way here, though I doubted the ringing of the bell on the hour would have allowed such a small creature any peace. It could not be nested here, just lost.

Startled, when the bell had started to ring.

It had dived after me, lured by the shine of my jewelry, perhaps. Had I not heard of some types of birds drawn to shiny, pretty things? They decorated their nests with them.

My eyes wandered, to the textbook I'd left on the ground.

A corner of silver adornment on the textbook's back cover was missing.

I looked around, as if I could spot the bird with its prize watching me from nearby. But it was nowhere to be found.

Enjoy it, I thought to the bird. *I have no need for it.* I twisted the ring even as my voice echoed out in a hollow prayer. *And when I vanish tonight, perhaps you'll return to take the rest. Stop the jewelry from being some Higher-Zone citizen's prize.*

Chapter Six

I had a modicum of free time after dinner.

A dinner I'd been served alone in a classroom. A meal I'd hardly eaten.

Even knowing it would be my last, I hadn't been able to swallow it.

My head swam, screaming at me to lie down.

I trudged my feet through the detritus instead, moving forward, enjoying the burning sensation in my legs.

There was a small woods at the far end of the courtyard, a place for gentry candidates to practice hunting, the sport many of them would enjoy in the other world. The rest of us were discouraged from wandering through the trees, for fear we'd be lost.

But I belonged here. Today, I was to be the prey.

Clutching my textbook to my chest as if it might prove essential as I wandered through the woods, I trudged forward, my thoughts frozen, my mind empty.

It was only the ringing of the bell that brought me back to the moment.

I stood still, an ocean breeze from out beyond the woods rustling through the trees, kicking up the fallen plant life and dirt and my billowing skirt along with it, sending it all twirling around me. My short strands of hair whapped across my face and I hugged the book tighter, tighter, the back cover against my chest, the part with the flaw, the scratched leather binding, the missing adornment.

There was some sort of light filtering around me. Glowing, like a sea of fireflies, only there were no insects to be found. A *strange* feeling seized me. For a moment, instead of being powerless... I felt power.

And then it was gone.

A flap of wings caught my attention, and my heart immediately clenched as I remembered the bird darting down at me in the bell tower.

Above me, a flutter of white.

The dove in its nest, a glint of silver.

I cracked a smile. It didn't seem to notice me this time.

I took a step forward, but my foot snapped a twig below.

The bird took off, shrieking at me.

"I won't hurt you," I said. "Nor your babies." Everywhere around me, the rot and decay of a winter thawed surrounded spindly trees just barely budding with leaves. I wondered briefly if it would be spring soon in that other world, or if their seasons didn't line up with ours. The subject had never come up in any of my classes.

"New life," I said, wondering if the bird's offspring were still just eggs in that nest high above.

"New life," I repeated, the clang of the bell tower stirring my feet into movement. "That's enough for me. That's enough," I said quietly.

The walk through the woods and back to the courtyard was hardly as treacherous as professors had warned it might be. There was no mistaking the direction of the bell's sound, the salty tang on the air from the ocean.

I broke through the last of the trees to the courtyard, filled with people marching toward the Academy. Toward the bell tower overhead.

I froze suddenly, my resolve weakened.

"Georgiana!"

Nora's voice anchored me back to the present.

She picked up her skirts and ran across the courtyard, taking me in her arms before I even had a chance to react.

The textbook jammed into my chest and hers as she embraced me harder.

"I've been looking all over for you!" she said, pulling back. Tears dotted her eyes, clear even in the waning light of the day. "My family is here," she said, her whisper harsh. "I don't know of any other servant candidates whose families get to attend to say goodbye. They don't know why they were summoned—"

"It was me." A smile tugged on my lips as she pulled back, her hands on my shoulders, as if to get a better look at my face and discover I was just teasing her. "I—You may hear things, Nora, but I doubt the veracity of them. It's just, I seized the opportunity and I made it so your family could be rewarded for my sacrifice. Instead of mine. Well, your family and my mom."

Nora's jaw dropped. "But you-you..."

"My dad deserved nothing," I said flatly.

Her mouth went into a grim line. She'd avoided him as much as she could as a kid, but she'd seen enough. Her father hadn't liked mine, either.

"Come," she said, as it was clear the crowd had started paying attention to us—or more accurately, to me, dressed as I was and marked as the pawn for the Sacrament.

She threaded her arm through mine, and I tucked the textbook under my other arm. She didn't have her book. No one in our class needed them anymore, least of all me. I supposed I'd just held on to mine for want of *something* to hold on to.

"They let you choose my family instead?" Nora whispered, her voice cracking and the tears in her eyes covering something like a spark of hope in her expression. She was happy, if just somewhat.

That was the most I could offer her, since she would

grieve me, I was sure. Long enough to step through the portal at least, before she forgot me completely.

Since I had no doubt she'd make it to that other world.

I chewed my lip, unsure how much to tell her. "My mom... *lied*," I said quickly. That was what I believed, anyway, and it hardly mattered, considering the result. "To cast my father out and save your family instead. And I happily agreed."

"Your mother?" Nora frowned. She probably wondered at the motivation my mom, the woman who hardly left her bed, would have to save Nora's family. It wasn't a motivation to save, but a motivation to punish the man who'd made her life hell.

But I wasn't sure, even as empathetic as she was, if Nora would understand that, considering the loving support of her own family.

I squeezed her hand. "Don't question it," I said. We stopped just shy of joining the crowd entering the Academy's main building. "Your family will enjoy a Higher-Zone life after I'm gone."

She smiled, but those tears wouldn't stop shining. "Thank you," she whispered.

She didn't question any more.

The crowd parted to make space for us as we ducked inside and followed the line funneling upward, toward the bell tower. To the side, Headmaster Banfield and Professor Harding stood at a center of a line of their fellow instructors, my mom and Nora's family lined up awkwardly a few paces behind them. The headmaster nodded at me curtly, Professor Harding's expression in its perpetual frown. My mom smiled stiffly at me, and Nora's family stared blankly, confusion evident on their faces.

I smiled back.

Professor Finch wouldn't meet my eye.

We reached the top of the stairs, and a short time later, as the line grew narrower, the conversations on the tongues of fellow students louder, we passed a single chair unoccupied outside of a classroom, the last one we'd pass before the bell tower. I glanced at the book in my hand and tossed it at the chair.

It hit the armrest and clattered to the ground with a crash, silencing conversations, bringing feet to a halt, and turning all heads in my direction once more.

Nora tugged on my arm, smiling widely, disingenuously at the leering eyes all around us.

"How incredibly uncouth," said a shrill voice from behind me.

Dinah.

"Ignore her," whispered Nora.

I turned to go, to urge those in line in front of us to keep walking, refusing to look behind me at where Dinah's ill-mannered remark had come from.

My fingernails dug into my palm.

Aylmer appeared from somewhere behind me as well, slipping past in his dashing attire and grabbing the textbook off the floor, settling it smoothly on the chair and running both hands over its white plume adornment. I wondered if he noticed the piece of the embellishment missing on the back cover.

"You'd think on the last day of your life, you could go out with your head held high and an ounce of decorum."

Dinah devolved into a shrieking laughter, joined by a couple of deeper chuckles.

"Georgiana..." said Nora, but even her usual pleading had lost some of its urgency.

I broke away from her and offered Aylmer a quick glance. Our gazes caught one another's. I bowed my head and he tipped his hat to me, and I moved through the students behind me, all moving to either side of the cramped hallway to allow me room, to reach Dinah and her followers.

"A lady isn't *heard*," I told her, knowing that any misstep in the other world's social etiquette would be the quickest, surest way to wound Dinah, obsessed with becoming the lady candidate all these years. "But rather seen." I gave her a quick onceover. True, she looked gorgeous, but I didn't let that stop me from implying otherwise. "And best to be *seen* at one's best."

It wasn't impossible to miss the quick chuckle echoing out from my left—I glanced around and saw Aylmer battling a smile on his lips—but Dinah's focus was entirely directed on me.

"I don't need advice from *you*. I shall be the ultimate lady." Dinah brought a paper fan she'd been clutching up to her face and hid everything but her eyes behind it. The narrowed eyes, the stark arch of her brow, though—those gave away the rage simmering beneath. "And you shall be dead."

Even Unity gasped at that, the students around us breaking out in whispers.

Unity tugged on Dinah's elbow, much like Nora often did with me. "Don't upset her." Her whisper caught in the air and reached my ear. "She needs to be ready to open the portal—"

Dinah closed her fan abruptly and tapped Unity's knuckles over her elbow. "I know how this works. My father's on the Board."

"Then you should know this is a sacred moment in time." Aylmer stepped forward, his hands clasped behind his back, his posture without fault. "A moment that will be chronicled in our history. And you *don't* want to be the reason why it all goes wrong."

He barely moved, but just the tension in his neck muscles was enough for Dinah to avert her eyes and snatch Unity's arm. "We're going to be late." She brushed forward past me, and then Thomas and William moved after them, their backs straight, a pair of scowls on their faces. William straightened his coat and actually elbowed me—intentionally or not—as he passed.

I wondered if they had enough brain cells between them to even understand what had happened.

"Are you all right?" Nora asked, her voice just a little

louder than the resumed conversations of the students on their way to the bell tower. We stepped aside into the doorway of the open classroom.

"Yes, I..." I shook my head. "I've been wanting to tell her off for a long time. No time like the present." I offered her a flittering smile. "Actually, literally *no time* other than the present for me."

Aylmer hovered behind Nora, and our gazes met.

What was it about him that made him such a likeable Higher-Zoner?

"Miss Radcliff, if I might have a word," he said. Behind him, the long line of students and now other people—Board members, no doubt, or other Higher-Zone citizens I wouldn't recognize—continued past and toward the bell tower.

Nora looked from him to me and back, but Aylmer just offered her a stiff smile for a moment, turning his eyes back to me.

She let out a deep breath and embraced me again. This time, one of her tears dripped onto my neck.

"I love you," she said, one sister to another. And perhaps our names would go down in history as "sisters," thanks to my mom's little sweet lie.

"I love you, too," I said.

I gripped her by the shoulders and pushed her gently away. "Now enjoy your new life. Head to the new world knowing your family will want for nothing, and that what I do will keep them safe."

She wiped away a tear and curtseyed just slightly, in perfect example of a servant candidate toward a gentry candidate. Aylmer nodded at her, and she joined the crowd headed toward the bell tower, walking backward to lock eyes with me, then slipping away.

I'd see her again during the Sacrament, but we would exchange no more words. I wouldn't see her go to the other world because I would *become* the gate. Or the gate would appear where I'd stood.

No one knew exactly how the magic worked.

"You've been kind to me," I told Aylmer, no nervousness in the presence of our grade's most handsome student anymore. My nerves meant nothing now. And besides, though I'd always been fond of him, though there'd been a period a few years back when just a glimpse of him had caused my breath to catch, I hadn't thought of him romantically in ages. There would be no romance for me now—not if I couldn't find any in the time leading up to tonight.

"You have been... extraordinary." Aylmer put a hand on my upper arm and I jumped.

A gentleman never touched a lady so wantonly.

"Patient," he continued, "and clever. Far braver than I."

"But you saved that student earlier today," I pointed out. My gaze kept slipping to his hand on my arm, the touch so minimal yet so strange. We were not friends, close enough to warrant such a touch. In the other world, among the gentry, no man other than a lady's father, brothers, or cousins might dare to touch her so casually. "You confronted Dinah—"

"To save you," he said bluntly. Saving? Had I needed saving? I hadn't been the one about to tumble down an oceanside cliff. "Miss Radcliff, I wish I'd spoken earlier." He took a deep breath. "My heart, it will not be silent.

"I am in love with you."

Chapter Seven

The words "I am in love with you" felt like strange echoes in my mind, familiar but so wrong coming from those lips.

To me.

"You can't be..." I cocked my head. "A character said something similar in one of the novels published in the other world." One of the Returned had brought back a stack of popular books several years back, copies of which had joined the curriculum at Bedlam Academy. They'd all been within reach when the return portal had appeared before him, he'd said, and so he'd thought to bring them. He'd been more willing to accept his duty than Professor Finch had been, clearly.

The tension across Aylmer's brow loosened, and he dropped his hand from my arm. His body crumpled just a bit as his eyes scanned the ground. "Not in those exact words, no."

"Oh, it's just..." I swallowed. Why was I focusing on *that* and not the fact that Aylmer Linden, *the* leading gentleman candidate, had confessed his feelings for me?

Because it didn't feel real.

Those words weren't meant for me. Least of all tossed out mere moments before my demise.

"I just had to tell you. Before the Sacrament." Aylmer swallowed, tipping his hat toward me, and turned to go.

I blinked.

"Wait!" I found myself clutching an extra pocket of fabric at his elbow. Most unladylike.

He froze.

I let go of his coat sleeve.

"You can't just... tell me that... and..." Behind Aylmer, the crowd headed toward the bell tower was thinning, curious looks spared our way less and less often.

"I am sorry," he said, turning back to face me. "I just knew there was a chance I was soon to forget myself, and I didn't want to erase that part of me. Not without acknowledging it first."

My words took on a sharp tone. "You do realize I'm about to *die*, don't you?" I folded my arms over my chest. Most unladylike, indeed. But what did that matter, considering my fate?

Aylmer's eyes flicked back up to mine. "I am sorry for that. I wish things could be different. For us all."

His earnest tone, his soft, open posture... It was difficult to stay angry with this man.

"You don't even know me," I whispered.

"I know enough."

I couldn't meet his gaze anymore.

"What do you like about me?" I whispered.

He clenched his fist at his side. "You aren't afraid."

That got me to snap my gaze back up. "Then I was right. You don't know me at all."

He looked as if I'd slapped him, and I sighed. These were *my* last few moments to spend, but to be fair, it may have been the last few moments Aylmer would *be* this Aylmer at all. An end to his life as well, in a less literal sense.

"Look, I-I appreciate your feelings. And I am... fond of you. Of all the students here, other than Nora, you've shown the most compassion, the most restraint. You've acted like a true gentleman should."

Of all the reactions I'd expected my words to have, I hadn't expected him to flinch, his lips pinching. As if I'd hurt him.

I'd been complimenting him, but I supposed I'd been rejecting him, too. But he couldn't have expected otherwise, confessing moments before the Sacrament.

My gaze flicked over his shoulder. The hallway was growing empty now. If ever there was a chance to throw caution to the wind and do something wild like—like kiss him, it was now.

But I just... couldn't.

He was handsome. Pleasing to be around. But I'd never let my heart open to such a possibility. At least not in the past few years. And back when I'd harbored a secret sort of affection for him, I'd never imagined it possible he'd return those feelings.

"I know I stand out," I said. "in more ways than one. I think that's all you may have found appealing about me. If you think about it."

"You're beautiful," he said, softening.

My mouth opened up into a little "O." "You're-You're kind to say. And of course you're handsome, but—"

"I didn't expect anything," he said quietly, his hand once more on my arm. "You don't need to say anymore. I wish you well... And I hope you find peace, wherever we head next."

This time, he turned too quickly for me to follow, for my brain to catch up.

"What are you still doing here?"

Headmaster Banfield's voice caused me to turn my head.

She hovered at the end of the hallway, the other professors forming a line behind her. Beyond them, I could just make out my mom and Nora's family.

Professor Harding's countenance was harsh in the dim

light. "Make haste and proceed to the bell tower." He would brook no argument, clearly.

Even if he'd just told me to make haste and proceed to my death.

I didn't hesitate any longer. Aylmer's confession had distracted me for a short time—and perhaps, now that I thought about it, I was grateful for that—but I had settled on accepting this.

I'd go out with my head held high, knowing I'd made things better—for Nora, for her family.

I rubbed my suddenly sweaty palms down the front of my bodice. Another unladylike gesture.

But this academy had put me in this dress, had made me seem different than the rest. It couldn't expect me to obey the same rules of etiquette.

I didn't look behind me, didn't chance one more glance at my mom. Depending on where she was positioned, I might see her again before Sacrament's end.

The murmurs of voices in the echoing tower up ahead stopped suddenly—almost as one collective breath—when I stepped through the door into the bell tower.

I clasped my hands together and was about to divert my eyes to the scuffed, wooden slats of the floor below when I remembered what I'd told myself.

Head held high.

In all the years I'd been here for the Sacrament as an observer, I'd never seen the pawn walk in with their expression anything but meek and sullen. True, there'd been sacrifices long before I'd joined Bedlam Academy, but I'd never heard mention of any of them throwing all humility into the wind as their ends had approached.

My eyes flitting over the crowd as I approached the center of the circle drawn beneath the great bell, I ignored most of them to focus on the small gathering of future pawns. I tried my best to smile at them, though the curvature of my lips felt like sharp knives cutting into my cheeks. I didn't know them

58

well—we didn't take classes together and received instruction from Professor Harding one-on-one—but I did know their feelings better than any of them. *"Your time will come too soon,"* I wanted to tell them. *"It feels like I'm buying you more time, and I will—but you'll blink and you'll be here beneath this bell."*

Would it have helped if other pawns had spoken to me so in the past?

No. Every pawn was too aware of the time remaining until their Sacrament.

The last of the crowd entered the bell tower, some of the professors barring the door shut behind a distinguished crowd of Academy Board members who'd filtered in after my mom and Nora's family. I recognized them from previous Sacraments. Always the last to enter, the first to leave. No one else should disturb the process once it had begun.

"Welcome, students, friends—graduates, to this year's Sacrament." Headmaster Banfield stepped as near to the circle drawn on the floor as she dared, her voice carrying out and up to the rafters. "We appreciate our guests making it here on such short notice." She nodded at the Board members, who kept their expressions stoic. Only a few bothered to nod back in acknowledgement.

Professor Finch clutched at her robe, squeezing it as a sheen of sweat dotted her brow. It was clear to me even from this distance and the flickering torchlight at the edges of the room.

"Today is a solemn day, but a joyous one, too," said the headmaster, her gaze only flicking to me briefly at the word "solemn" as she paced around the edge of the circle, past the row of people gathered in a single-file line against the wall. She smiled as she stood in front of Dinah, and I finally looked down in order to avoid having to see the wretched academy bully anymore.

"We've prepared our graduates for this day," said the headmaster. "Let each pass through and reveal their fates."

My gaze flicked back up as the headmaster started to move. Aylmer was staring at me, his focus unbroken.

I tossed my head back and concentrated on the wall over his head.

"We wish you all well. May your path in the other world —should you get there—aid our appointed lady candidate in accomplishing her task." The headmaster stopped once more in front of the Board and clasped her hands together in prayer. "Let us begin."

Professor Harding's gaze narrowed on me as everyone else closed their eyes and put their hands together in front of them. My mom gave me one last glance, a frown tugging on her lips before she echoed everyone's posture.

I did the same, the words I'd practiced with Professor Harding for this moment lost amidst the same words coming from the crowd.

"We practice the Sacrament," we all said as one, "to join the other world with this one. May fate guide Bedlam Academy graduates to their destinies. May the other world's bountiful energies save our world from ruin. Year after year. Until the end of time."

Eyes opened, hands lowered, and mouths went silent. It was time for me to finish the prayer on my own.

"Op-Open the way," I said, my voice cracking. A glint of silver sparkled from the bracelet at my wrist to the bell up above. "Other world, accept my sacrifice. Choose your new denizens and weave them into the fabric of your reality. Destiny awaits."

A chirp distracted me from up above. A white feather fell down in front of me, my gaze flitting upward to catch sight of the bird I'd met here and in the woods before.

Professor Harding cleared his throat.

I took a deep breath. "Open the portal!" I said, just as the feather hit the ground.

Something warm burrowed out and up from inside me, and I went to scream, but I'd lost my voice. My hands went to my throat—it was impossible to breathe—but the warm,

warm force just wouldn't stop. My eyes were covered in white, blinding light.

My ring clattered to the ground, the bracelet and necklace following suit. They hadn't broken. They'd just slipped right through me. I tried to dig my nails into my palm. I couldn't feel a thing.

The last thing I saw before the warmth burst out and through every particle of me was the little bird, sitting up there on the giant bell's clapper.

Chapter Eight

I was alive.

At least, I *assumed* I was alive.

This place around me was beautiful, but so was the Bedlam Academy campus. Beauty didn't preclude a darker ugliness beneath the surface.

Would the afterlife be such a place? I'd always assumed... the Sacrament was the end. For the pawns. That nothing awaited me on the other side.

I stood, brushing off my dress. The same dress I'd always worn since becoming the pawn for my graduating year. Only it was covered in grass and thistles and little petals. It was further along in summer here—wherever "here" was. And it was morning—late morning, perhaps, judging by the position of the sun. I was shaded under an apple blossom tree full of fruit, the green leaves floating down like feathers all around me in the tepidly warm breeze.

Like feathers... The Sacrament had not been in a dream.

There was an afterlife. There had to be. I had no reason to expect my destination to be anywhere else, if not oblivion.

And this was not that.

I took a deep breath of fresh air. There wasn't the saltiness I'd come to expect from the ocean breeze at Bedlam

Academy. There wasn't an ocean anywhere in sight. A field as far as the eye could see in front of me, a forest at the horizon in one direction.

And in yet another direction, far off... There was a house. Brick and quite large—larger than anything afforded to a Lower-Zoner regardless of the size of one's family—but somehow cozy as well. Two stories, perhaps allowing for four or five bedrooms. Nothing so grandiose as houses we'd studied at the Academy, the ones belonging to the richest of the gentry in the other world, but definitely something only the gentry could afford. A gentleman without much fortune, perhaps, subsisting mostly on the reputation of a family long past its prime.

I chuckled to myself as I headed in the direction of the house. As if my lessons would come in handy here. Then again, perhaps my lessons had shaped this place?

An afterlife that was warm and cozy, elegant but not ostentatiously so. Was this what my subconscious had yearned for? A place in "that other world" that was comfortable but not too extravagant? Had I been worthy of being rewarded with such a treat?

My feet kicked up through the calf-high grass, frolicking. What would I find in the house? Other spirits?

Was this where all pawns went? Perhaps it'd been a tad self-aggrandizing to assume the afterlife would have conformed to my vision of coziness. Perhaps it was just where we all went, in our time.

I was in the middle of the field now, the house getting larger in my view. There was a garden here at the back of it. Flowers in blues and reds grew up around a small cobblestone path, bushes demarking the borders of a pathway, a gazebo and an archway covered in vines the highlight of the sight.

Yes, a remarkable vision, indeed. A home beyond what I could ever hope for. Was this to be my final resting place? Could I have been so blessed?

Was all of my life's suffering just a price to pay?

I reached the arch, stepping inside the garden. Smoke rose from the building in front of me, and the scent of something delicious lingered in the air. There was a kitchen at one end of the building, its doors and windows open, something mouthwatering being prepared inside.

My stomach growled and I froze as I took a step on the stone path.

Was I still to eat in this afterlife? True, it could be pleasurable—and the aroma of whatever was cooking promised it would be—but I had never imagined even a peaceful afterlife to be so… grounded in the other world's rules.

Little matter. If there was food cooking, there was someone cooking it. Perhaps a soul had loved cooking. Perhaps this was their idea of paradise.

I worked my way through the small garden path, my fingers grazing the soft petals of flowers on my right. I headed for the open kitchen door.

"Hello?" I called out, peering inside. A fire roared, a pot bubbling over it. Otherwise, sunlight lit the place, no candles to be found.

A figure loomed ahead, bent over. Other figures darted in and out of a side door, unclear in the shadows of the room.

I wasn't alone. I could spend my life here—happy and not alone.

My foot knocked into a crate I hadn't noticed, my knee banging up against it. I shouted out, bouncing, and cradling the injured limb.

Pain. Pain still existed here in this afterlife.

The figure bent beside the fire stood around, a dead, plucked bird of some kind dangling from one hand.

It was Nora.

"Miss Radcliff?" she asked. "Do you need something?"

She looked at me, her eyes darting to just below my face, as if she didn't know me.

"No-Nora." The name stumbled past my lips. This

couldn't be the real Honora, could it? Nora should have been in the other world, living a new life.

Or back home, having failed to pass through the portal I'd created with my death.

"Yes, Miss Radcliff?" she asked, a cheery smile on her face. She set the bird down on the table and wiped her hands on her apron. She was wearing a similar outfit to the one she'd worn at school, but the colors were more muted, the fabric faded as if it'd been washed time and time again. The white at her collar was starched and sat sharply at her collarbones.

"What-What are you doing here?" Had I conjured a copy of her to keep me comfort in my afterlife?

Would I have pushed her into the kitchen, even if she didn't mind cooking? She'd been educated in the servant class at Bedlam Academy, but I wouldn't have *wanted* her to live a life of toil and hardship.

"Where else should I be?" Nora laughed.

I looked around. I wouldn't have sent *anyone* here to my cozy, ideal afterlife. We wouldn't even need food. "But did you need me, miss?" She picked up a knife and sliced the bird's head off.

I startled.

I would *not* have incorporated slicing off bird heads in my afterlife paradise.

"Your mother was in here not ten minutes ago looking for you," Nora said, her knife continuing to chop, tugging on a wing of the fowl.

"My mother...?" It was hard to focus on her words when she was slicing the bird right in front of me.

Nora had had cooking classes without me. Was this the type of thing they'd gone over in those classes? I clutched my stomach at the remembrance of roast pheasants and potpies the servant classes had made that the Academy had served at the lunchroom.

Nora didn't notice the odd cadence of my question. She reached into a bowl of flour and sprinkled it over the wing.

"Yes. She guessed you'd wandered off again, but I told her I hadn't seen you." She pointed one shoulder toward a basket of strawberries in the corner. "There are berries if you came in here for a snack. Mary picked them this morning."

My stomach rumbled again. Yet somehow, I had no appetite. I walked over toward the berries and picked a leaf off the first one I grabbed. I didn't know a Mary. My mom was not someone I would have imagined here with me, either, despite our uneasy truce of sorts at the end.

But that hadn't been the end, had it?

My voice grew hushed as Nora hummed to herself and went back to dissecting her bird. An image of the bird atop the bell's clapper flashed before my eyes, and a pain seared across my chest as I stared at that dead fowl. "Nora, did you pass through?"

She stopped humming and looked up. "Pardon, miss?"

"What happened after I vanished?"

Her knife stopped moving. "Miss? I don't follow."

She took me in from top to bottom, as if searching for the source of the behavior she seemed to find so odd, and cocked her head. "Where did you get such a dress? And your hair!" Her jaw dropped. "You've lost it all!"

My hands flew to my head, but they came back holding the clumps of hair I'd expected. Skirting just above my shoulders, thick and dark brown.

"It's... here?" I said. Now it was my turn to furrow my brow and stare at Nora quizzically.

"Nora, is Mrs. Stone back yet from the market? I wanted to run over tonight's dinner courses..." A woman walked into the kitchen from the direction of the house.

She had dark-brown hair tucked under a white cap edged in lace, though several ringlets dangled outside of it. Her arms were thick and her figure full. The dress she wore was something belonging to the gentry, though it was also a touch faded.

She clearly wasn't my own emaciated mom, but... she looked a lot like me. Just older, with a bit more weight.

Her jaw dripped, a tinge of pink darkening her pale cheeks. "Georgiana Radcliff, *what* have you done to yourself?"

I took a step back, such was the intimidating force of this woman, whose shriek made even Nora jump.

"Pa-Pardon?" I asked as my back slammed into the basket of berries. The sweet treats went scattering across the dirty stone floor.

"Oh, dear," said Nora, scrambling to pick them up. "Wait!" I said, stopping her. "Wash your hands first."

She cocked her head, but I took the moment offered by her hesitation to bend over and start gathering the berries myself. Half were still in the basket at least.

She'd just been touching the raw bird. Our world had regressed somewhat from its pinnacle, but there were a few things we knew better than denizens of that other world. Like germs and bacteria and washing one's hands after handling raw meat.

"Georgiana, what are you doing? Let Nora handle that!" The woman *tsked* and came around the large table at the center of the kitchen, but I was almost finished. Nora retreated quietly back to preparing her bird.

"Nora, can you be sure to wash these again as well?" I asked her, ignoring this woman who continued to stare at me, her mouth agape. I was used to stares, though. "Wash your hands and then the berries."

"In fresh water?" Nora asked.

"Yes. Different water for your hands and the berries."

"If you wish, Miss Radcliff." She arched a brow and shrugged.

I shook my head, trying to reorient myself. Why was I even telling her this? Nora knew this. She wouldn't remember her training in the other world, true, but it was supposed to be ingrained deep in her mind. She was supposed to know without remembering.

She certainly knew how to prepare a bird.

But then... This couldn't have been Nora, could it? This was just... my dream of her.

"*Georgiana*! I will not be ignored!" The woman grabbed me by the arm. She gasped. "What is this? This dress? It's... so thick and... Are those little embellishments around the edges? Where could you have gotten such a thing, my child?"

That made me look at her closer. "Mo-Mother?"

"Of course I'm your mother." She rolled her eyes to the skies. "The things this one puts me through. Not like my angel of a stepdaughter. If only your father could see the disobedient child you've become—"

"I'm eighteen," I told her.

"Yes, and old enough to be married! Yet still a child." Her voice cracked and a tear formed in her eye. "And your hair! What have you done? How will you get married like that?"

"Am I... due to get married?" I asked.

"Is there something you should be telling me?" She glared at me. "Because last I knew, fortunately, you had not secured yourself a match, for I fear any marriage that might have been arranged already would be at an end should your betrothed get a look at that hair." She started fussing with my hair, holding the length of it at the back. "Perhaps we can salvage it. Pin it back." She rapped a finger across my wrist. "But cut it again at your peril, do you hear me? It needs to grow. It won't be unnoticed you won't have much hair collected at the nape of your neck." She ran her fingers over her temple. "Whatever am I to do with you? My goodness! Your father just received a letter. We have been *invited* to a very important ball this Saturday and oh—your hair will take *months* to grow! Months!"

"I don't... I don't understand." My mind latched on one word. "'Father'?"

"Your *stepfather*, you strange thing!" She placed the back of one hand across my forehead. "No fever." She tossed her hands in the air. "Off to your room. Take off that silly play dress—you look like the lady in some sort of tale of knights and quests and chivalry! Minus that hair." She *tsked* again but started shoving me toward the doorway through which she'd entered. I spared a glance over my shoulder one last time at Nora, but she was back to humming, not paying me any mind at all.

We went down a dark, narrow hallway and entered a brightly lit entrance area, complete with narrow staircase leading up.

There was a table near the door, on which sat a tray holding a few letters. Calling cards?

Sunlight streamed in from the nearby sitting room, couches surrounding an unlit fireplace. There was someone seated on one couch, facing the fireplace, a hand tugging at a needle and thread popping up into view.

"Up, up," said this woman—my "mother" in the afterlife, because perhaps I'd needed a new one—as she shoved me, two hands on my back, toward the stairs.

I slowly put one foot in front of the other, grabbing the handrail and taking in the place. It was as simple and quaint as I'd imagined—cozy and comfortable without being so expensive to seem breakable at the slightest touch.

"Up with you! My goodness, Georgiana, how you are testing me this day! Worse than any other day!" Mother let out a deep sigh.

"Mother? You found Georgiana?" A feminine voice drifted up out of the living room.

I stilled at that voice.

Stopped halfway up the stairs and turned to look down.

Out of the sitting room stepped Dinah Sinclair. Her bright-colored eyes snapped upstairs to look at me.

And she smirked.

Chapter Nine

"Dinah...?" Her name cracked on my throat.

Of all the strange details to appear in my afterlife, *she* was the strangest. I certainly never would have imagined some copy of her here, in my home, if it were up to me.

"What did you do to your hair?" The gasp that escaped her lips seemed almost playacted, her delicate hand moving dramatically over her mouth. "And what are you wearing?" She dropped her hand again, a genuine arch of her brow conveying her puzzlement.

She was puzzled?

I stepped back down the stairs. "What are you doing here?" I snapped.

Mother laid a hand over her heart. "Goodness, Georgiana. Watch your tone around your sister! You may be many things, but I never took you to be so rude!"

My foot froze on the bottom step. "'Sister'?"

Dinah exchanged a look with Mother. "Is she all right?" Dinah asked.

"Heaven help me if I know." Mother hustled over to me and started directing me back up the stairs again. "That's it. Change and to bed with you."

"She'll miss dinner," Dinah said.

"So be it," Mother said, and her forceful push did manage to make me stumble back upward. This time, she walked behind me, a moving wall keeping me from turning back around.

I let her escort me to the top of the stairs, my eyes catching Dinah's one more time as I headed down the darkened hallway on the landing. She shook her head and went back into the sitting room, out of my sight. Sunlight streamed in through open doorways, but it left the spaces between each of the four doors up here swallowed up in the dark.

"*What* has gotten into you?" Mother asked. I passed one room to keep looking around and Mother caught hold of me by the shoulders, directing me inside the first room.

"*Your* room," she said.

It was small but pleasantly decorated. Smaller, perhaps, than my dorm at the Academy. There was a four-poster bed and a sheer sort of linen hung down and was pinned off to the side of one post. White blankets covered the plush bed, which looked far more comfortable than any bed I'd ever known.

"Do you remember *anything*?" Mother shook her head and directed me to sit in front of the mirror, pushing hard on my shoulders to force me down in a bit of a rush. "Honestly, I swear you're *trying* to be noticed. In all the wrong ways, I might add. If your father were here—"

"Where's... my father?" This woman was so different from my mom, I wondered if my new father would be, too.

"If you mean your stepfather, he's out riding. But I was referring to the man who passed away when you were but two years of age."

I whipped my head around. "My father's *dead*?" She'd spoken of a stepfather, yes, but... I hadn't thought about what that might mean. Divorce didn't seem like something that would exist here. It was rarely allowed back home.

Still... Hadn't we all died to get here? At least, hadn't I? How could anyone be dead *in* an afterlife?

Mother's eyes widened. "Don't be so coarse, Georgiana! Honestly. John Sinclair is as good as your father, anyway. I married him only the next year. A widower, with a daughter of his own your very age."

"Dinah," I said softly.

"Yes, Dinah. She gets something right!" She stared up at the ceiling, as if speaking to an invisible force. God—the one of a specific form of worship—was important to those people in the other world.

In the other world.

Where the likes of Nora and Dinah were supposed to have gone. Where they would slide into lives practically created for them, lives they'd somehow always lived since birth, with no memories of the world from which any of us had come.

Any of *us*.

Here. In the other world.

Mother fussed about the room, pulling a dress more suited to the gentry out from a trunk at the end of the bed. It was a pale-blue color and it had seen better days, but it was still attractive. And suited for that other world.

"Put this on," she said, looking at me. She snatched a brush off the table—a brush covered in dark hair, as if whoever had owned it—me, somehow—had been using it for years.

She started pulling at my hair, practically yanking my entire head back. "I'll ask Mary what she can do with this. You still haven't explained to me why you cut it. What were you thinking?"

I grabbed a chunk of it. It had been allowed for me at the Academy because I'd never be coming here.

Yes, here.

Instead of dying, I'd been sent, along with the chosen graduates, to the other world.

The Sacrament had sent me to the other world—and with my memories intact.

After a period of rest, which Mother had insisted I take, I was not doomed to miss dinner. So long as I started acting like I wasn't entirely confused about my surroundings.

Mary was a maid shared between all three ladies of the house, I learned, in addition to performing her cleaning duties and whatever else she needed to do. This household wasn't quite rich enough to employ a dedicated lady's maid. I didn't see how one would do better, though. She'd done a good job of pinning my short locks back, the whole presentation resembling, at a glance, a hairstyle suitable for a young lady who was "out" in Society in this world.

"Need anything else, Miss Georgiana?" Mary asked. She smiled at me in the mirror—quite a pretty smile that lit up her sallow complexion—and tucked in a stray coil of dark hair that had snuck out from beneath her white cap.

"No, thank you, Mary." I studied her again for a moment, wondering if I could place her among Bedlam Academy's graduates, past or present, but I could not. Another person, like this "mother" of mine, native to this world.

"Dinner should be ready shortly," she reminded me before she retreated out the door, shutting it behind her.

I stared at myself in the mirror, the short strands of my hair pulling on my scalp rather tightly, but the dull discomfort served as a sort of reminder that this was real.

I wasn't in some blissful afterlife.

I was in a quaint country house with real people—including Nora and Dinah. Dinah, who had no place in any cozy retirement of mine.

I was wearing a pale-blue dress that flowed out from under the bust, a fine, white collar tucked in at the open neckline. I reached for my clavicle, where no necklace awaited. No ring on my finger, no bracelet on my wrist. The theory was that those adornments acted as a sort of conduit for the energy, which was why they clattered to the ground and were left behind when a pawn vanished.

My jewelry hadn't come here with me, so that much may have been true.

But what else had the Academy gotten wrong? Were all the pawns here, not dead? Did they all remember their past lives?

Were they here to help the graduating class's goal?

And what did that mean? I was to help... Dinah marry the viscount's son? I looked around me at the cozy room. This family was gentry, but it was hardly possessing a fortune to attract the highest level of suitor.

I sighed... But then, if it were true that other pawns had made it here, why had none of the Returned told us back home? Could it really be whoever was chosen to come back never crossed paths with the pawn? True, while here, they wouldn't *remember* they were interacting with the pawn, but once they saw the portal and their memories flooded back, wouldn't they realize they'd seen the pawn here?

My hand gripped the handle of the hairbrush on the vanity. Professor Finch had seemed so discomfited about her vision foretelling this year's goal.

What if her nervousness meant something had been wrong about her dream? What if... I was the first pawn to actually make it to the other side?

"Georgiana!" A knock at the door was followed by Mother's voice. "Come downstairs."

"I'm coming," I told her quickly.

I was here. Nora was here—and her loved ones back home were counting on this year's leading lady candidate marrying a viscount's son.

I could help Dinah accomplish that.

I stood and stared at the candle flickering on the vanity. Did I blow it out? Why hadn't I paid attention to such details in class?

...Because I'd been sure I wouldn't need them.

Better to light it again than burn down the house. I blew it out.

Stepping out into the hallway and heading down the stairs, I took in the sight of the house by soft candlelight rather than sunlight. I'd spent the rest of the afternoon in my room, "resting," but really thinking, learning what I could from Mary once she'd been sent up, searching the contents of the room for any clue of what to do. And finding nothing.

The softly lit home still stirred my heart—perhaps even more so than before. A fire roared in the sitting room, but it was to the dining room I dragged my feet.

The room was modest but still wide enough to hold a table that could seat six. It wasn't full. Mother sat at one end, speaking with a woman dressed as a servant—a woman about her own age, about the same pear-shape as her, with a ruddy complexion and hair hidden beneath a cap entirely. The servant was placing a plate full of fowl and potatoes and parsnips in front of the mistress of the household. At the other end of the table sat a man, older than Mother by perhaps a decade, his gray hair noticeably thinning, and a thin nose that almost seemed liable to slip off his cragged, rosy complexion. He smiled at me as I entered, his eyes piercingly blue, and I was taken aback by the genuine sense of welcome he conveyed to me.

"Georgiana, dear, take a seat," he said.

The cook stepped away from Mother and slipped out the door as Nora entered and put a plate piled with food in front of me.

"Don't you 'Georgiana, dear' her," Mother said. "I told you what she'd done." She *tsked*.

I was smiling at Nora, hoping to get some sort of acknowledgement from her, but she smiled only politely, her eyes never reaching mine, and retreated.

This man, whom I presumed to be my stepfather, examined me. "I can't even tell."

"Oh! Don't let her fool you. Mary has clearly done her

best, but the hair is so much shorter! What if a man expresses a desire to court her and then gets a good look at that *hair*?" She covered her mouth, her voice a tremble.

My stepfather chuckled. "Well, as he ought not to see it down until *after* the marriage, he will just have to divorce her."

Mother shrieked, so hard, the fork I was in the process of picking up slipped from my fingers. "Oh, Mr. Sinclair! Please do not even *joke* about such a thing. The scandal! Oh, the scandal."

"Calm down, dear." Mr. Sinclair stabbed at some of the roast bird on his plate. "There are only a handful of divorces each year, and I've yet to see Parliament grant one based on the wife's shorn locks." He leaned toward me and lowered his voice as Mother continued to make a grand display of her grief over my hair. "If it were an allowable excuse, I imagine half the women in this county would have cut their hair off long ago."

"I *heard* that, Mr. Sinclair, and you will not get a rise out of me!" Mother sniffed, her bottom lip trembling, as she stuck her nose in the air.

"Is Father claiming Mother ought to divorce him already?" A voice carried from the doorway. "A bit early in the evening for that, is it?"

"Oh, I tease, dear. You do know I love to tease." Mr. Sinclair winked again. "Now sit down."

Dinah shuffled inside with soft steps, taking her place across from me. She locked eyes with me, but only briefly. I detected no annoyance in her glance.

"Now that you're both here," Mr. Sinclair said, dabbing his lips with a cloth napkin, "I can share my news."

Mother's demeanor changed rapidly, her sullen sulking vanishing as she clapped her hands together, making me jump again.

"We've been invited to a ball! This Saturday!" she shouted. The cook who'd brought in Dinah's plate nearly dropped it at the sound of her squeal.

Mr. Sinclair sighed, but he was clearly biting down to hide a smirk. He leaned back in his chair and threw his hands up. "Well, you've spoiled the surprise, haven't you?"

Dinah leaned over and squeezed his hand across the corner of the table. "She already told me earlier today."

"Me-Me, too," I said, trying to keep up. Trying to believe I could play this role of a daughter who belonged here. With this strange family. I kept a wary eye on Dinah as I ate, thinking of the bird I'd seen Nora handling earlier today. Even after studying this world for so long, this life seemed so removed from me.

"Well," said my stepfather, folding his hands over his chest, "I suppose you know it all, then. The fact that the ball is to be held by the viscount, who recently acquired Wycliff Manor to be his country estate."

Dinah gasped. I swallowed hard. The viscount. The viscount... and his son.

"No, she seemed to have *forgotten* that detail," said Dinah, her lips pursed in Mother's direction, but her eyes twinkling. She was the perfect lady candidate, I realized with a start. Beautiful, friendly, witty... Not a trace of her cruel self. Not that I could see.

Losing her memories had rebirthed her as a person.

"Now, I know, Georgiana may have an advantage," said Mother, suddenly serious. "Your father being who he was, and the amount he set aside for your marriage. Five—"

"Let's not get crass, darling," said my stepfather.

"Yes, well. Despite our circumstances, Mr. Sinclair also has set aside a small amount for you both."

Five hundred, had she been about to say? That was a decent, if not unparalleled fortune to bring into a marriage, I knew. It wouldn't make me the most highly-sought-after for fortune hunters, but it was certainly worth a second look.

"What about Dinah?" I asked, panicked. *She* was the one who needed an additional boost.

Mr. Sinclair's smile dropped and he squeezed his daughter's hand. "I've done the best I can for her. For both of you." He didn't name a number.

"She should have my share," I said quickly. "She can have the money from my father too."

Dinah's arched brow reminded me sharply of herself at Bedlam Academy. "You are really strange today, you know that?"

"Don't be silly," said Mother. "Your money from your father is yours and that can't be changed." She narrowed her gaze at me. "Besides, it's clear of the two of you, it is *you* who needs the additional reason to catch a man's eye." I opened my mouth to object, to insist, then, that whatever else Mr. Sinclair may have contributed had to go to Dinah instead, but Mother continued. "Now, the grubby business of money aside, you are both gentlemen's daughters." She smiled widely. "And you have as much a right as any to secure a gentleman's hand. The richer, the better." She looked upward. "Perhaps, then, you can take care of your poor mother in her old age."

"Ah, planning to kill me off again, are you?" Mr. Sinclair said.

"*Mr.* Sinclair!" Mother shook her head. "Oh, how you tease me so! Instead of worrying about how your poor widow should get on without you—"

"I always imagined you'd secure yourself another husband," he said dryly, though he exchanged a knowing look with me, as if I were privy to this type of conversation on the regular. "As you so brilliantly secured yourself me."

"Oh, Mr. Sinclair. I will be an old woman by then. No one should be interested." She nodded at Dinah and me and turn. "Besides, I should not find the will to throw myself at suitors with two daughters unmarried. Their marriages must come first."

"You hear that, girls?" my stepfather asked. "You must thank providence that you shall not have to compete with your mother for suitors. Or the best one shall be taken."

"That is *not* what I meant!" Mother let out a scoff that was almost a sigh.

"I shall be glad of your support, Mother," Dinah said, finally picking up her fork and starting to dig into dinner. "Perhaps we can run into town and buy a new ribbon to go with my best dress?"

"Yes, we should do that tomorrow." Mother beamed. "Perhaps we'll stop by Mr. and Mrs. Dowding's while we're in town. See how she and her daughter are preparing. *Surely,* they got an invitation as well."

Dowding? Could that mean that Unity, Dinah's perpetual shadow, had made it through as well? That was her surname, even in my world.

Well, I suppose I'd expected that.

Mr. Sinclair smacked his lips. "Ah, see? She's already scoping out your competition."

"Unity isn't *competition*, Father," said Dinah succinctly. "She's Georgiana's dearest friend."

I nearly choked on the lump of potato I had in my mouth.

Chapter Ten

It was another beautiful day in this town I'd learned was called Hemlock, the only place referred to by name, other than "the city," which Mary had eventually revealed to me to be called "Londyne," and another large city nearby for rest and relaxation of spirits—at least among the gentry—called "Bathe." We'd studied the two larger cities in class, but the town I was in was new to me. There'd been too many known smaller villages for the curriculum to focus on, I supposed.

We lived about a thirty-minute walk from Hemlock proper, a collection of thatched roof-buildings amid pebbled pathways. But Mother and Dinah had been excited about the walk—ecstatic, even—as we'd made the journey across well-trod paths of worn-down grass between our home and the village. We'd passed the church, a modest collection of brick with a cross that soared into the skies and was unmiss-able even at a distance, and greeted the clergyman, a young, friendly man who'd practically run out the front door to express his well wishes for us to have a good day. There had been a few more homes along the way, but most of the path had been verdant green, a sea of trees, which in and of itself had a sort of charm to it that I'd found in my past life only by the ocean.

"Georgiana? Well? Which color?" Dinah held up two strips of ribbon, one a pale-rose color, the other yellow. Her head was tilted as if studying me and I wondered if she'd already asked me this question.

"Oh, um, the yellow." I nodded at it, my own white-gloved hand caressing a pile of lace ribbons.

Mother walked over from where she'd been examining a hat and took the yellow ribbon from Dinah. "Yes. Yes, that color brings out your eyes." She held the ribbon up beside Dinah's face and nodded. "We'll weave it into your hair and pair it with the white dress."

"Oh? The white?" said Dinah. "But I thought I might wear the green one."

"The white attracts more attention," said Mother firmly.

"Miss? Is there anything in particular you're looking for?" The shopkeeper, whom Mother knew by name, was a middle-aged woman with brown hair threaded with gray and small spectacles over her eyes.

"No, I'm fine, thank you." I gazed out the shop window and caught sight of a familiar face. Unity looked as beautiful as ever, donning a forest-green dress and a straw-colored bonnet. She was beside an older woman I didn't recognize, just as lovely, with matching dark hair pinned up beneath a hat.

"Mother? Isn't that Unity?" I asked, as if I couldn't recognize her myself.

Mother checked outside and beamed, running to the door and opening it. "Oh, Mrs. Dowding! Mrs. Dowding, we were just about to call on you! Please join us."

The shopkeeper laughed nervously, and I felt mortified at my mother's behavior. I'd never been mortified by such a silly minor aspect of a parent's behavior, but the coziness of this world had lowered my guard, it seemed.

"I'll speak to Unity outside," I said quickly, passing by Mother and heading out the door.

"Georgiana! You haven't picked out anything!" Mother chastised.

"I don't need anything," I told her over my shoulder, offering her a small smile. She spoke as if money were tight, but she tried to bedeck me with unnecessary ribbons. Besides, it was Dinah who'd need all of our family's resources. This other world should have made her an heiress with a fortune that couldn't be ignored if we were to have a high chance of success.

I nodded at Mrs. Dowding, the woman I was supposed to know well but had never met before, and stopped in front of Unity outside the shop.

"Georgiana!" She took both my hands in hers, which also donned white gloves. "It's all the town can talk about—tell me you got your invitation to the viscount's ball!"

"We did." I smiled awkwardly, the light in her dark eyes so genuinely dazzling. "Mother hopes to marry Dinah off to the viscount's son."

She hadn't said that specifically, no, but that was *my* goal, anyway. It was supposed to be the goal of any graduate from Bedlam Academy this year.

Unity's mouth fell open into an "o." "*Dinah*?" she echoed. "And why not you?" She playfully tossed her nose in the air. "Though take heed—Mother has already declared I should try for him."

I bit my lip. She was testing me, it seemed, but at the same time, I couldn't *feel* any sense of urgency from her. Subconsciously, she ought to know to aid in getting the leading lady candidate to marry the viscount's son.

Unless... How could I be sure Unity hadn't been chosen to complete the task?

"What fortune do you bring to a marriage?" I asked her suddenly.

Unity giggled, finally dropping my hands. "How *crass*, Georgiana." She spoke so seriously, I was almost certain I'd committed a great breach of etiquette. But she lowered her voice. "We both know you have the greater fortune. Your father's wishes being for you to have it, and his cousin

82

George being so generous as to allow it when he took over the entailment of your father's estate."

I hadn't known the details of my small fortune. But that made sense—only male heirs could lay claim to a man's title and property, even if related by some distance.

But that aside, that meant this world had not set Unity up for an easy way to attract the viscount's son, either. Still, I'd have to observe them both.

How was I to know which was the one who was supposed to marry him?

Weren't they supposed to at least be subconsciously acting in such a way to make it clear which lady was supposed to wind up with him?

"Walk with me," Unity said, slipping her arm through mine. "And let me astound you with this little bit of gossip."

Despite this sudden proclamation, we didn't have time for gossip the first few minutes of our walk, as there were so many villagers to greet.

"Good afternoon, Mr. Byrd." Unity nodded at one such resident, a cheerful, rosy man arranging an assembly of breads of all shapes in front of a bakery.

He tilted his head toward us both. "Afternoon, Miss Dowding. Miss Radcliff."

I smiled at him. This village was just another extension of a cozy dream. If I hadn't remembered our home world, I would have happily settled in here, I was sure of it. I wouldn't even have known to suspect anything duplicitous from Dinah.

Still, I was cautious. She may not have had her memories of that other life, but there had to be something said for one's nature.

I glanced at Unity out of the corner of my eye, wondering the same of her. She'd always been quiet, passive, even, willing to participate in cruelty by association, if not direct deed, but here she was... effervescent.

"You said you had some gossip?" I asked her.

"Shh," she said. Though her dimples on display indicated she wasn't unamused. "Wait until we have a corner to ourselves. Busybodies are always listening."

Once we'd reached the edge of town, Unity guided us to a bench with a lovely view of the path through the woods leading back to my house. I wondered where Unity lived, if we needn't call on them after our visit to town today.

Unity launched right into her story, as soon as we'd settled down. "My father just returned from Londyne, where he spent an evening at the house of Lady Fitzroy." She spoke perhaps as if I wouldn't know this woman, but I couldn't be sure. "*She* knows Lord and Lady Gillingham quite intimately."

I nodded, though I was still utterly lost.

"Well, Lady Gillingham—that is, the viscount's wife—has been planning this ball in Hemlock for some time, but Lord Gillingham wasn't even sure he wanted to move *into* the place. Even if just for the off-season."

The viscount... So this was his title. I found myself at the edge of the bench, clenching the wood beneath my palms, soaking up every word she had to say. Anything I'd need to see this year's goal through.

For whatever reason, I was alive, and here, with my memories intact. It was my duty to identify if either Dinah or Unity were the one who would have to marry this man's son.

"And his son?" I prompted. "How old is he? Is he staying with them?"

"Look at you, interested in the man. Is some of your mother rubbing off on you at last, then?" she teased.

I rolled my eyes. "Oh, please. I ask for Dinah, not myself."

Unity frowned. "If any of us in Hemlock has the chance of securing the interest of the viscount's son, it's you." I didn't interrupt her, instead chewing on the inside of my cheek. "But I doubt he'll take interest in anyone here, despite our mamas' keen expectations. Lady Fitzroy says Mr. Richard Gillingham, the viscount's son, may have found himself an heiress during a recent trip to Bathe. The engagement is as good as an announcement away."

My heart sunk. "But... But the viscount has other sons, surely?"

Unity laughed. "No. My mother was quite particular when it came to affirming that with my father. But she also said until the man's engaged, he's *not* engaged, now, isn't he? So she said I should try for him." She nudged my arm with her elbow and I was reminded with a sudden, painful jolt of Nora and I spending time together at school. "But I'd rather help you attract his attention. Like I said, you're the only one in Hemlock with a chance."

"Why do you think that?"

"Your fortune, for one."

"It's not even *that* much!"

She blinked—hard. "I wasn't aware you set your expectations so high. Your father's cousin has ensured you'll have a fortune of five thousand. Something my father has said time and again you're quite lucky he was willing to allow, your father's wishes or not."

Five... thousand? But that... That was sure to turn the heads of a few suitors. Even five hundred was certainly worth a look in this other world, if I remembered right.

And I'd misunderstood my mother entirely.

I was the most eligible lady in all of Hemlock by far.

"In *any case*," said Unity, no longer so bothered by my embarrassing proclamation that an apparent large fortune wasn't "that much," "the viscountess finally convinced her husband, and thus the short notice for the ball. It's been practically in the works for weeks. Lady Fitzroy says Lady Gillingham always gets her way. In the end." She looked around us, though there was no one nearby. "And there's a rumor that Lady Gillingham is unhappy with her son's choice of bride. She has fortune, you see, but her father is a... merchant." She lowered her voice on the last word. "Made his fortune in textiles or some sort." She nudged me again. "See? We shall see you married to the viscount's son yet."

"Unity, I'm not going to marry—" My breath caught.

No, it was impossible.

But me *being here* was impossible.

Me *being alive* was impossible.

Professor Finch's odd behavior had made me so certain something was strange about this year, but everyone had brushed aside any concerns I'd had. Earlier Sacraments, though rare, had happened before. No person who Returned could clearly visualize precisely the nature of the graduating class's goal that year. It was all not unusual.

"*I'm* supposed to marry the viscount's son," I said aloud.

Almost as soon as I'd spoken, a group of birds burst out of the boughs on the trees up ahead, a veritable flock of white doves who soared out and upward and into the deep-blue sky.

Unity raised a hand to her face, covering up her tittering giggle. "Well, what a fright you gave those poor creatures with your declaration. See? I knew you'd see it like I do. You'd be a perfect match for a viscount's son—if Lady Gillingham does indeed get her way and ends her son's engagement. You are, after all, a baron's daughter."

I nearly choked on my haste not to state, "*I am?*"

Another characteristic this world had crafted in my favor. "Of course, let's hope the viscount and his wife aren't so conceited as to look down on the fact that you're living in a title-less man's house." So a baron was the birth father I'd heard so much about. Titles—or estates—never passed on to daughters, though some daughters of the highest-ranking men had titles of their own at birth. So why not make me one of those, a "Lady Georgiana"? Why kill off my baron dad? I couldn't think of what possible advantage putting me in a comfortable, if not ostentatious life, instead might be if I were truly the leading lady candidate.

Other than I personally found it remarkably charming.

"Is there something wrong with my father's house?"

Unity and I whipped our heads behind us to find Dinah,

adjusting her bonnet atop her head. Her lips were curled into a frown, her eyes narrowed on Unity's specifically.

"Miss Sinclair!" she said, jumping in place and looking remarkably cowed. "No, of course not. My own father has no title. I would never mean—it's just that we both know Georgiana is destined to make a great match. Since she's had so few opportunities to visit the city, I just thought that with a viscount coming *here*—"

Dinah plopped down unceremoniously on the other side of me, taking up the smallest space left on the bench. "She's had *so few* opportunities because my mother and father are rightfully frugal with their money," she said, stroking the new yellow ribbon she'd woven through her bonnet that dangled beside her cheek. Her chin dipped, like she realized the hypocrisy of her words faced with the new, if small, purchase. "Georgiana's fortune is tied up exclusively in her marriage."

I chuckled nervously and pulled my bonnet off my head, if just for a moment to let Unity see. "Mother said I've ruined my chances of securing a husband." I gestured to my head.

Unity's brow furrowed as she took a closer look. "Your hair! It's shorter."

I put the bonnet back on. "I cut it. Apparently."

Nobody commented on that last word, Dinah scuffing her shoe across the stones in front of us. "She could be bareheaded and gentlemen would come flocking. Nothing matters but that fortune."

"Which is *why*..." I said, sliding one arm through Unity's and the other through Dinah's. Dinah's eyes fluttered, as if the simple gesture had startled her. "I'd much rather focus on marrying one of you off to the viscount's son. Take advantage of every opportunity and all that." I looked from one to the other, waiting for their subconscious mission to point out the audacity of my latest line of thought. I couldn't be the leading lady candidate, despite all evidence.

They would think it over and surely point out which of

the two of them had to marry the man—or risk destroying the world we'd left behind.

Dinah patted my arm and offered me a sad smile. "You're kind. Please don't say such things because you've mistaken me. You are my sister. I am happy for you." She reached over and embraced me. "A viscount's son would make the perfect husband for you. And I'll do everything in my power to help you secure him."

She pulled back.

Unity nodded. "I was just telling her, though, there's an obstacle. Mr. Gillingham—"

"Might be betrothed," said Dinah. "Yes, your mother told ours in the shop just now." She looked over her shoulder and then stared straight at me.

"I don't care. You're going to marry him, Georgiana." Her gaze didn't waver. "You have to."

Chapter Eleven

Letting out a sigh, I wandered through the house and into the kitchen. Mrs. Stone and Nora were hard at work, cooking up dinner to keep us all fed before tonight's ball at our new neighbor's, the grand Wycliff Manor, country estate of the Viscount and Viscountess Gillingham.

I'd spent the past few days in a sort of daze, trying to wrap my head around Unity's and Dinah's attitudes. I'd played the role of this world's Georgiana Radcliff as best I could, found myself sliding into this largely happy family as if they were a warm, cushioned bed. It'd be so easy to just *live* this life. Ignore matrimony. A few crushes aside, I'd never needed romance. My heart had flittered as I'd thought of Aylmer's confession for the first time in days. I wondered if he was here.

But I knew *someone* else who'd made it to this world.

Someone else whose subconscious mind would tell her exactly which person was supposed to be marrying the viscount's son to save the world back home. Even if her role as a servant could only be limited in helping achieve such an endeavor.

Though if I thought about it, what possible help could she offer Unity, as a servant in another household? Dinah was the only other candidate if Nora's placement at all mattered.

"Oh, Miss Radcliff, you startled me." Mrs. Stone had turned around and put a hand on her chest as she took me in. "I'm just about to serve tea. Surely, a lady can wait, especially with all the excitement of the ball this evening." She sent a discerning look at Nora. "Unless *somebody*'s been letting the young ladies of the household sneak in a few extra snacks?"

Nora stopped pounding the dough on the table in front of her with her knuckles. "I didn't—"

I remembered her offering me the berries.

"I'm not here for a snack," I said quickly, to end the argument. "I just wondered if... I might have a word with Nora?"

Mrs. Stone studied me curiously but nodded. "Go on, then. Just a few minutes, mind you. I'm about to serve tea."

Nora wiped her hands on her apron, following me outside to the back of the house.

"What can I do for you, Miss Radcliff?" She tugged on her ear before wiping her hand on her apron again.

It was another sunny day. The weather was quite beautiful here. Warm without being too hot—though I supposed it was late in the summer season regardless.

"I just wondered if... Well, one woman to another. I was hoping you might have some advice? On how to help Dinah secure herself a husband at this ball?"

Nora's jaw dropped. Then she blinked. "Miss? Why would you ask me that?" She laughed.

"I just thought—"

"Well, I don't know anything about a lady marrying her gentleman, I can tell you that much." She frowned. "What sort of husband did you have in mind?"

This was my chance to gauge her reaction to the precise nature of our goal as graduating class. "The viscount's son, of course. The most eligible gentleman to come to Hemlock in ages—"

"The *viscount's son*?"

A bang of a pot falling to the ground echoed out from the kitchen behind us.

Nora covered her mouth and lowered it, speaking quieter this time. "But, miss, the whole staff is certain *you're* the one, if any, to attract his attention this evening."

My hand went to my head, searching for a lock of hair to twirl before I remembered it was pinned tightly back.

"Oh, don't you worry about your hair. Mary fixed it so you can hardly tell it's all missing." She smiled broadly. "Besides, we all know you have the better odds of making an impressive match."

"But Dinah deserves the viscount's son," I reiterated. I knew nothing about the man. A week ago, in another world, I wouldn't have cared a wit for Dinah's happiness. Now I was desperate to believe there was a chance I was wrong. That *I* wasn't at the center of this.

"No," said Nora firmly, clutching her hand at her side. Then she cocked her head and loosened her hand, as if puzzled by her own behavior. Her eyes darted to the ground, her voice growing quiet. "That is... I... I'm *sure* it's you who should be with the viscount's son. Yes, I'm sure of it." She frowned. "Not that it should matter. And we should all be glad to see you both well matched, it's just..."

"Something inside you tells you I have to marry the viscount's son."

Nora's face lit up. "Yes! Why, yes, that describes it perfectly." She started humming. "I'm sure I'd be quite happy if that were to come to pass."

We stood there a moment in silence, my thoughts racing wildly. There was no reason for Nora to particularly care about whom Dinah or I married, not unless her subconscious was directing her to help reinforce the path that would save our world back home.

"Nora! The bread!" Mrs. Stone called out.

"Excuse me, miss." Nora did a little partial curtsey and stepped back inside the kitchen.

I stared out at the field in which I'd found myself when I'd first woken up in this world.

I'd felt like I'd stumbled into some sort of undeserved reward then.

Now I realized once and for all that I'd been thrust straight into another hapless fate. Lives depended on me still—and I had no choice but to walk in the path set forth for me by others.

"Now, girls, remember, smiles on those pretty faces." Mother leaned back in the carriage, gesturing at her comically wide grin on her own face. It seemed as if her lips were trying to break through her dimples.

Dinah and I exchanged a look and I suppressed a chuckle despite myself.

"Now, dear, if the three of you walk in like that, with such *dazzling* smiles, I'm afraid it wouldn't be fair to the other ladies present." Mr. Sinclair patted his wife's leg. He cut a debonair figure in his formal waistcoat, and Mother, too, looked attractive in a dress perhaps just a touch out of date, if I remembered my fashion lessons accurately. She'd tried to make it seem new with fresh ribbons woven through the lace at her collar and cuffs.

The smile fell off Mother's face and she playfully whapped her husband on the arm with the fan she kept clutched in one hand. "Mr. Sinclair, I know you are teasing me. You cannot help yourself."

"Oh, I can't, can't I?" He arched a brow at his daughter and me. "Then I simply must continue."

"Oh, *you*..." Mother flapped her fan rapidly over her face and looked out of the carriage. "If you spent *half* as much time helping me get our daughters suitably matched as you did *vexing* me!"

"Then we would find our daughters one and a half suitors for each, and I don't think Dinah or Georgiana would be fond of dancing with just a man's dress shirt or breeches." He winked.

Mother let out another exasperated gurgle and I tried to stop myself from smiling, hiding my smirk by leaning forward to look out the window.

So this was the grandest estate in Hemlock. Wycliff Manor. It grew larger as the carriage moved up the drive, a sprawling, two-story wonder far beyond anything a sketch in a textbook could do justice to. I felt as if, the closer we got, the more encompassing the estate grew, its shadowed stone almost sparkling in the moonlight.

As we came to a stop, a footman opened the door and held out a hand. I was nearest, along with Mother across from me, so I got out first and looked around.

We weren't the only ones still milling about outside or spilling out from the grand, open entryway. Unity and her parents were exiting another carriage, just as Mr. Sinclair finished getting out of ours and it began driving away.

"Georgiana!" Unity whisper-shouted, coming over toward Dinah and me, grabbing my hands. She looked elegant in a lavender dress that was something like the fashion that was the height of the season, based on some observations Mother and Dinah had made in town when passing the tailor's. "Doesn't this surpass even your wildest dreams?" She gazed up at Wycliff Manor unabashedly.

"I *know* you've been to finer parties in Londyne," said Dinah. "At larger houses, surely." She tugged on her rose-colored dress that brought out the fine gold of her hair. My stomach sunk at the fact that I was paying Dinah a compliment, even just in my own head. Even if she was so altered in character as to be unrecognizable in this world.

"No estate is as grand as this in the city." Unity pinched her lips as her eyes flicked up and down over Dinah. "There simply isn't the *room*! But I realize you wouldn't know that. Since you've traveled so rarely."

Dinah's face pinked, and she seized on the opportunity

offered as Mother called out for us to join her and Dinah's father.

"Sorry," Unity whispered, leaning toward us. "I ought to hold my tongue. There's just something about her..." She *tsked*, staring at Dinah a few yards away as Mother fussed with her stepdaughter's dress. "I can't explain. She's done nothing to deserve my contempt. And yet..."

I frowned, wondering if Unity was accessing some sense of her former life. Had she resented Dinah for her bullying behavior—even if Unity herself had always gone along with it?

"I wish you would get along better," I said, unclear, exactly, on the dynamic they'd lived in made-up memories over nearly two decades in this world that I simply could not remember. It was as if holding on to the memories of the lives we'd left behind had afforded no room for the energy of this world to give me the memories of a Georgiana Radcliff who'd always lived in this place.

"For your sake, I shall do my best."

"Girls!" Mother called out, Mrs. Dowding beside her, as Unity's and Dinah's fathers engaged in conversation. "We have to be announced!"

Unity took me by the hand, her smile just as wide as Mother's demonstrative one had been, but far more genuine, and we settled in line beside our families, joining the town's gentry—and even some unrecognizable faces from towns beyond.

The viscount really *had* brought Society to this small town of Hemlock. If I weren't here on a mission, though—if I really were just the Georgiana Radcliff of this world, I wondered what I would think of it all. My heart had warmed at my cozy country home. Did I need anything grander than that?

And this was far grander, indeed. Our line moved inside to the long entryway, ending at an open doorway flooding the hallway with light. We waited there a while longer, until at last, Unity's family was introduced first.

"Mr. and Mrs. Oliver Dowding," said a portly butler at the door to the ballroom, announcing Unity's parents. "And Miss Unity Dowding."

The room was packed with people—at least a hundred, easily. I was used to seeing crowds in the halls of Bedlam Academy, and Dinah should have been accustomed to groups of people, too, but she clutched my arm tightly, a bead of sweat at her forehead.

"There are so many people," she whispered.

This Dinah wasn't used to crowds.

"Mr. and Mrs. John Sinclair," the servant bellowed out. Mother thrust her head back and beamed, though only a handful of people were staring at us.

"The Honorable Miss Georgiana Radcliff and Miss Dinah Sinclair."

Dinah still clutched to me for dear life, but she threw on a wide smile, too. I forgot until it was almost too late, until we'd overstayed our moment in the doorway.

"Girls," Mother hissed from in front of us.

Dinah tugged on my arm and directed us to a group standing several feet away, facing the guests as they entered.

A man and a woman, perhaps in their fifties or forties, stood side by side, each dressed in colorful finery that reeked of fortune. White threaded through their honey-colored hair, the gentleman's complexion a touch tanned and the lady's almost devoid of color entirely.

It wasn't either of them who drew my attention for long, however, or even the younger man dressed in a maroon waistcoat and sharp, crisp matching breeches beside them.

It was Aylmer Linden a little ways behind the three of them.

It shouldn't have surprised me to see Aylmer in this world. Of course it shouldn't have.

But still, my heart jumped into my throat for a moment as his gaze locked on mine.

He looked finer than he had even at the Academy, in a

dark-green waistcoat and with dark hair that seemed purposely shaggy.

He stepped up beside the younger gentleman with the maroon waistcoat and leaned over to him, whispering in his ear.

As our parents greeted the viscount and viscountess—as it seemed clear they were now—Unity took a step back and spoke softly to Dinah and me. "Now *that's* a fine gentleman."

Dinah nodded. "Any idea who he might be?"

"Papa has socialized with his father at a gentleman's club in Londyne. That's Aylmer Linden. No title, but not without fortune." She left suddenly, as her mother signaled for her to join her in front of the host and hostess of the evening's gathering.

I finally had the force of mind to focus on the man with whom Aylmer had been speaking—just in time for the stranger's eyes to meet mine.

He was tall, pale, and though somewhat nondescript in face, he wasn't entirely unremarkable. He shared the honey-blond hair of the people I presumed to be his parents, and it swooped just so in front of his brow to add a dash of character to his expression that his thin lips and pinched nose might not have otherwise lent him. His light-colored eyes were perhaps the most defining feature of his visage, and they were unabashedly staring straight at me now.

I tried to look away, but that only made me look at Aylmer, who nodded approvingly, as if there were some understanding between us.

An instinctual understanding to match me with the viscount's son, if I judged things right. I almost laughed at the idea that this man had confessed to having feelings for me himself not so long ago. He wouldn't have remembered that, and there was nothing to confirm that he felt the same now, as he bowed slightly and stepped back to cede the floor to his friend.

"Thank you so much for having us in your lovely

home." Mother's voice grew louder, and it drew my attention back to the introductions going on in front of us. "These are my daughters, Miss Georgiana Radcliff and Miss Dinah Sinclair."

Lady Gillingham barely moved her head in a slight nod in our direction, Lord Gillingham focused entirely on speaking to my stepfather instead.

It was the younger man, Mr. Gillingham, who bothered to speak to us at all. "Charmed. Ladies, thank you for joining us." His smile was wide, and there was no denying a sense of roguish charm in his comportment. The man knew how to work with what he had.

He took first my hand and then Dinah's, offering a quick peck to my hand and a sly wink, followed by what could only be a lingering look at Dinah as he took her proffered hand. It was as if he were noticing her for the first time.

I frowned. Was I wrong, then, despite everything? Had Aylmer pointed the man's eyes in Dinah's direction?

That would have suited me just fine, of course, but I had to be sure.

Richard Gillingham had dropped Dinah's hand, but he was assessing her now more fully, his mouth parted. "Perhaps you'll honor me with a dance this evening?"

Dinah blinked hard and looked toward me.

Aylmer's jaw dropped slightly as he stepped back up beside the viscount's son. "The dark-haired one," he said softly, quickly, though I heard it loud and clear. He glanced my way but refused to look at me for long, turning his back to me. "She is the baron's daughter. The other has nothing."

I wondered if Dinah had heard that, but her cheeks were pink again, her gaze dropped to the floor.

Mr. Gillingham turned to me. "As I said. Please, honor me with your first dance? Miss Radcliff?"

"Oh, uh, yes," I said quickly, digging through the pouch strapped around my wrist to bring out my dance card. "I'll make a note of it."

"Dear, we have other guests to greet," said Lady

Gillingham to her son. Her voice was high-pitched but somehow quite commanding.

He nodded, then turned his smile on Dinah and me. Dinah refused to look up at him, though. "Until later."

Dinah slipped her arm through mine and practically whirled us away into the crowd, taking us away from our parents and settling us near Unity.

"What was that about?" Unity asked as we neared.

"Mr. Gillingham asked Georgiana for her first dance," said Dinah.

I chewed my lip, taking out the little writing instrument that would allow me to pencil in the viscount's son's name. It would be improper to have more than two dances with the same man, but I wondered if I should bother making myself available to other men for the other dances. I had a specific goal in mind, and I could not fail.

Aylmer's words had reaffirmed my theory. *I* had to woo this Mr. Richard Gillingham. I checked with my Bedlam Academy graduates one more time. "I rather thought he was asking Dinah at first. He seemed more interested in her than me."

"Not true!" Dinah said, almost a touch too loudly. She covered her mouth and lowered her voice. "He asked you."

Unity nodded. "Yes, yes, of course it should be you. It *would* be you." She thrust her head back. "If you'll excuse me, I asked my papa to give me a proper introduction to Mr. Linden." She dug her own dance card out of the pouch around her wrist. "I have a mind to fill my card soon, too."

I looked around, searching for more familiar faces, but there were none that held particular meaning for me amidst the crowd. There were students I'd never been close to, sure, but I thought I would have at least recognized them at a glance.

They could have been servants somewhere. Or perhaps only a small number had made it through the portal this graduating class. Anything was possible, considering I was here at all.

"Shall we let our parents make introductions for you, too?" Dinah asked me. "You can fill up your dance card entirely. I think perhaps Mr. Gillingham will be even more intrigued if he has competition." She winked. My gaze floated back to the viscount's family, still greeting guests, and already, I saw Mr. Gillingham taking excessive time to pull away from kissing another young woman's hand. I frowned.

There was no need for the man to fall in love with me, correct? Nor I him. I barely knew him, and the thought of making a romantic match settled heavily in my stomach. There had to be a reason why my lineage and fortune due upon marriage would draw his focus, even if he was not without prospect of a title or fortune himself. Aylmer had been trying to direct the man's eye to me. We'd *have to* make a match.

"Let's find you some dance partners, too," I said.

"Oh, no, I don't need to dance." Dinah took a seat at the edge of the room. "I can watch you from here."

"But Mother wouldn't like—"

"Please." Dinah offered me a flittering smile. "Don't encourage her."

I cocked my head. "You don't want to get married?"

Dinah fluffed away my comment. "Let's worry about your marriage first, all right?"

I nodded slowly. That made sense. Her focus would have been on the goal.

The goal to wed me off to... I sighed, looking at him. His gaze followed after a young lady's backside as she giggled and stepped farther into the ballroom, and his mother had to bump her elbow against him to draw his attention back to the older couple in front of him.

"I need some air," I said brusquely, walking out before Dinah could object.

I found a quiet spot just outside, an open door that led out to a lovely garden that no doubt blossomed in wild colors in the light of day. I slipped behind a rather tall hedge, just hoping for a moment to myself, and stepped backward, keeping my eye on the door. I knew from lessons that a lady ought not to be outside unaccompanied, at least not so far out of sight of the doorway and the multitude of chaperones at the ball. But my heart was thundering, and the reality of my plight was strangling me. I just needed some air.

"Watch it," said a deep, gravelly voice from behind me. My back bumped up against something hard and firm—another person.

I whipped around.

The person I'd bumped into was striking, even in the dim moonlight.

My breath caught in my throat.

Chapter Twelve

The man before me towered over me by at least a head, and he filled out his dark waistcoat quite nicely. Most noticeable were his strong, thick calves poking out in stockings from beneath his breeches.

He had dark hair and pale skin, the hair curling in thick waves around his brow and at his cheeks. A thin shadow of burgeoning facial hair clung to his chin below the carefully-coiffed sideburns, which were a bit shorter than was custom.

And I realized just then I was staring entirely too long, entirely too obviously.

He smirked, just the slightest bit. The lopsided grin drew my eye to a beauty mark just below one ear.

"I'm afraid you've caught me unprepared to deal with company." He flicked his gaze over my head, toward the open door leading back to the ball. "Where's your chaperone?"

"Oh." Yes, the impropriety of being caught alone with a gentleman in the garden. My heart clenched. Forget *impropriety*. It would be a downright scandal. "Inside. I'm afraid I must get back. You understand." I oughtn't even to be *talking* to this man without a proper introduction.

"Of course." He put a finger to his lips. "It'll be our secret."

My breath caught. The heat rising up from my toes to the very top of my scalp warred with all logical nerve centers in my brain. I needed to leave. And pray no one saw us alone together.

But I didn't want to go.

That made no sense whatsoever.

I turned on my heel and started making my escape.

"Wait," he called, and I stilled just at the end of a towering hedge.

I turned around. There was more space now between us, but the air seemed warmer somehow in the emptiness.

"I just wanted to know what drew you here." He grew unnaturally still, pasting on another charming smile. "It's not every day a lady seeks solace in a moonlit walk."

"I..." I folded my hands together, fighting against the warning to escape blaring inside me. Escape back to the ball-room, where I and all the other successful graduates plotted to marry me to a man who did nothing to stir my affection. It oughtn't have mattered. It *didn't* matter. But yet... "I just needed some air."

"A safe answer, though not an untrue one." He looked up at the bright moon in the sky. "I could say the same for me. I don't often go to gatherings of this nature." He chuckled darkly. "As you may be able to tell from my complete lack of social grace."

"I wouldn't say *complete lack*," I said, smiling despite myself. "You did warn me we shouldn't be out here alone together."

"So I did." He stepped closer, swallowing as he looked down at me. "And yet I stopped you from leaving with my inane questions."

"They're not inane," I whispered, unable to hear my own voice over the throbbing in my chest. "I just don't know if I can fully explain myself."

"Try me," he said softly. "Despite my poor showing at

such gatherings, I do admit I find human nature fascinating."

I arched a brow at him. If only it were all just a matter of human nature. I sighed. "I have a role to play."

"The young woman in search of a husband."

"More or less," I admitted, shaking my head. "Though it's hardly as simple as that."

He leaned forward, his lips slightly parted. "Now I *have* to know more."

Laughing nervously, I took a step back. I felt as if I might instinctively lean forward if I didn't. "A woman must have her secrets."

"So long as they're not scandalous ones." He grimaced and looked over my shoulder. "Perhaps it's best you—"

"Yes," I said, letting out a small sigh. Music started up from the ballroom and I jolted. How long had I been out here?

The stranger reached a hand forward, and I expected him to snatch my hand. Instead, he took hold of the dance card in my grip and opened it up.

"I see you have a gentleman waiting for you." He blinked rapidly. "Not just *any* gentleman, but the son of our host and hostess."

"Yes," I said quickly, snatching the card back from him. "So if you'll excuse me." I shoved the card back into my pouch and made a quick exit out the garden, clutching to my skirt as I took awkward steps.

I couldn't help myself, though, as I approached the door leading back inside. I stopped and glanced over my shoulder.

But he wasn't in sight. Still hiding behind the hedge.

Perhaps it was for the best.

That way, no one would see us step inside together.

But I had to admit. My heart felt like it was caving inward just a bit as I left him behind.

"Where have you been?" Dinah met me near the door leading out to the garden, though fortunately, no one else seemed aware that I had just stepped inside the house unaccompanied. "Mr. Gillingham is looking for you."

I didn't have time to apologize or make excuses. I simply allowed her to escort me to where Richard Gillingham awaited and let her take the pouch around my wrist from me so it wouldn't get in my way.

"Miss Radcliff," said Richard. Though I knew we were not so intimate for me to call him by his given name, at least in my own thoughts, I would allow myself to drop the formality around this man. I was used to referring to my classmates by their first names, even if it wasn't the convention in this world. And he was hardly any older than them. He smiled broadly, a little too falsely as he held his hand out for me to take.

"Mr. Gillingham," I said back to him, remembering perhaps a beat too late to put on a smile, too. I took his hand.

Then, as the musicians began to play, I panicked.

We'd had dance lessons at Bedlam Academy, but I'd never given them much import, considering what I'd assumed to be my fate. And then there was the fact that we only knew whatever dances the latest professor who'd returned thought to add to the repertoire. Trends evolved, surely.

In any case, I found myself tripping over my feet, lagging a step or two behind, as I looked wildly to all the women on either side of me and tried to copy their steps.

Richard arched a brow, though his clamped lips told me he found my fumbling amusing at first. I was doing a decent job of keeping up with the routine, if just a beat or two behind, but the longer the performance went on, the more I drew the attention of those around me. I could feel my brow dot with perspiration, my breath grow shallow as all the eyes around the dance floor seemed, at least in my head, to be focused on me. Every coy whisper was about me. Every lighthearted laugh.

There was a moment where the couple beside us was

apparently due to swap partners with us for just a moment, and I fumbled again. The man, a somewhat older shorter gentleman with brown hair threaded in gray, sneered as I looped around him and back to my starting position.

Richard swallowed then, his gaze darting to the stranger beside him.

"So," he said, raising his voice to be heard over the music—though likely only just by me. We'd learned at the Academy that dances were one of the rare opportunities ladies of the gentry had to converse with gentlemen without threat of causing a scandal or a chaperone hovering close enough to hear. "I see your dance tutor has been remiss?"

I blanched. The dance was beginning to repeat, the chords of the music a refrain, and despite myself, I was beginning to pick up the pattern without needing to focus so much.

"There aren't many opportunities to dance in the country," I explained to him. Since I couldn't remember this Georgiana Radcliff's life before about a week before, I couldn't be sure that was true, but everyone had certainly acted as if the ball the Gillinghams had been about to throw were the event of the century. The event I was currently the spectacle of.

Richard chuckled as our hands met again and we pushed toward one another and back. "I would have thought a baron would have employed all the finest tutors for his daughter."

Perhaps he would have. But from all accounts, this version of me would have been too young to need them before his passing.

"My *stepfather* did his best," I said. I had no idea what kinds of tutors my parents had employed. Perhaps I should have inquired. But either way, Dinah and I were too old for such things now. We'd been left to our own devices when it came to enriching our lives.

Besides, I'd had some of the finest tutors at Bedlam

Academy. I just hadn't realized I'd needed to pay better attention to them.

I was dancing far better already, hardly stumbling at all, even when we did the loop with the couple beside us again. This time, the surly man didn't scoff at me, though he didn't smile, either.

Every time I looked out at the crowd around us, I was relieved to find their eyes wandering, their backs to me. Perhaps I'd been paranoid and was just now regaining some confidence, but it did feel as if I'd recovered from my literal and figurative missteps. There was Dinah, sitting to the side. Her eyes were still on me. She winced as I stumbled once more. I looked for Unity and realized she was down at the end of the line of dancers, partnered with Aylmer. Both kept glancing my way. Unity dropped her partner's hand to gesture at her face, displaying a broad smile.

Of course. Smile. Converse. One, two, three, one, two, three, four. Match the beat, follow the steps.

The music grew louder and then it came to a stop.

The song was over already. And I'd barely spoken to the viscount's son, beyond focusing on my inability to dance.

He clacked his heels together and nodded curtly. "Miss Radcliff."

Then he was gone, retreating through the crowd and making his way to where Dinah was seated.

I'd failed to make a good impression during our first dance together.

Even aware of my fortune overshadowing Dinah's, he'd retreated to his clear preference for her over me.

If we danced again, I'd just be learning new steps and fumbling all over again.

Oh, if only I'd paid closer attention in class. Or been aware enough to realize I'd needed a refresher in the week leading up to this disaster.

What could I do? Apologize for my clumsiness on the dance floor? Swear to improve, when I knew full well the next dance would present the same issue?

Wringing my hands, I headed back to Dinah, our mother making her way there as well from a cluster of middle-aged women gathered to the side.

"I, um…" Dinah fingered the dance card dangling from her wrist.

"You're already engaged for this dance?" Richard asked her.

That would be the only excuse for a polite lady to turn down a dance with a gentleman, assuming it was the first time he'd asked that night. That, or, perhaps…

"I'm afraid I'm feeling a bit unwell." Dinah smiled flittingly as her gaze caught mine. "But my sister could certainly dance a second time with you—"

Richard turned on his heel and glared down at me. "Yes. Your sister." He sighed. Actually *sighed*.

"Girls, girls!" Mother slipped into the chair beside Dinah, putting her hand on her stepdaughter's knee. "Oh, Mr. Gillingham. Didn't you make a fine figure out there on the floor with my daughter just now." Her eyes turned sharp as they glared at me. My incompetence had not gone unnoticed. "It took her a moment to find her steps, but yes, the two of you looked quite grand, I must say."

Richard grimaced and held his arm out to me. "Shall we?"

Two dances. In a row. At the top of the evening.

We'd be sending quite a message to those around us, that our interest in one another was serious.

If I'd failed so miserably, as I'd feared, surely he wouldn't have wanted to risk such a thing.

Then again, there was the matter of my five thousand pounds. Thank the skies this world had conspired to provide me that advantage.

"Thank you. I'd be delighted." I offered a quick curtsey before taking his proffered arm.

I tried to ignore Mother's giddy, little giggle, the whispers as we approached the floor again, this time joining the line just at the last moment, at the very end of the dancers.

Swallowing, I looked down the line to find even my fellow dancers whispering. Unity was with a younger gentleman I didn't recognize, Aylmer with a lady a few couples down from them. They were the only two who looked wholly delighted to lock eyes with me, their smiles practically reaching their eyes.

The music started. Richard bowed quickly, his back stiff. I curtseyed and straightened back up to take his hand.

This was our second dance. Our last for the night if we cared at all about propriety. I couldn't mess this one up.

It started slow, and the steps even seemed familiar. Perhaps one of the dance lessons had stuck inside my mind, after all.

"So, how do you like our town of Hemlock?" I asked, eager to start the conversation off right this time.

"Rural." Richard's nose stuck up in the air as he wove around the man beside him and came back again.

I hesitated a beat too long to do the same with the woman beside me, and there was no missing the unpleasant curl of Richard's lips as I came back to him.

"You prefer the city?" I asked quickly. My chest hurt. It was hard to watch what the others were doing and focus on this conversation, especially with such an unwilling partner.

"I must say I do. There are things here I find quite beautiful..." Richard's eyes went over my head as we slowly spun, and I caught sight of what he'd been looking at: Dinah sitting on the side, her gaze demurely downward. "But the Society is a bit... lacking. Unsophisticated."

My eyes fluttered quickly. That was an insult toward not just the town, but to me in particular. I bit my tongue to stop myself from making some remark about his rumored "lower-class" heiress. It would destroy my chances with him, and besides, I had nothing against the woman in question, supposing she existed. As a Lower-Zoner, I knew too well what it was like to be considered "lesser."

"The vistas are quite stunning," I said instead, pouncing on his remark that some of the country was beautiful. I wondered if he actually thought anything but a particular lady or two was beautiful here.

"There's sport to be had," he said as we stepped toward one another in a jig. He smiled a bit devilishly as he looked over my head again. "I shall certainly find myself entertained before I head back."

"My stepfather enjoys shooting," I said, though I hadn't even really talked to him about it. It was this world; he was the gentry. More likely than not, it was among his occupations.

"Yes, shooting. And riding." Richard was playing along, but he was bored.

The music's beat picked up and I was lost again, struggling to follow the ladies' lead a beat or two behind. One, two, one, two, and smile. Smile.

Richard drew in slow, steady breaths, a vein at his forehead bulging beneath a thin layer of his wavy hair.

I stumbled again, this time nearly falling into him. Instead of stepping in to catch me, he actually stepped *back*.

"May I cut in?"

I was shocked to find I hadn't fallen flat on my face. Richard was pointedly too far to catch me.

I looked up. My hands were splayed across the broad chest of the man to whom I'd spoken in the garden.

Richard put his heels together again, his hands behind his back, and offered him a curt nod. "Sir Lawrence. Very well."

And then he was gone.

My jaw was open, my eyes locked on Richard's abrupt retreat as this man—this "Sir Lawrence"—took his place across from me.

He leaned in just slightly as the other men stepped forward toward their partners. "Follow my lead."

His voice sent shivers down my spine.

Chapter Thirteen

He'd told me to follow his lead. I did.

The dance was already half over, but with my hands locked in this man's—Sir Lawrence's—I found my steps growing far more relaxed, my faded memory of the patterns easier for me to slip into.

"There you are." He smiled broadly, and my breath caught—not an ideal reaction when I was already growing short of breath focusing on the jaunty tune. "A true gentleman leads his partner." A flash of something darker flittered over his face as he glanced to the side of the room.

The "Honourable" Richard Gillingham was speaking with a group of young gentlemen, his back to the dancers, having moved on from the disaster of our dance entirely.

My stomach roiled. I *had* to woo this man. I had never been meant to be his bride, but here I was, all signs pointing to me being the one tasked with fulfilling's this year's goal. The pawn, doomed to die, instead here, dooming the world from which she'd come.

"He's not worth that look of sadness, surely," Sir Lawrence offered as we did a little twirl around the couple beside us and came back to face one another.

"Oh? I..." I cleared my throat. "Thank you for coming to my rescue. Literally and figuratively."

"'Literally *and* figuratively'?" he echoed back at me. "My, you are a delight to converse with."

I smiled despite myself. "I think Mr. Gillingham would disagree."

"Hmm, well, Mr. Gillingham and I would disagree on a lot of topics, I'm afraid," he whispered. Our hands locked together again as we moved toward one another. "And in matters of taste."

His breath was so close, the slight heave to it bringing a hearty flush of red to his pale cheeks, that I found my legs struggling to keep me upright.

A sobering thought occurred to me. "Do you think people will assume we've been properly introduced?"

"Since we're dancing together, I would imagine so." He tilted his head toward Richard. "We'll just say our mutual friend Mr. Richard Gillingham introduced us at some point —if anyone asks."

"Your friend?" I asked. He was certainly not mine.

Sir Lawrence's lips clamped together as the music wound down. "Acquaintance," he corrected.

He took my hand in his and lifted it, stopping just short of kissing it. "Sir Lawrence Fitzroy," he said softly, so that none of the others around us would hear he was only just now giving me his full name.

The family name rung a bell. But it was the convention of calling him "Sir" that made me take a guess. "The baronet?"

He chuckled. "One and the same. But you?"

Oh, of course. I'd never given him my name. "Georgiana Radcliff," I said quickly, darting my eyes downward.

The applause died out and Sir Lawrence dropped my hand.

I looked up at the loss of contact, suddenly quite bereft, but the warm expression on his face as he studied me, his eyes roving... It made me quite forget myself.

"Miss Radcliff," he said softly. "I know a George Radcliff."

"My cousin," I said smoothly, running my hands down my dress. I was quite hot, and Sir Lawrence seemed to notice immediately, offering me his arm and guiding me toward some refreshments. "Or my father's cousin. He inherited his estate. I live with my mother and stepfather and stepsister now."

"Oh," said Sir Lawrence, his eyes growing wide. "A baron's daughter."

I reached for a glass full of something red. "Well, I was. I am. I suppose." I swallowed my embarrassment with the drink. It was quite heady and tart, making the room spin more wildly around me.

"I can see now why Mr. Gillingham was so keen to dance with you twice." Sir Lawrence's brow arched as he stared down at me.

I slammed back the rest of the drink and set it down. Sir Lawrence was shaking his head slightly, though his eyes sparkled with a sense of amusement.

I suppose I'd just been *very* unladylike.

"It wasn't enough to overcome my faults," I said sheepishly, gesturing to the cup. "My eccentricities," I explained, trying to come up with a reason why I kept fumbling.

"On the contrary." Sir Lawrence took a step closer, leaning in toward me. "I would think such a thing could only enhance those *eccentricities*."

My breath hitched and I clutched the table behind me for support.

"Georgiana!"

It was Unity's voice that compelled me to turn. Away from the table. Away from Sir Lawrence.

Toward the very displeased friend of mine currently glowering in my direction, a fan going unused resting in her palm.

Unity spent a moment glaring at the striking man

standing a few feet behind me, expanding her fan and raising an eyebrow.

By rights, it ought to have been her father or at the very least her mother making the introduction, but they were nowhere in sight. Besides, there was the fact that technically, I hadn't been properly introduced to this man myself.

"Sir Lawrence," I said, turning to the man behind me. "This is Miss Unity Dowding. Unity, Sir Lawrence Fitzroy."

The tension dropped out of Unity's body as she made a simple curtsey. "Sir Lawrence? The baronet?"

Sir Lawrence smirked, his hands behind his back as he offered her a small bow. "I would have to be, I suppose. But if you meet the Sir Lawrence who's a fishmonger, I'll be glad to have a chat with him about how we keep getting mixed up."

Unity and I exchanged a look, but I was already stifling a chuckle. The fact that he was merely joking must have been evident on my face, as Unity whapped her fan rapidly in front of her mouth and pasted a smile on her lips, letting out an obviously-forced giggle.

"*Sir Lawrence*," I said, stopping just shy of whapping him on the shoulder. I curled my fingers into my palm instead, though my intention was far too obvious. "You mustn't tease us."

I lowered my hand slowly, too aware of both their gazes following its trajectory downward.

Sir Lawrence turned away for a moment as if to collect himself, then turned back, his spine straight and his eyes on Unity. "I've heard of a Mr. Oliver Dowding."

"My father," she said, her eyes lowering demurely as she blinked rapidly. "He and my mother have been acquaintances of your mother in Londyne." She peered around the crowd, as if she could pick out the woman herself with a glance. "Is she here? I'm sure they would like to pay their respects."

"No, unfortunately not. Mother isn't as keen on traveling as she used to be."

"Oh, that's too bad." Unity clapped her fan together and showcased her dazzling, white teeth in a penetrating smile. Her dance card dangled most perceptibly from her wrist, which she thrust forward demurely. "I should be keen to hear how she's doing so I can relay the information to my parents."

"She's very fine, considering her health often troubles her." Sir Lawrence didn't seem to understand the hint to ask Unity for a dance—or if he did, he'd decided to outright ignore it.

Unless his entire evening's dances were engaged elsewhere, it was a touch rude for him to not ask Unity for at least one dance once there'd been an introduction made.

But I was hardly the arbiter of social decorum. Even eight years of classes focusing on how to act and blend in to this world had done me little good.

I wondered if it was naturally easier for my classmates because it was all subconscious for them, or if it was simply because they'd paid better attention.

To be fair, *they* had had a chance of coming here in the first place, though. I wondered if I'd ever discover why I was really here—but for now, there was one thing I had to do...

My heart sank as my eyes darted over the ballroom to find Richard huddled in a group of young men, Aylmer among them. Aylmer spoke to Richard, his eyes darting in my direction.

So his role was to infiltrate the viscount's son's social circle and constantly steer him back to me. Just as Unity was here, no doubt, to remind me that I had no business being so happy dancing with another man. And to maybe make a play for the baronet herself, considering she had no duty to aim for a specific partner.

I swallowed roughly.

"Georgiana!"

This time, it was Dinah making her way to us, her expression lit up just so.

"If you'll excuse me, ladies," Sir Lawrence said, making quick, curt bows to us both. "I'll leave you to your gossip."

I did a double-take as Sir Lawrence turned to go without hesitating for even a moment.

I didn't even have a chance to thank him once more for his rescue on the dance floor.

"Who was that?" Dinah asked as she approached. There was a strange flush to her complexion, and if I didn't know better—for I'd seen her sitting nearly all the while—I would have assumed she'd just finished dancing herself. She passed me my pouch and dance card she'd held for me and I slipped them both around my wrist again.

"Sir. Lawrence. Fitzroy." Unity spoke the words slowly, as if each successive one deserved special attention all on its own. "I believe Mother told me he's worth ten thousand a year! Ten thousand! And he has a title, albeit just that of a baronet."

I winced. I had no idea Unity was in a position to be so discerning.

"Oh!" Dinah laughed. "I should think he wouldn't care too much about finding a wife with a fortune, then. And since he's *already* baronet and not an heir waiting for his father to pass on the title, I would say he's overdue for a baronetess, wouldn't you?"

Since stepping into this world, I'd never seen the two of them getting along so swimmingly. Actually, back at Bedlam Academy, I'd hardly ever seen the two smile when it hadn't been due to the suffering of others. And even then, Unity had at least had the grace to hold back.

I glanced around, suddenly keenly aware I needed to be on the lookout for Thomas and William. But I found them nowhere, not among Richard's friends or off to the sides of the room. I let out a deep breath. Perhaps the dunces hadn't been chosen to make it to this world at all.

A few hundred feet away, the servant who'd been announcing names of guests spoke again, even though the last of the guests were supposed to have arrived by now. At least if they were adhering to any sense of decorum.

I only just caught sight of it because I'd been searching for signs of the two who would have rounded out Dinah's little group of bullies. Perhaps their absence accounted for some of her changed personality?

"Mr. Edward Smith," said the servant, his back stiff as the town's vicar stepped out, unaccompanied.

I'd seen him briefly earlier in the week, on the way into town. He'd spoken as if he'd known me practically my whole life, but that was true of just about everyone here.

He was somewhat plain in appearance, though there was something about the way he smiled even through the whispers and judging glances that brightened his entire comportment. He was tall and a touch overly thin, his evening clothes practically hanging off him. He had fine, reddish-brown hair and a ruddy, opal complexion, and his hands were rather worn.

Mother appeared out of the crowd, Mrs. Dowding alongside her leading a number of the town's women their age, all walking over to greet him. The viscount and his wife would have to be sought, I was sure. They had already done their duty waiting in the wings to greet guests; this one would owe them an apology for his late arrival.

It was a wonder he hadn't just forgone the visit at all.

I turned back to Unity and Dinah and was about to speak of other things, but Dinah was leaning around me, trying to get a better look, practically bouncing on her heels.

"He promised he would come by eight," she said, her breath hitching. "And he did! I knew he'd keep his word."

I turned around to look at where she was so eagerly staring. Then turned back to Dinah. Unity, too, studied my stepsister as if she were making a spectacle of herself.

"Excuse me," Dinah said, nodding at us both. She paused briefly in front of me, then leaned in and whispered, "You looked happier dancing with Sir Lawrence. I hope you won't forget it's Mr. Gillingham who deserves your attention."

My jaw dropped. And before I could respond, she was gone, weaving her way through the crowd to the fairly young vicar.

"Is she *still* in love with him?" Unity laughed, flapping her fan again. "Will she ever see reason?"

"Pardon?" I said, my brain processing what she'd just said.

Dinah—my "sweet" stepsister, whose very form reminded me of Bedlam Academy's snobbish tormentor at every breath—was in love with the town's clergyman?

Chapter Fourteen

I hadn't even *thought* to pick up on any clues when I'd last
seen Dinah and Mr. Smith together. The event had been
so unremarkable, my stomach still in knots over the
prospect of being the lady candidate assigned to save my
world, that I hadn't even remembered much about the brief
meeting.

Mr. Smith had been friendly. Mother and Dinah had
been happy to see him and had inquired after him. I
supposed I knew he was unmarried, as Mother had teased
him about finding a wife at the upcoming ball.

Why couldn't I remember how Dinah had reacted to
that?

"He's the third son of a gentleman from Devynshore,"
Unity said, flapping her fan again. "Assigned the living
outside of town two years past by the rector. There's definitely no money to speak of—and Dinah isn't exactly secure
in her fortune herself. I've always thought it a rather bad
idea, for her to be so *clearly* focused on him."

I stared after Dinah, her flushed appearance suddenly
given new meaning, as she looked up at the tall clergyman
with a grin that couldn't be contained. Mr. Smith looked
down at her, all smiles, but he'd been all smiles since enter-

ing. I wasn't sure I could pick up on any specific sign that he returned her affection.

She was a gentleman's daughter, so she would have been suited for him, if her parents had no objections. Which, to be fair, they might, since he offered a wife no fortune.

Perhaps he aimed for a wife who *could* bring him a fortune, but since he had so little to offer in return... He ought to be glad of the interest of any woman of the gentry, surely.

"And to be *so late* to the ball," Unity added. "I wonder why he attended at all."

I turned back to Unity. She was pacing a little now, her nose wrinkled. It was as if all of Dinah's actions at Bedlam Academy had bled into her subconscious, and *she* was channeling the judgmental behavior that belonged more appropriately to her friend.

Dinah should have been affronted at the idea of marrying a third son, a clergyman without fortune.

Then again, Dinah would have been affronted at being anything less than the chosen lady candidate.

"I, um... She doesn't talk to me about that," I said truthfully. I wondered if, in their collective false memories, Dinah and Unity had been talking about it for some time. Then again, they were hardly close companions here.

Had Dinah woken up in this world, already in love with this clergyman for two years, even if she'd appeared here only recently, when I had?

Was that fair, to take away her self-determination like that?

"No wonder," said Unity. "If I were her, I'd be ashamed of my affections, too. And yet to flaunt them so openly!"

Did Bedlam Academy *Dinah* deserve any less than the scorn of her peers?

Biting my lip, I looked over again. Mr. Smith was escorting Dinah to the dance floor, *after* she'd excused herself by citing ill health to the son of the very host of this gathering.

"Well, if Sir Lawrence could not understand my meaning, I do at least have several other dance partners waiting." Unity frowned as she looked over at me. "It's a shame you've squandered your two dances with Mr. Gillingham already." Ever so slightly, she raised her closed fan in the direction of Richard and his friends, and Aylmer, already looking our way, seemed to catch her meaning directly. "I did ask Mr. Linden if he might learn some things from Mr. Gillingham that could improve his opinion of you. Perhaps he'll tell you while he dances with you himself."

"Oh," I said, straightening. I had not expected to have to dance with Aylmer.

It shouldn't have mattered at all—it didn't, really—except I couldn't get his intense regard out of my head.

The way he'd held my arm, his eyes boring into mine, and confessed his affection for me.

Whatever magic was at work, it would have erased those feelings, I was sure. Dinah's own affections toward the clergyman were proof of that.

Unity excused herself as Aylmer grew closer, and my eyes darted around wildly, my fingers clutching the front of my dress to wipe off the sweat, trying to avoid looking at Aylmer as he neared.

That meant, however, that I managed to see Richard leading a dark-blonde young woman I didn't know by the hand toward the dance floor. And his gaze was—every single step of the way—on Dinah, his nostrils flaring.

So he'd noticed her health had "improved" in time for the late arrival, too.

"Miss Radcliff." Aylmer knocked his heels together and offered a slight bow, then held out his arm. "May I have this dance?"

"Of-Of course," I said quickly. "If you won't be embarrassed by having me as a partner." I took hold of his proffered arm.

He leaned in, his breath warm on my face.

"I won't let you make a spectacle of yourself," he said. "I

am to make you the marvel of the dance floor, so that Gillingham might regret he's used up both dances with you."

I didn't have time to protest before Aylmer practically *dragged* me to the end of the line of dancers.

I would have told him that was simply not possible.

I supposed I had whatever magic forces were at work to thank for Aylmer's unfounded confidence in my abilities.

Aylmer was true to his word, though, doing perhaps an even better job than Sir Lawrence at guiding me through the dance routine that was only vaguely familiar. Sweat glistened at my brow, and the pouch at my wrist got in the way a few times, but I wasn't the only one who still carried her dance card as she moved across the ballroom floor.

"The steps are coming back to you, I see," Aylmer said, a little out of breath as he took my hand and we moved toward one another and then a little apart. He winked.

My skin tingled at the sudden thought.

"Do you remember our lessons?" I asked him as we drew nearer again.

Remember the lessons at Bedlam Academy, I meant.

A lighthearted feeling invaded my body, and it wasn't just the little jumping jig my feet did in echo of Aylmer's dance and that of everyone around me.

I might not be alone!

Aylmer laughed. "Of course I remember my lessons. I may not be the child of a baron, but my instructors were not remiss in keeping me abreast of the latest dances."

He let go of my hand and I noticed it was time to weave around the couple beside us. The movement took us perilously close to Richard Gillingham and his new partner a few couples down the line.

I smiled at the viscount's son, but a moment too late. My heart was too weighed down by the dashed hopes. For a moment there, with Aylmer's sly wink, I'd thought he'd meant I'd remembered my dance classes. At the Academy.

Richard scowled as he saw me, pointedly looking away, and I bit my lip as I came around to Aylmer once more.

"My first impressions have been disastrous," I told Aylmer. I doubted I even needed to elaborate.

"Give him time." Aylmer looked down the row at Richard, a furrow working its way through his brow. Richard wasn't glancing our way at all, though he wasn't exactly looking much at his partner, either.

Several couples beyond them, there was Dinah, her face flush, but her eyes sparkling as she moved in perfect time with Mr. Smith, the both of them bouncing jauntily.

"I don't know if I can draw his eye like Dinah can without even intending to." I gasped for air. Even though the melody the musicians were playing was quite exciting, my heart was sinking and my steps were slowing.

The dance came to an end, and Aylmer and I bowed to one another, my leg back in a slight curtsey.

We both applauded, but Aylmer's focus was elsewhere, his eyes squarely on Dinah, who was laughing quite rapturously at something Mr. Smith had said as he leaned over toward her.

"Perhaps Miss Dowding's mother can arrange a trip to Londyne," he said. "For your sister."

I almost asked *why*, but the need to remove Dinah from town became clear soon enough. Richard immediately abandoned his partner on the dance floor and made his way straight to Dinah, practically squeezing himself in between her and Mr. Smith. No doubt once again requesting a dance.

Aylmer offered an arm and escorted me toward the side of the room, closer to the subjects of his undivided attention.

I found myself looking around, seeing unfamiliar face and familiar alike engaged in gossip with their neighbors. But I couldn't find Sir Lawrence. He hadn't been on the dance floor.

But why did I *care* where he was?

"Miss Sinclair." Richard clopped his heels together, his

arm already out toward Dinah as if expecting no resistance now that he'd just seen her dance. "Will you do me the honor of the next dance?"

"Oh, um..." Dinah's eyes darted to me as I approached, then to Mr. Smith beside her, then to the ground. "Thank you, Mr. Gillingham." She accepted his arm, keeping her touch feather-light. Aylmer frowned as the pair passed him.

"Miss Radcliff?" a cheery tenor voice asked to my left. "Shall we take to the dance floor together?"

I turned to see who had invited me to dance. It was Mr. Smith, of course. I'd almost forgotten he was there, despite everything.

Clearing my throat, I dropped Aylmer's arm and did a quick curtsey. "Of course. Thank you, sir."

Aylmer blinked and leaned closer before I was able to take Mr. Smith's offered arm. "I hope, Miss Radcliff, that you might regale us with a song this evening? Lady Gillingham has a most beautiful pianoforte set up in the adjoining room. I plan to draw my friend Gillingham there as soon as the next dance ends."

Our eyes connected and I swallowed. What fiendishness was this now? First, I'd made a fool of myself on the ballroom floor, now to do the same in the parlor?

I nodded all the same. I'd taken classes in music as well. There were many talents at which a refined woman of the gentry was supposed to be accomplished, and that included pianoforte. If only I hadn't found it all rather pointless.

We joined the line of dancers right next to Richard and Dinah. Dinah's head lifted up, a jolt of brightness dancing across her face as she and Mr. Smith exchanged a look.

Richard turned to stare at Mr. Smith from head to toe, his lip curling with greater revulsion than it had with any cold look he'd thrown my way thus far.

I stared at my partner. He wasn't unpleasing, but there did seem to be a bit to be desired in the way he held himself —slightly hunched over—and the general state of his attire.

A thread dangled noticeably from the tip of his sleeve as he held his hand out to start the dance.

This one was slower than the last, the steps lending themselves less to mistakes.

"Mr. Smith," I said, doing my best to seem amiable should any of Richard's glances direct my way. "Fine-Fine weather we're having."

"Why, yes," Mr. Smith responded. "Fine weather, indeed."

And then there was silence, woefully awkward as we completed a few more steps hand in hand. We turned toward Richard and Dinah, who faced forward, their backs to us. Dinah leaned in toward Richard and spoke softly, but whatever she had to say didn't seem to erase the scowl off of his face.

There was no hearing what they had to say, the music too loud, the conversations all blending together. I just had to trust she was doing her best to put me at an advantage with her partner. My stomach sunk at the thought.

I turned back to my partner. "I didn't expect you to come." I hadn't thought about him at all, really, but I couldn't say that. "I mean, not after we didn't see you here earlier in the evening."

"Oh, yes, that. Most unfortunate." Mr. Smith shook his head slightly, his expression serious. "Mrs. Clark, in town? She was doing poorly and I stayed longer than I meant to when I paid her a visit."

I racked my brain for a Mrs. Clark, and I didn't remember her. Still, if he was visiting an ill parishioner, that meant he was attentive in his role as curate. "How kind of you. Do you call on members of the parish often?"

"Oh, yes," he said. "It's, frankly, difficult fitting so many duties into my day."

I glanced to Dinah beside us, a small smile affixed tightly onto her face as she looked at her partner's chest rather than his face.

"If you had a wife, perhaps she'd help share the load?"

Mr. Smith laughed. "She would, indeed." He studied me up and down as the dance came to an end, a deep and prolonged gaze that ended somewhere around my lips. "I am afraid I have been rather remiss in putting myself forward to the ladies of consequence in this town."

My throat tightened, the words so at odds with the—albeit, admittedly, only newly formed—estimation I'd had of his character. Then again, he *was* a gentleman, even if one without much consequence himself. It stood to reason he'd be looking for a lady wife.

He took my hand and held it, a moment too long, applying just a touch too much pressure for my liking. "Perhaps, Miss Radcliff, you'll honor me with a second dance?" He leaned over slightly. "I should be very interested to hear your thoughts on how I should procure myself a wife."

A shiver bolted down my spine.

Dinah stepped over, Richard being pulled back by Aylmer a few feet behind her.

"Georgiana!" she said, quite out of breath. Her eyes darted to the vicar. "Mr. Smith." She held her arm as if to fan herself, the dance card dangling down from it most obviously on display.

"I, er..." A second dance? In a row—with *Mr. Smith*? I hadn't even considered such a thing. "If you'll excuse me. Mr. Linden was quite insistent I join him in the parlor."

I didn't wait to see what he said, slipping away from the ballroom and in the direction I'd seen Aylmer drag his reluctant friend.

I didn't have time for the distractions of the local vicar and his inexplicable charm in the eyes of my strange stepsister. Instead, I had to fill my brain with the musical pieces I thought I remembered how to play, leaving little room to even wonder how much more of a fool I could make of myself before the evening was over.

Chapter Fifteen

"Georgiana." Unity appeared at my side as I headed toward the parlor, slipping her arm through mine. "How was it dancing? With *Mr. Smith*?" She spoke the name as if asking how it had been dancing with a wriggling leech.

I would have thought the judgment unfair, but in those last few moments we'd had together, there'd been something unsettling in Mr. Smith's disposition.

"You know, if he's to marry *anyone* in your family, he'd want it to be you," said Unity, confirming my burgeoning beliefs. "Since all the town knows about your dowry." She wrinkled her nose and leaned closer. "Of course, you would never dare entertain such a thing."

"*No*," I said quickly. I glanced over my shoulder. Dinah had convinced him to take her to the dance floor a second time, and he didn't have wandering eyes for the moment, at least.

"Do you think he likes Dinah?" I asked Unity.

We paused in the doorway and she looked back. "Maybe. But he'd be a fool to marry her—and she'd be a fool to throw herself away on him. It's not like she has *nothing* to offer a man of better standing."

"Some men are already showing a clear regard for her," I said, turning toward the parlor. Richard was there, along with Aylmer and some other young men I didn't recognize.

But there... just a short distance away from them, skirting the outside of the group, was Sir Lawrence.

His attention was on the pianoforte, where a young woman was playing, her fingers moving rather quickly over the instrument. Her mouth moved, some sort of song escaping, but she sung so quietly, I couldn't hear her.

Almost no one was looking at her, outside of Sir Lawrence and a few older people, dressed in such finery, it only made sense they didn't dance, as I wondered how they could all even move, seated in rows behind the instrument being played.

Though it was only Sir Lawrence's abject stare that made my stomach sink so.

The song ended, and those paying attention clapped, followed by polite clapping from those who'd gathered around and spent the time gossiping rather than regarding the entertainment.

The woman—who wore glasses, a curled lock of her light-brown hair flapping across her face as she stood and turned to curtsey—grew suddenly red at Sir Lawrence's stern, fixed stare, and excused herself, disappearing into a group of women about Mother's age over in the corner.

"Who was that?" I asked Unity.

She patted my arm and dragged me farther inside, keeping her voice low. "That, my mother tells me, is a Miss Hatfield, from Devynshore." She leaned even closer. "Rumor is she was the former baronet's natural daughter."

I blinked. That meant she'd been born out of wedlock, a secret child usually shoved aside and sent to a boarding school if the father was feeling particularly generous.

"That'd make her Sir Lawrence's sister, then?" I asked, sure to keep my voice equally low as we staked a spot a short distance away from Aylmer and Richard and their friends.

"Yes. But he's taken her on as a ward. Even though he's

not more than two years older than her." Unity giggled a little. "Lady Fitzroy lauds him for his kindness. Explains she's the orphan daughter of a distant relation of her late husband's."

"I see." My eyes flitted to Miss Hatfield, who'd taken to sitting in a chair behind the front row of gray-haired people nearest the pianoforte. No one spoke to her.

That was, until Sir Lawrence exchanged a few words with the young man beside him, nodded, and headed across the room in her direction.

I watched, eager to see how their interaction might go—surely, they both knew of the rumors, whether or not they were true—but Aylmer stepped in front of me, blocking my view.

"Miss Radcliff." He gestured toward the pianoforte. "Perhaps now is the right time for you to honor us with a song."

My spine stiffened.

I'd almost forgotten about this promise of a new humiliation.

I was not allowed to stay frozen. Unity guided me to the pianoforte, a wide smile revealing her teeth. She thrust her shoulders back and seemed so proud of me as I sat down.

There were sheets of music there, and my brain scrambled to remember how to decipher it. I blinked, then it all sort of started to make sense, but then my fingers hovered over the ivory keys in an attempt to transfer the sheet music to the instrument.

Unity looked over her shoulder—and there was no avoiding noticing whom she was looking at. Richard wore a hard expression, leering down his nose at me as I sat there, stunned.

"Perhaps it's best as a duet," said Unity, quickly closing her fan and sitting down beside me, pushing her way onto the bench. Her fan on her lap, her hands hovered over the keys. "Perhaps you can sing?" she asked, a lightness forced into her voice, which was altogether too tightly pushed past her lips.

She began to play with ease, her skills in music more impressive than Dinah's in every Bedlam Academy lesson.

My back straight, I took a deep breath and sang.

The song wasn't familiar to me, but I struggled to think of one from our lessons that truly would have been. No matter. All that was in my mind at that moment was the song.

It was a sweet tune, centered on regrets about love and the hope of a happy resolution. My tongue stumbled on occasion as the melody shifted, but my lessons allowed me to follow along with the notes on the paper, and I made sure to turn the pages for Unity at the right moments. I was nearly finished when I realized I was projecting my voice louder than Miss Hatfield had before me. The room was quieter, which permitted me to hit the higher notes with more impact.

To my left, there was movement, and my breath caught as I realized Richard was moving closer, a sort of small, pensive smile on his lips, a visible swallow at his throat as he settled near the pianoforte on the side where Unity was seated.

But at least he was looking at me.

At the last second, I remembered to smile at him, tossing my shoulders back. His intense stare was completely unexpected at this point, even if it could only mean good things for me and the graduates' goal, and I suddenly became engrossed in the last of the music, changing the final page. When there were no more pages to turn, I looked away to my right, the side opposite Richard.

There was Sir Lawrence. He'd snuck up beside the pianoforte entirely unnoticed by me. He touched the edge of the instrument, firmly pulling himself closer as the song ended and my throat went raspy for the final note.

His glance darted to mine, then to the crowd gathered behind me as they broke out into enthusiastic applause.

Unity heaved just a little as she picked up the fan on her lap and leaned toward me, giggling.

"Well done," she whispered.

"Thank you for playing," I said back to her. Somehow, my singing had been enough not to bungle this entire endeavor, even though I was quite positive the most impressive lady candidate would have been able to put on a performance including both pianoforte and vocals.

Aylmer slipped in beside Richard, and I found it suddenly easier to look at the viscount's son, as the prospect of looking at Sir Lawrence made a lump form in my throat.

"Perhaps you'll gift us with another song, Miss Radcliff? Miss Dowding?" Aylmer asked. He looked at his friend. "Gillingham found it quite riveting, I must say."

Richard frowned. "The song reminded me of something, that's all. Excuse me." He nodded at Unity and me, then turned on his heel quickly, exiting the room. The smiles dropped off both Aylmer's and Unity's faces in an instant.

"But he seemed to be enjoying our performance," said Unity softly. She turned over her shoulder, watching Richard's retreating back as he blended into the crowd still in the ballroom.

"I'll go after him," Aylmer said quickly. "You keep playing."

I stood as he darted out of the room. But my feet wouldn't allow me to drag myself after him.

"Georgiana, perhaps we should play and they'll return—"

"I, um..." I'd interrupted Unity, but I suddenly had no excuse to give her. There was no point in continuing to play if the viscount's son wasn't here to hear it, and there were no more sheets of music within sight. If Unity started playing something from memory, I was afraid I wouldn't be able to sing along with it.

"Miss Radcliff." Sir Lawrence extended his arm out to me. "Perhaps Miss Dowding can continue to play on her own? I would love to introduce you to someone."

I couldn't think straight. My heart fluttered at the sight of Sir Lawrence, and I knew the entire room was sure to be looking my way.

I took his arm, suddenly grateful for the escape. My hand on his arm, even through the clothing, tingled, my heart beating faster as he escorted me to the corner of the room.

I didn't turn around to face any objection from Unity, and just as we settled in a quiet corner of the room behind the rows of chairs, she went back to playing music. Perhaps keeping the seat warm, hoping that I—and more importantly, Richard—would return.

For my part, I felt suddenly sure she'd wait in vain. I'd expended all of my energy on this night and then some—and even when I'd finally made some semblance of progress toward securing Richard's favor, it hadn't been enough.

I didn't know how much more of this I could take.

"Excuse me if my intervention was unwarranted," Sir Lawrence said softly. "But you looked a little faint."

"'Faint'?" My eyes widened. It was as if he were putting to words what I only just now realized about myself.

He laughed. "I hope you won't, if you can help it. Here, have a seat beside my ward. Miss Radcliff, Miss Arabella Hatfield," said Sir Lawrence, and I realized we were standing in front of the timid young woman who'd performed before me. "Arabella, this is Miss Georgiana Radcliff."

Finding my anchor in a night where I'd often felt adrift, just floating wherever the tide would take me as I scrambled to achieve my goal, I nodded, focusing on the woman in front of me. "A pleasure."

I took a seat beside her.

She mumbled something. Or at least I thought she did. Her mouth moved.

"Arabella, what did I say about proper introductions?" Sir Lawrence's lips were in a thin line, though even with his serious eyes, he didn't seem overwhelmingly stern.

The way Arabella jumped, though, I would have

believed he'd spoken in a thunderous tone that couldn't be ignored.

"It is a pleasure to make your acquaintance, Miss Radcliff." She straightened in her chair and looked toward me, but her eyes were more fixedly pointed at my shoe. "You sang most eloquently."

Sir Lawrence smiled and nodded.

Arabella turned back to staring at her own shoes.

"I didn't walk in until the end of your number," I said quickly as the conversation grew quiet, "but I was most impressed by your talent."

"My cousin has had me playing all evening," she said. "He tells me it is good practice."

"And so it has been," said Sir Lawrence. He chuckled, his hands behind his back. "And I would hardly say I had you at the pianoforte *all evening*, Arabella. I made a point of asking you to join me for a dance as well."

She shuddered. "And trip over my feet in front of... all those people? I could never."

Sir Lawrence studied her as she looked away, and I cleared my throat.

"You couldn't have made more of a fool of yourself than I did." I threaded my fingers together. "Nerves. But Sir Lawrence rescued me from the worst of it."

Sir Lawrence's breath hitched and he brought a fist to his mouth, suppressing a cough. "Yes, well, a better gentleman wouldn't have had a lady in such a position to be rescued. But there you are, Arabella. Testimony that I would have assured you'd not have made a fool of yourself."

Arabella hardly seemed convinced. "Yes, but then you would have sent some of your friends to dance with me."

"Well, I couldn't very well monopolize you for the entire evening. It wouldn't be fair to the other gentlemen."

Arabella scoffed. She spoke softly, but I was sure she said, "As if I were such a prize."

"It's not so bad," I assured her. "I have a friend who

could have danced with you, too. He helped me to dance most elegantly."

"A friend?" Sir Lawrence asked. His muscles grew suddenly tight. "I must have missed—"

"I don't *want* to dance," Arabella said flatly, still staring at her feet.

"Well, I'm afraid you must if I am ever to find you a husband." He broke the statement—said most firmly—with a little laughter.

Arabella mumbled something and played with the material of her dress over her legs.

"What was that?" Sir Lawrence asked, stern once more.

The young woman straightened and stared up at her guardian she'd called her "cousin." I knew that to be a broad term people of this world applied to any distant relation, though it was hardly what one would call one's brother or sister. Then again, that was just a rumor, and even if true, one unlikely to be acknowledged.

"Perhaps I shall not get married," Arabella said, her back straight.

Sir Lawrence guffawed, one time, loud and barking. His shoulders shook slightly as he looked from me to his ward and back. "It was my father's wish you be taken care of," he said.

"And I suppose you don't want an old maid on your hands." Arabella jumped up and walked out of the room, without giving either of us a chance to reply.

Something about her circumstances reminded me of when I'd been forced to be Bedlam Academy's pawn.

Only I hadn't had the strength of character to rally against my fate as this timid young woman did.

And I'd thought I'd been facing death. Did Arabella view her fate to be a gentleman's bride one day to be as grim a goal as that?

Chapter Sixteen

"Arabella!" said Sir Lawrence quickly. He turned on his heel, glanced down to me, and then looked at her retreating back.

Sighing, he took the seat his ward had vacated, pushing back the tails of his coat as he moved. "Well, I don't suppose I have to worry about that one getting into any trouble."

"No unescorted walks through the garden for her?" I asked, teasing.

"Actually, that sounds exactly like where she might be headed. So long as she doesn't run into any ruffians who foolishly take walks alone there and put a lady's reputation in question—albeit unintentionally." He exhaled again, looking across the room at the group of young men beside whom he'd stood fairly recently. "There isn't likely to be another gentleman who spurns the company of his fellow man at this gathering. I will give my ward some time to think on her actions. Heaven knows I've tried everything I could think of to encourage her to dance. Perhaps if I stop asking, she'll suddenly have a mind to do it." He grimaced.

Unity was on her second song by now, though she didn't sing along with it, as if hoping I'd return. Some of the younger gentlemen had wandered closer to the pianoforte now, staring appreciatively at the lady playing, though a number of others broke off and retreated to the ballroom.

"You, um, have a ward," I said, for lack of anything else to say. I still had no desire to retreat to the ballroom myself to search for Richard or to join Unity at the instrument. At this point, I felt I might get in the way of her own admirers. "For how long?"

"Ever since my father died. Five months now." His voice grew thick with emotion. "It was his dying wish that I take her from the finishing school to which he'd sent her and introduce her to Society." He shook his head. "On that, I have largely failed."

"That can't be true." I gestured around us. "Hemlock may be small, but she's here at the height of Society we have to offer."

"Without my mother," he said grimly. His jaw muscle twitched. "My mother has not been fond of me taking the girl on as my ward. I could use a lady's help in this endeavor, but she offers only the barest of assistance. Only what social decorum demands." He pursed his lips, and I found the serious contortion of his facial features strangely attractive. "She doesn't *approve* of the relation."

There was more evidence that Arabella was Sir Lawrence's secret half-sister. But I knew there was no way I could express such an observation, not least of which because I hardly knew the man and it was none of my business.

Let the tongues wag at such gossip. Where I came from, people were unfaithful to their spouses with unsurprising regularity. I did not believe my real mother when she'd named Nora's father as my own flesh and blood, but no one had found it utterly impossible. Nor had Mom been suddenly stricken as an outcast.

There was little my home world got right in comparison to the idyllic life offered in this place. But that didn't mean that everything this place offered was justified.

"What about a wife?" I asked—and only too late did I

realize the question was far too blunt. I rushed to explain myself, squeezing my hands together. "I only mean, you are unmarried, correct? A wife might be nearer Miss Hatfield's age and could help you instruct her—"

"Not to mention I'd be setting an example of matrimony for her." Sir Lawrence's eyes positively twinkled as he smirked at me. "The thought had crossed my mind, yes. Might there be someone you think I should consider?"

My breath caught in my throat, my skin suddenly too hot. I couldn't look away from him. I had to clutch my hands slightly together because all I wanted to do was reach over and—

No.

This wasn't why I was here. "Unity—Miss Dowding," I said quickly, looking back to the pianoforte. "She's accomplished and genteel. Any man would be lucky to have her as his bride."

I chanced a look back. Sir Lawrence's face had fallen.

"Have you danced with anyone else?" I asked him, pretending the look on his face hadn't knocked the wind out of me.

"No." Sir Lawrence sat back, putting just a bit more space between us. But it was noticeable, the air suddenly grown colder. "Between overseeing Arabella and continuously bumping into someone in need of rescue at every spare moment I found myself free of my ward, I have not yet had the pleasure."

I laughed, but it was hollow. He'd kept *rescuing* me—from the very thing I needed to face.

"Well, there's my stepsister, too, Dinah Sinclair. Though her affection might already be engaged. We're not sure..." A sudden idea struck me. Dinah clearly had Richard's attention, and there was something about Mr. Smith that I did not like, even if I wasn't of the belief that his low position in Society and lack of fortune alone should have kept the two apart. But I couldn't *be sure* of his affection for Dinah. "Perhaps you might dance with her?"

If Sir Lawrence were to court Dinah, then perhaps Richard would be more likely to give up on her than he was when she was just being courted by a country vicar.

"If the lady would like that," Sir Lawrence said curtly. "I will see if I can make time."

"And Mr. Gillingham?" I rubbed my sweaty palms against my dress. "You seemed to know him when you mentioned the son of our host and hostess, and when you took over from him for our dance. Perhaps you might put in a good word for me? I know I danced dreadfully when I had my chance with him and I—"

Sir Lawrence's eyes grew cold and he stood—so abruptly, I nearly cried out. There was a tightness in his expression as he turned and bowed at me, his heels clapped together. "I'm afraid I can't help you," was all he said on the matter. "Now if you'll excuse me. I've let my ward wander long enough."

And then, he was gone.

For the first time since arriving in this other world and realizing the life Bedlam Academy had claimed had not, in fact, been stolen from me, I felt utterly alone.

In some ways, I had been the moment I'd awoken in this place. Familiar faces kept popping up, but that was all they were. They didn't share my memories. They barely even acted like the people I'd left behind.

A pit sunk in my stomach.

I wasn't equipped to fulfill this year's goal.

I didn't *want* to fulfill this year's goal.

I'd spent this dance flaunting myself in front of the viscount's son to no avail.

If I had no memories, would I feel the bitter sting of failure? Or would I rally onward? Would I simply *want* to marry the viscount's son? Would I struggle so?

Perhaps Mr. Richard Gillingham would have been impressed by a lady candidate whose every instinct led her to him—without the weight of everything that went along with failure hanging overhead.

Had other graduates struggled? The professors who'd returned from this place... they had never seemed happy. But I'd always thought that was because they'd tasted life in this place—and had had it ripped away from them.

When they'd been sent back to our world. That depressing, strange place.

Not that I'd ever experienced much of it, outside of Bedlam Academy. There hadn't been much to do in the Lower Zone.

My chest tightened and I found myself wincing as I moved to stand. Unity glanced over her shoulder as she finished a song, and the thought of her headed my way, threading her arm through mine and dragging me back to throw myself desperately in front of Richard made the pain worse. I moved quickly out of the salon, back into the ballroom.

The music there was dizzying, the pounding footfalls of the dancers a short distance away like blows to my temple. I sought out my mother here, in this world, this friendly if fretful woman who'd slipped into the role like an actress in a pantomime. I'd played the mother once in a scene in class, where we'd pretended to be enjoying a meal from this world together so we could practice our manners. I hadn't been so talkative. I'd only been eleven, and I'd relied on the example my own mother had set.

Professor Wraxall had accused me of not wanting my classmates to succeed in their endeavors. I hadn't been trying hard enough to embody the role. Mothers in this world weren't sullen like that.

I spotted her, at the edge of the room, gathered with a group of women about her age, though all from town, including none of the guests Lady Gillingham had invited from Londyne and towns elsewhere outside of Hemlock's borders. In the room just beyond her, there were men and women at tables, in groups of four, playing card games. We'd practiced those, too, at the Academy.

"Mother?" I said, tapping on the shoulder of the woman

more a stranger to me than even my own mother. "Might we leave? I'm not feeling well."

Mother turned an ear in my direction, but her eyes were still on Mrs. Dowding in front of her. "What, dear?"

I spoke louder this time. "I asked if we might go home—"

"Nonsense!" Mother smacked her fan in my direction. "The night is still young." She snatched the dance card that stuck out of my pouch at my wrist and glanced at it. It was entirely blank after the first few entries. "You've barely been on the dance floor. Look! Your sister is there now. We can't leave."

She tucked the dance card back into my pouch and I followed her line of sight. Dinah was dancing—with Sir Lawrence. As I'd asked him to.

My stomach grew heavier at the sight.

Had he not found Arabella, then?

"Your father is busy at cards," Mother said. "Step outside and get some air. It'll refresh you."

"Might there be some way I can head home?" I insisted, fighting down the waves of nausea. Nothing felt right anymore. And I wasn't certain it was entirely due to my continued failure.

"Oh, Elizabeth, why not let her go home with Mr. and Mrs. Brown? Mr. Smith went to arrange a carriage for them. Mrs. Brown thought she could handle the evening, wanted to get out a bit, but her feet are swelling, and Mr. Brown thought it best they get home."

"Oh, nonsense. Georgiana doesn't want to head home with a couple of *old people*," said Mother. "She's in the prime of her youth! She—"

"Yes, I think if there's room in the carriage, I'll head home with them," I said quickly. "I'll see you at home, Mother."

"Georgiana—"

I ignored her and headed for the front door, weaving

behind the crowd gathered around the dance floor in hopes Dinah wouldn't notice and head over to stop me.

Or that Sir Lawrence wouldn't...

What did I care if he noticed me? He certainly wouldn't feel compelled to stop me.

I headed past a servant near the entryway to the hallway, finding the hallway itself quite deserted. The door was ahead. Mr. and Mrs. Brown would be waiting. I didn't know them that well—did I know anyone here?—but I knew they'd pass our home on the way to their place in the heart of town, and I was sure Mother and I had exchanged pleasantries with them at the market the other day. I just had to catch them before they left, and Mr. Smith...

The footmen opened the doors as I approached.

Mr. Smith. I froze in place just inside the door. Mrs. Dowding had said Mr. Smith had been arranging the Browns' carriage. And sure enough, he was there now, helping an elderly Mrs. Brown up into a small, closed conveyance.

I'd entirely forgotten the slight discomfort I'd felt around Mr. Smith had been among the many unpleasant aspects of this evening.

He hadn't noticed me yet, standing back to let Mr. Brown rather slowly help himself in after his wife.

It wasn't as if Mr. Smith would be joining them in the carriage, though. And it wasn't as if I could explain, exactly, why I didn't want to be around our village's vicar. Dinah liked him, clearly. Yet...

"Miss?" the servant holding the door to my right asked. He did his best to hide his annoyance on those thin lips of his, but even from a rather short height, he seemed to be glowering down at me, asking me to make a decision.

Mr. Smith turned around, and somehow, that made the decision for me. "Oh, thank you, just checking..." I mumbled nonsense then, purposely not finishing my sentence, turning on my heel and heading back down the hallway. The doors closed behind me, but just as I was about to return to the ballroom—the light bleeding into the darkened hallway so bright, I had to squint my eyes and put an arm over them—the doors leading outside opened again, Mr. Smith no doubt returning, and I panicked.

I ducked into a room with a door ajar just slightly, quickly slipping inside and flattening my back against the door, my breath stilling, as if Mr. Smith could find me if he heard me.

Footfalls continued down the hallway unabated, not even pausing at the open door.

I let out a deep breath and shook my head, a small laugh escaping me.

As if the entire evening weren't proof enough... I couldn't handle any of this.

"Did you hear that?"

Someone's soft voice carried out from the darkness. There were no candles lit in this room, no lantern.

"Hear what?" This voice was deeper, distinctly devoid of the anxiety that characterized the first. "The sounds of the ball?"

"No, not that. I thought I heard... laughter."

They both grew silent. I covered my mouth with my hand. I knew I wasn't supposed to be in that room.

"You fret too much," said the man after a moment. "Our time together is so limited. Would you ruin it by frightening yourself with things you've only imagined?"

"I suppose not."

"Come here. Let me hold you."

This was definitely my cue to exit. I may have been bound by the rules of this Society myself, but I didn't need the complication of catching a couple unsupervised in a compromising position.

I picked up my feet, as quietly as I dared, biting my lip as I stared at the beam of light that trickled from across the hall in that crack in the door. My silhouette would be visible if they looked my way, but I had to risk it.

The sudden burst of sobs from the woman in the room

arrested my steps. I turned despite myself, on nothing more than instinct, and blinked, my eyes adjusting to the dim moonlight flooding the room from a large window at the other end. It appeared to be an office, and the clandestinely meeting couple was standing in front of a desk. The woman faced away from me, her head buried against the man's shoulder.

I gasped.

The man was Richard Gillingham. The viscount's son. Torn away from his crowd of gentleman friends—to meet a lady unaccompanied in a room off-limits to the party guests.

This, I had to see. If this woman was to be an obstacle for me, I had to know.

A sudden determination to see my graduating class's goal through filled me, a second wind rousing me to action. Crouching, I snuck closer, hiding behind a large globe.

"There, there," Richard said, patting the woman's back. "I promised you, didn't I?"

She pulled back quickly. "You swore you loved me. You would take me to Bretna Brown if that was what it took."

I stilled. I knew that place. We'd been taught about it. It was just over the border into the neighboring country—a place where two youth could get married without their parents' permission. Scandalous, though still better than running off together with *any* other destination in mind.

"I know I said that." Richard's voice was soothing, but it still made me bristle. "But circumstances have changed."

I'd bet. He'd had this woman all along and had spent the evening staring at Dinah—and what about the rumors about a betrothed in Bathe? The one whose father was a merchant? Was that just rumor? Or was this she? Perhaps because his parents hadn't approved, they were going to elope.

I had to commit her face to memory. Leaning forward, I gripped the globe, peering around Richard's back to get a better look at the woman in question.

"I don't believe you!" she said, her voice quiet but almost hoarse. "Or you would have—"

The globe slipped from between my hands and my face fell forward, my jaw hitting the hard ball with a *thunk*.

Richard spun around at the sound, and the woman peered around him.

Arabella. Arabella Hatfield was clinging to the viscount's son.

Chapter Seventeen

"I knew we weren't alone!" Arabella gasped, covering her face, but peering at me from between two fingers. "Ruined! We're ruined!"

"Calm yourself," Richard said, gesturing for Arabella to quiet. She was being more quiet than he was, though.

Rubbing my jaw, I got to my feet. I didn't think it'd bruise or anything.

"Miss Radcliff?" Richard's mouth hung agape before pinching into a thin line. "What are you doing here? This is my father's study."

"Miss Radcliff?" Arabella squeaked. "Miss Radcliff, oh, no. Oh, no, no."

Richard glared at her, but she ignored him.

"I-I got lost," I said quickly.

"You followed me," said Richard. His brow narrowed in the moonlight. "You've had your friends direct me toward you all night, and when that didn't work, you *followed* me."

"I most certainly did not." I straightened my back. Then I scoffed. A quick thought crossed my mind about how I'd accepted my fate to *die* for my world to continue existing and yet here I was, faced with the chance to live—but with the prospect of having to marry this man to save my world instead. Which was the greater punishment?

"My *friends* were just looking out for my happiness," I said quickly, my nose in the air as I adjusted my dress. "And they led me to believe you were a man of such esteem, I should be lucky to gain your favor. But I can see your *favor* is already engaged elsewhere—"

"You were clearly hiding," Richard said.

Arabella still mumbled incoherently, beginning to pace.

"As were you two. So, I'll admit, I grew a bit curious as to what I was witnessing. But that was all." Sweetness hadn't worked with this man—and I was in no mood for it. "Miss Hatfield, does Sir Lawrence know where you—"

"You can't tell him!" Arabella was in front of me then, clutching both of my hands in hers. "Please. Swear it." Her lip trembled, her eyes glistening with tears in the moonlight.

"A friend of Fitzroy's?" Richard asked, giving the man no proper title. He *tsked*. "I should have guessed."

"I only just met him this evening. And you should *know* we became acquainted, seeing as how he took over from one of our dances." I frowned. Here I'd thought I'd made a terrible first impression. Maybe, until now, I hadn't made much of an impression at all, aside from Aylmer and Unity doing their best to direct Richard's attentions my way.

"You mustn't tell him," Arabella repeated hoarsely. "Please."

"I won't tell him." I squeezed her hands. "Is it really so frightening a prospect? Did he not just say he'd *like* you to be married?"

Behind Arabella, Richard smiled tightly, as if hiding a wince.

That was it, then. He had no intention of marrying her —and I wasn't sure if she had a fortune. She'd been poor at one point, said the rumors, but Sir Lawrence had since taken her on as his ward. Could she have been the same woman Richard was said to have engaged himself to in Bathe? But her father wasn't a merchant. She didn't have a known father, right? So was that another woman entirely?

Would this man's roving eye ever be halted? How cruel of this world to demand such an impossible feat from me. The only thing special about *me* had been the fact that I'd been chosen as a sacrifice. And even *that*, I'd managed to blunder somehow.

Arabella looked over her shoulder. "Richard won't—"

"My parents would never allow it," he said simply. "Besides, she's too young, as I've told her. We have to wait a few years." He patted her shoulder.

"My cousin will marry me off *before* then," Arabella retorted, the first bit of bitterness in her tone since she'd snapped at Sir Lawrence. "As I've told you. He doesn't think me *too young*."

Richard cleared his throat but didn't answer.

"Miss Hatfield—*Arabella*," I said, trying to assure her she could confide in me, that we were poised to be friends. "How did you even meet Mr. Gillingham?"

Richard adjusted one of his sleeves. "My father has a place in Devynshore. Miss Hatfield attended school there."

I grimaced. I could already picture success in my endeavors—a husband who could barely stay home, his eye wandering to every fresh, young face that crossed his path. I'd never allowed myself the hope of love, but... That pit sunk deeper in my stomach.

"We older girls attended a ball there," Arabella said softly.

"Hardly a 'ball.'" Richard rolled his eyes. "A very small party."

"He asked me to dance—twice." She smiled over her shoulder. "Oh, Miss Radcliff, you must forgive me. I saw you dancing with Richard earlier in the evening, and I grew terribly jealous. When my cousin wanted me to meet you, I-I'm afraid I wasn't the most charitable."

"You have nothing to apologize for," I said quickly. I couldn't possibly have guessed when I'd met her what had been going through her head. I dragged her to stand beside me, the both of us facing Richard as I patted her arm. "Your secret's safe with me." I could feel Arabella relaxing under my grip, but Richard's jaw set, and he narrowed his eyes on me.

I felt like I'd backed him into a corner—and he knew it, too.

"But wait a minute, Richard, my cousin told me when I asked that *you* were the one to introduce him to Miss Radcliff. Were you not?" She looked from me to Richard and back again, a childlike innocence decorating her face. I flinched.

Richard's tight lips curled into a smile. "Oh? When I passed Miss Radcliff off for a dance, they already seemed *quite acquainted*."

I'd been out in the garden with Sir Lawrence unchaperoned, true, but that was *hardly* the same thing as what I'd caught Richard and Arabella doing.

Richard thrust his head up. "Well, Miss Radcliff. It seems poor *Miss Hatfield*'s fate is in your hands. We've been quite chaste, I assure you, in all of our dealings." Arabella shrunk into her shoulders, her eyes batting. I wondered if that was a lie or if she was shy even about holding him chastely in the dark. "But I wonder, if I dug a little deeper, if *your* fate might be in *our* hands, too."

He had *not* just turned this around on me.

But somehow, I really felt like he had.

I turned to the tense young woman. "Arabella, I feel it best you return to your cousin. But I won't press you on the matter."

I had nothing more I could think to say to either Richard or Arabella, couldn't even bear to see them looking at me any longer, so I made a quick exit before I could hear her reply. Exhaustion overtook me. I'd half-feigned the need to leave before, but now, I was tired of these dances—both physical and mental—at the ball of Wycliff Manor.

I dreaded returning to the ballroom, to the students of

Bedlam Academy who would be pushing me toward the very man I'd fled, the one who held the threat of disgrace over my head somehow almost as expertly as I'd tried to hold the same threat over his.

I dreaded seeing Sir Lawrence, knowing what I did about his cousin, and being unable to tell him—quite sure I didn't *want* to ruin the poor girl's reputation in the first place.

I dreaded explaining myself to my mother from this world, now that I'd missed the carriage the Browns had taken back home.

Fortunately, my stepfather was exiting the card room on his way to the drawing room, where some of the ladies were gathered for the rest of the evening.

"Father," I said.

He smiled. "Are you having a good evening?" He leaned closer. "Will it soon be that your mother will stop fussing about finding you a husband and instead start fussing about planning a wedding?"

Just behind him, Lord Gillingham himself lingered, talking to Mr. Dowding and a few other older men I didn't recognize. The viscount's hard glare flickered my way, and I wondered if, despite my stepfather's efforts to stay quiet, he'd heard what he had said. It was almost as if he *knew* that I had to woo his son. And he didn't approve.

But there was no cause for the man to know. Still, I couldn't help but feel he'd prove another obstacle I'd have to overcome.

As I massaged my temple, my stomach hardened, and the horror must have been evident on my face because my stepfather's smile dropped.

"Dear, you look unwell. Should you be resting?"

"I'd really like to go home. Mother said I could go, but I missed my opportunity to join the Browns in their carriage."

"Then we'll set off ourselves." My stepfather took hold of my upper arm and I flinched on instinct. My own father's touch had never been so kind.

He frowned but dropped his grip and gently ushered me toward the door without making contact. I couldn't explain. I wasn't his stepdaughter. Not really. Whomever he'd known all these years had vanished. As I should have.

I felt the need to fill the silence. "Mother wasn't ready to go and Dinah—"

"We'll head home," my stepfather said succinctly.

And that was that.

"We left *far* too early," said Mother, an everlasting echo of herself before, during, and now after the carriage ride back.

We all lingered in the hall, removing shawls and gloves and, as far as the ladies went, setting down the little bags we'd carried with us throughout the evening's festivities. My dance card slipped out of mine as I placed it on the table, and it wasn't the sight of Mr. Richard Gillingham's name twice that caused the sharp pain at the back of my throat as the pressure behind my eyes seemed to mount. It was Sir Lawrence's, which I'd scribbled in afterward rather than before, as a record of sorts of the evening's activities.

Of all the impediments to me achieving this year's goal in this other world, it was the baronet who kept rising to the surface of my mind.

His cousin's secret—and Richard's threat to expose my accidental, improper meeting with the baronet, as if the two even compared.

His charming smile as he'd rescued me from embarrassment on the dance floor.

The way he'd watched me as I'd sung at the pianoforte, as if he were actually witnessing something *spectacular*.

He'd been there everywhere the viscount's son should have been, if I were steadfastly focused on my role here instead of... instead of... the baronet.

"Georgiana? Are you even listening to me?" Mother asked.

I shook my head softly.

Mother scoffed. "Why am I even surprised? Off to bed with you. I need to draft a letter to our gracious hosts, excusing our early exit—"

"There were so many people there, I'd hardly think anyone would notice," said my stepfather.

Mother let out a gasp. "But that would be even *worse*, don't you see? Now, *really*, dear, do you have *any* idea of the *difficulty* of what I have to accomplish? Two daughters of marriageable age, and a lack of suitors in the area on any other occasion."

Dinah slipped by, her lips in a tight line, though it seemed she was trying not to smile.

"What would you have me do?" Mother said, clearly about to jest. "Have me marry one of them off to the impoverished town vicar?"

Dinah stiffened as her hand reached the bannister.

"No, I think even Old Widow Clark could do better than Mr. Smith," Father said, heading into the drawing room. "Ah, Mrs. Stone. Yes, we're back early. No need for fuss."

I didn't hear the rest of his instructions to the housekeeper, though. Dinah's breath hitched and she bolted up the stairs, and no one seemed to notice but me.

"Dinah?"

I knocked on her bedroom door. Our parents' voices carried from downstairs, but neither seemed about to head up here, even if they were both still dressed for a party.

I looked down at my own dress. The bright design had made me feel a bit cheery, hopeful, earlier this evening. Now nothing was as it needed to be and I didn't know the way forward.

My only help was a number of people with no memories of why they'd even want to be of assistance.

The door opened a crack and Dinah peeked out. Her eyes were watery, but she didn't seem about to spill her tears yet.

I'd never seen tears on that face. At the Academy, she'd always seemed above such things. As if she'd viewed it as weakness.

Sighing, she stepped back and gestured for me to come in, closing the door behind me. A single candle lit up the dark room, resting on the table beside her bed.

"You noticed." Dinah squeezed my hand and directed me to sit beside her on the bed. She'd let her hair down, and it tumbled over one shoulder in golden waves. "It's hopeless, Georgiana. Father will never accept Mr. Smith and me."

I blinked. So I *knew* about this intended courtship? Or the Georgiana who'd lived here before me had, I supposed.

Still. I couldn't be sure how much she knew—or even how much there was to tell. And I wasn't sure what would happen if I started acting suspiciously, particularly to those who'd come with me from Bedlam Academy. Perhaps it might jog their memory, though...

I cleared my throat. I didn't need to resort to acting strangely just yet. I knew the fact that I had never been the star pupil at the Academy meant I was surely slipping up here and there in ways I didn't even realize. No need to compound matters.

"Are you sure this is what *you* want?" I asked her. "Mr. Smith didn't seem to show you particular favor at the ball—"

"Of course he didn't." Dinah dropped my hand and pulled back, her face hardening as if I'd slapped her. *There* was the Dinah I was more familiar with. "No one can suspect. Not until I secure my father's approval, and you know they won't—" She swallowed, her face going softer. "Besides, Edward won't dare ask for it yet."

No one could suspect... Did that mean there was an *understanding* between the two of them?

"But he has no fortune," I said. "The vicarage is even smaller than this house." I almost laughed as the words left my lips. This house was comfortable beyond anything I'd ever lived in—even if it paled in comparison to the viscount's manor.

"Why do you think I'd *care* about that?" Dinah huffed and crossed her arms tightly over her chest. I couldn't tell her she'd been very proud of her Higher-Zone status in the other world we'd lived in. I wouldn't know how to even begin. "Have you forgotten your promise?"

"My... promise?" When my words caused a furrow in Dinah's brow, I realized there was no way her stepsister would forget such a thing. Not unless she'd been replaced by a different person entirely. "I don't know if I can keep it," I said, wincing as a I spoke. I had no idea whether I could or not, but I figured claiming I couldn't might get the promise repeated.

"But you have to!" Dinah jumped to her feet, wringing her hands. "You know Edward can't marry me without that! You *have to*! You promised!"

I blinked, trying to think what she could mean, despite the multitude of things weighing me down after today. Mr. Smith had been a little too familiar with me tonight in my opinion, even if we'd clearly known each other a long while. I'd suspected he'd have preferred to marry me over Dinah if he'd had the chance—though I knew he'd be reaching high above his station to presume he could. But I figured it was the matter of my dowry more than anything.

"Money," I said simply, more to myself than to her. "He won't marry you without more money."

"We've been over this," Dinah said, sitting beside me on the bed so quickly, the mattress bounced beneath us. "It's not that he's greedy, but he *has* to have money. His family could not provide much for their third son, and his position offers so little..."

"And your dowry won't suffice?" It wasn't as if she had *no dowry* to her name.

"I knew it. I knew you'd turn cruel." Sulking, Dinah threw herself back against the bed. "You promised you'd marry rich, and then your husband wouldn't even *need* your dowry and you'd have money to spare to add to mine, but of course, you have to dither and take your time. And now you tell me you don't think you even *can*."

"But when I offered to give my dowry to you, you didn't seem interested."

She shook her head. "What a preposterous solution. You can't even *access* that money until you're wed. And the richer the man, the less likely he is to need your wealth."

"Is that why you want me to marry Mr. Gillingham?" I asked. Was that the rationale she'd given herself in this world, where memories of Bedlam Academy and its goal for the year were forgotten?

"Who better?" Dinah said, jumping back up. "It's not as if many wealthy gentlemen frequent these parts."

"There's... Sir Lawrence, too," I said. Surprised I'd even said such a thing out loud.

Dinah fluffed a hand in the air. "His home is hardly close enough to count, and besides, I think the baronet may be out of your reach."

"A viscount is even *more* of a reach," I argued.

"But not his son."

I tilted my head, about to point out Richard was a *future* viscount, and so his prospects of marriage—assuming he actually did what his parents likely wanted of him—were just as scrutinized as a baronet's might be, perhaps more so, but there was a knock at the door and Dinah shushed me with a wave.

Whatever remained of the Dinah I knew—a person who danced at the edges of this stepsister of mine's behavior— would likely not accept me aiming for anyone but Richard, regardless of whatever logic I used to argue with her.

The knock repeated, and it was quiet but urgent. Not at all what I expected from Mother or even Father in this place.

Dinah got up to approach the door, but before she could, a letter shot out from underneath it, gliding to her feet.

Chapter Eighteen

"Who sent that letter?" I asked, passing Dinah as she walked back toward her bed, a smile on her face, her shoulders relaxing. "Who put it under the door?" I opened the door and looked down the corridor to find Nora —in her nightgown—headed up the attic steps to where the servants' quarters was located.

"Nora?" I whispered.

She froze, a candle in hand that cast an orange glow over her face as she turned.

"Come back in and shut the door," Dinah hissed.

Nora quickly picked up her feet and headed upstairs. I hesitated, wondering if I should follow her, but Dinah didn't seem surprised by the letter, so I resolved to ask her.

There were footfalls on the stairs from down below, and Mother's voice echoed out over the corridor. "In the morning, make those biscuits of yours, Mrs. Stone, to make sure we have something to go with the tea for our gentleman callers."

I pushed the door quickly—then thought better of it, making sure to shut it closed softly.

Dinah kept her finger to her mouth as I moved back toward her and sat on the bed. We waited for Mother's voice and footfalls to quiet, for the sound of her own door shutting, before I glanced down at the letter in Dinah's hand, open now, the writing tight and slanted. The letter began with "Dearest Dinah."

Dinah noticed me looking and brandished the letter in front of my face, though I had to take it from her to angle it in the limited light better.

"And here you insisted Edward *doesn't love me* without money." Dinah thrust her shoulders back.

I read the letter to myself:

Dearest Dinah,

To see you this evening, so beautiful, so radiant, stirred my heart in ways no mere mortal can put into words. Our conversation during our dance could only be cordial, for one never knows what the ears of one's neighbors might be attuned to. Rest assured, my heart remains yours, and I pray every night that the day might come in which I may call you my wife.

-E.

"'E'?" I said aloud.

"Edward, of course." Dinah snatched the letter back, staring at it dreamily, as if more words might appear the longer she looked.

"And Nora knows?" I asked, thinking back to the letter's

messenger. I jumped to my feet, headed for the window, but though it overlooked the lane, there was no sign of carriage or shadowed figure.

"She knows he sends me letters," Dinah explained, folding the letter and tucking it in the bodice of her dress. "But she can only guess at the contents."

"Who brought the letter?" I asked, still searching the window for sign of any movement. Whoever had brought it was gone.

"Probably Mrs. Bates, his housekeeper. He often sends me letters after we meet." She scoffed. "It's not as if you've never seen them before."

I couldn't explain that there was no chance of me remembering anything that had happened before I'd truly arrived.

I chewed my lip as I turned back to the bed. "I don't think it wise to involve the servants. If our parents were to find out Nora kept such a thing from them, they might dismiss her."

Dinah rolled her eyes. "If they found *that* out, I'd be a little more worried about myself. I might have to run off to Bretna Brown with my beloved before they lock me inside this room and toss away the key." She flung herself back on the bed, sighing, her hand to her breast.

"You would go that far?" I asked, wringing my hands.

"Of course." She sat back up.

"And Mr. Smith... would too?"

Dinah adjusted her bodice, her face growing cold. "You don't understand. If you knew love as I did, Georgiana, you wouldn't be so callous."

I didn't really know Mr. Smith and was basing my opinion on one unremarkable interaction in town I scarcely remembered, followed by his shallow behavior at the ball. But I was still sure I wasn't wrong about him.

Running off to marry a woman in Bretna Brown was the last thing a man concerned with his reputation would do.

Then again, so would writing secret letters at the risk of being caught, and he'd done that. Though signing them "E" did leave room for deniability.

"But you understand I don't want to resort to that." Dinah took my hand in hers and I sat back down beside her on the bed. "And I hope to avoid poor, little Nora suffering for this, if it can be helped. I would have this whole messy, secretive business behind us. A proper engagement, and no one need know about the secret arrangement."

"He has given you his word?" I asked, thinking of Richard's promise to Arabella. There seemed to be so little advantage for the viscount's son there—and besides, I could not let him marry her. Not if I hoped to keep those back home safe.

"My lack of fortune is the only thing standing in our way," Dinah said. Not fully answering my question, I noted.

But if it worked to motivate her to help me harder... "I will marry Mr. Gillingham," I said boldly, bolder than I felt. But no one had failed Bedlam Academy's annual goal before this. "I just need help in persuading him."

Dinah's teeth flashed as her eyes lit up and she embraced me. "I'll do everything I can. Oh, thank you, sister. Thank you."

I patted her back. Under the enchantment of my reserved, kindly stepsister, I'd almost forgotten the vicious bully beneath.

If Edward Smith turned out to be a terrible husband who showed little regard for his wife—who was I to stop Dinah Sinclair from putting herself into that situation?

Still, even as I thought it... I knew the satisfaction would be hollow. If Dinah never remembered her other life, did this really count as comeuppance?

I would have expected to spend the night tossing and turning, but despite the whirlwind of my thoughts, exhaustion won out and I was asleep as soon as I closed my eyes—only to feel as if I'd opened them to bright sunlight mere moments later.

"For Heaven's sake, child." There was a knock and the door flew open before I could even answer. Mary was on Mother's heels, both fully dressed for the day while I lay beneath the linens in my nightgown.

"I let you sleep in since your *illness* sent us home early yesterday, but you really must be well today." Mother drew back the curtains, and I shielded my eyes with an arm for a moment while I blinked to get adjusted to the light. She whirled on me, clapping her hands together. "Tell me you're well."

"I—" My voice cracked, almost belying what I'd been about to say.

Mother let out a little cry. "Oh! The doctor—the doctor! Mary, send for—"

"Mother, I'm fine." I sat up. "Much better, thank you. Mary, there's no need to send for the doctor."

Mary paused in the doorway, looking to my mother for confirmation that I, in fact, did not need a doctor.

"Yes, very well. All the better." Mother waved a hand, drawing Mary nearer. "You've missed breakfast," she said to me. "But you cannot miss our callers. You must get ready."

"'Callers'?" I yawned, stretching one arm over my head as I swung my legs off the bed.

"Yes, *callers*." Mother *tsked* and took a handful of my shoulder-length hair in her light touch. She didn't comment on it, but I knew it still pained her to see it. "Every gentleman who danced with you two last night is expected to pay a visit." She shook her head. "I know it's been a while since your last ball, but surely, you could not have forgotten such a staple of polite Society."

"No," I said, though my mind sorted through my memories, searching for the lesson that touched on what happened after a ball. Perhaps there had been something of the like in those lessons—there had to have been—but admittedly, I hadn't paid close attention.

"Get her ready. Get her ready." Mother gestured wildly at Mary, who thrust herself into action, arranging my brush at my vanity and then dashing to my trunk.

"No, not that one," said Mother, pointing to whatever dress selection Mary had made. "The burgundy one. The one that looks so fine with the green Spencer. Yes."

"Mother?" Dinah's voice called out from the corridor. "Mother, a carriage is arriving!"

"Oh!" Mother shrieked just a little and both Mary and I jumped. "I should never have let you sleep in. You have your father to thank for that. 'Now, dear, if she is to be her brightest for your little game today, then you must let her rest after last night's ordeal.' Little *game*! The nerve of that man. Hurry, hurry." She waved both hands at Mary and me, then turned on her heel and exited, her voice carrying out louder than ever through the closed door. "And *do* not shout up the stairs, Dinah! You'll strain your throat. And what if one of our callers heard you? Most unladylike!" Her footfalls echoed down the steps, louder than anyone's.

Mary and I stared at one another as I finished wiping my face with a cloth dipped in the washbasin, and I was the first to smile. Mary threw a hand in front of her lips as if to hide her own.

"Thank you, Mary," I said as she helped me out of my nightgown and into my first layer of clothing for the day.

"You're welcome, miss."

We moved in silence after that, me sticking my arms up and out almost on instinct and then heading toward the vanity so she could pin my hair back. I was still waking up a bit, and now I was finally settling on the list of men we'd be expecting if what Mother explained had been true and every gentleman who'd danced with Dinah and me was expected to pay a visit.

Mr. Smith. No way I could forget him after Dinah's revelation.

And Richard himself. If he *dared* after how we'd left things.

I hoped he did. I still had to marry him, even if I was sure to be more miserable than Dinah if she actually did marry her impoverished vicar clearly unsatisfied without a fortune to his name.

Aylmer. "Mr. Linden," as I ought to call him in this place.

And... Sir Lawrence.

I let out a gasp.

"Oh, sorry, miss," said Mary, who'd tugged a bit on my hair to pull it back. I offered her a flittering smile in the mirror, unable to speak just then.

The dance between Sir Lawrence and I hadn't been planned, though. It was my own hand that had scrawled his name on my dance card. Perhaps that excused him from the visit?

He'd danced with Dinah, too, though, I'd asked him to. He wouldn't ignore a social call to our household, surely?

But why did I care?

How was I to look him in the eye, knowing what I did about Arabella, and say nothing?

But in fact, objectively, wasn't it better if I told Arabella's guardian? It would take her out of the running as my rival for Richard's hand entirely, and Richard himself wouldn't suffer much for it. Not enough to make him any less desirable a match for a woman in my station.

It'd ruin Arabella, of course...

But that wasn't important in the broader picture of my homeland's fate.

There was a knock on the door, and a familiar voice followed. "The misses wants Miss Georgiana down this instant," said Nora through the door. "The first caller is here."

"I'm coming!" I cried.

Mary patted my head and nodded at me in the mirror.

"Like nothing's missing," she said, likely referring to the length of my hair.

"Thank you," I told her, unable to voice my real thoughts at the moment. That something inside me—whatever it was that was supposed to gravitate toward the viscount's son and not the baronet—was missing, indeed.

Chapter Nineteen

"Mr. Linden, so good of you to join us." Mother's voice was an octave higher than usual, an almost song-like quality to her words.

My heart lightened as I headed for the landing. It wouldn't quite be the Aylmer I'd known back at Bedlam Academy—though perhaps that was for the best, considering how we'd left things—but he was an ally to have in my corner, someone whose face could only make me smile.

Mother and Dinah were already in the drawing room as I reached the bottom of the steps, Nora on her way from the kitchen with a tray full of tea and biscuits.

"Nora," I whispered in a hushed tone. She froze as I stepped up beside her, just outside the drawing room door. "About last night—"

Nora's eyes darted to the ground. "Miss Dinah's business is her own, and she promised me it was in the service of your own pursuit of matrimony." She looked up, then, smiling broadly. There was the friend I missed. If she weren't balancing a large tray in front of her, I might have reached over for a hug, but it would be a hollow echo of the comfort I'd had back home. In that place where everything had seemed harsh but this other girl's light.

"Nora? Where's the tea?" Mother appeared at the doorway, her eyes widening at the sight of us standing together. "Don't keep us waiting, girl!" She flapped her hands wildly to encourage Nora to step in, then slipped her arm through mine and positively tugged me inside the room.

"Here she is," Mother said, back straight, her singsong voice back in place. "Georgiana, dear, come welcome our guests."

Guests? More than one?

My breath hitched as we stepped inside and encountered Aylmer *along with* Richard seated together across one of our settees. They both stood, and Aylmer's expression softened, his eyes positively sparkling as he looked from me to his companion. Richard smiled as well, but there was an edge to the corner of his lips, a shake of the head that conveyed his amusement at seeing me squirm when we locked eyes.

I didn't find it the least bit attractive, despite his objectively handsome face.

"Come, sister, sit here." Dinah held a cup of tea in one hand, a saucer in the other, and gestured at the seat beside her—which would put me between her and Richard as soon as the viscount's son was seated.

Nora offered a quick bow, an encouraging grin behind the gentlemen's back, and exited without a word.

"Good morning, Mr. Linden," I said, offering Aylmer a little bow as I made my way to the seat Dinah had indicated. "Mr. Gillingham," I said, knowing I was supposed to greet the higher-ranking man first, so I took note of his reaction expressly out of my peripheral vision.

He flicked the tails of his coat back and sat down, that irritating smirk refusing to dissipate.

I grabbed for a cup of tea already poured as Mother busied herself by pouring another and passing it off to Richard. "So kind of you to drop by." An awkward silence descended over the room as Mother poured another cup for Aylmer and then for herself without anyone speaking.

"Biscuit?" Mother asked after a moment, lifting the plate toward the gentlemen.

"Thank you," said Aylmer stiffly, reaching for one.

Richard shook his head.

"They're quite good. One of our Mrs. Stone's specialties," Mother promised. When Richard still didn't move, taking a small sip from his teacup, Mother put the tray back down.

"Quite good," she repeated quietly, then she took one for herself, biting down on it.

No one had anything more to say.

I glanced at Dinah, then Aylmer. Were they not here— was Aylmer not together with Richard—in order to help me?

However did anyone from the Academy accomplish any task they'd set out to do? If those who lost their memories could not even rely on instincts to push themselves forward...

"Where's Father?" I asked, setting my teacup back down.

Dinah raised an eyebrow at me, and Mother laughed. "In his study. As a gentleman not paying calls would be this time of morning."

Another misstep. Only ladies accepted visitors this time of day?

"We were sorry to see you leave the ball early." Aylmer finally jumped in to cover for me, finishing eating his biscuit and putting his teacup down on the small table beside him. "You both were missed." He looked to Dinah and me in turn.

Dinah hid behind a sip of her tea, and I finally noticed Richard staring steadfastly at her.

Why did this world have to throw *this* additional impediment to my task? Why not make Dinah the leading lady candidate, then? Only *if* she'd get over her obsession with Edward Smith, of course.

"I would have thought Mr. Gillingham was rather happy to see me go," I pointed out.

That got his attention.

"What a silly thing to say," Mother said quickly before Richard could respond. He stared at me, though, his jaw twitching.

I shot a dazzling, fake smile at the man of the hour and threaded my hands together over my lap. "I only meant since I made such a spectacle of myself during our dances."

Richard's furrowed brow softened and he laughed—once and hard, without feeling. "Yes, of course." He leaned toward me. "You are forgiven. It was quite forgotten after the other dances of the night." He stared at Dinah then.

She set her own teacup down and reached over to grab my hand. "*You* were hardly far from my *sister*'s thoughts, sir."

"I told him," said Aylmer, almost giddily. "I told him he had made *quite* the impression on Miss Radcliff."

Richard arched a brow and placed his teacup down on the table, barely touched. "Of *that*, I had little doubt."

I forced a laugh. He smiled widely back at me.

We were caught in a stare-off, seemingly competing for who could hold, for the longest duration, their awfully forced smile.

"Mr. Linden," I said, breaking eye contact first and picking up a biscuit. "I'm afraid I didn't get to say goodbye to one of my new acquaintances. Did you happen to see if Miss Hatfield enjoyed the rest of the evening?" I bit off a bit of biscuit. It *was* quite good. Less sweet than the treats the cafeteria offered at the Academy.

Aylmer cocked his head. "Pardon? Miss Hatfield?"

"You aren't acquainted with her?" I took another bite of the biscuit, making a point of enjoying each chew for a deliberately long moment as a rush of red colored Richard's temple. "I would have thought Mr. Gillingham would have had a reason to introduce her to all his closest friends."

Aylmer looked to Richard, his forehead wrinkling.

"Miss Arabella Hatfield," said Richard quickly, a vein popping at his forehead as I finished my biscuit. "Sir

Lawrence's cousin. His ward." He smiled at everyone in the room but me. "If there were any introductions to be made, I would have left those to her cousin, of course. I hardly know the young woman herself. I'd just heard of her from Sir Lawrence before last evening."

Right.

He locked eyes with me. "Then again, it is of no surprise to me that he introduced her to so few at the party. I know the baronet to be wildly imprudent when it comes to proper introductions."

Laughing, I looked away. If he thought to ruin *me* with his accusations, he could do less damage than he thought. All I cared about was his own opinion, and he'd made it clear whatever he imagined had gone on between Sir Lawrence and me meant little to him—other than to use as something to hold over my head.

Then again, his parents *would* care. And I had little hope of encouraging this aggravating man beside me to run off to Bretna Brown to override their wishes.

I picked up my teacup and stared out the window, defeated for the moment.

"Mr. Gillingham," said Mother after the room went quiet once more, "you must express again to your parents how impressed we all were with the ball. Your mother outdid herself."

"Yes, thank you, Mrs. Sinclair. I'll be sure to tell her. Your presence was most welcome." Richard directed this comment at Dinah, who stared down at her tea. He straightened his coat and looked to Aylmer. "Perhaps we should get going. We do have other calls to make."

"So soon?" said Aylmer and Mother at the same time.

"Mr. Gillingham," said Dinah, her voice louder than it often was in this world, closer to the commanding tone she'd often taken at the Academy. Richard sat, rapt, at the edge of his seat. "I was wondering if you might... clarify something."

"Of course," said Richard, though his gaze darted toward me, a slight narrow to his eyes that had me guessing

166

he wondered if I'd unloaded the truth of last night to my stepsister. I wondered now if perhaps I should have. What was it that had stayed my tongue? Not concern over poor Arabella, surely?

Dinah offered a friendly, perhaps even flirtatious smile. "Rumor has it that you are engaged to be married."

The color drained from Richard's face.

Dinah spoke quickly. "It's just a rumor—I think. Forgive me if I'm being impudent. I only wished to... congratulate you if that were the case?" Her voice rose at the end.

She was trying to find out if the rumors about his betrothal to an heiress from Bathe were true, I presumed. For my sake.

"No, it's, uh..." Richard looked to me and I gave him a slight shake of my head.

"Before you even arrived, the whole town was gossiping. The viscount's son betrothed to an heiress in Bathe," I explained.

Richard let out a deep breath. Then he chuckled, and it seemed genuine. "Oh, that... Well, I *was* engaged," he said quickly. Dinah's mouth dropped into a little "o" and he held a hand up, smiling. "For just a fortnight. The lady in question changed her mind, you see, as was her right, when her father pressed a marriage to a son of a friend or some sort. So you see, nothing much to it at all."

He hardly seemed broken up about the end of the engagement. To not even know the details of the way he'd lost his presumed beloved...

I cocked my head. But when had he entered into an arrangement with this heiress? Presumably after he'd entered into one with Arabella.

Though perhaps he would have gone through with the marriage to the heiress. She had a fortune to recommend her.

"His parents were not particularly fond of the lady," said Aylmer quickly. "It all worked out for the best, I say." Aylmer knocked a polite elbow against Richard's side. "This man reads too much poetry. He finds love in far too many a pretty face."

"A poet. Guilty as charged." Richard locked eyes with Dinah, then, and she looked at me. He frowned. "Though there are times when a pretty face can prove equally vexing."

He directed this comment to *me*.

"I'm in complete agreement," I said back.

So it wasn't a fact that he found me unappealing on the surface. I'd just messed up my first impression terribly, or perhaps Dinah was more to his tastes. I studied my stepsister. There was a bit of Arabella's look in her.

"Oh! It looks like we're about to have another visitor." Mother jumped up from her seat, staring out the window. We all turned. There was a carriage headed down the lane, slowing as it approached our front door. "I don't recognize..." Mother said softly.

Richard jumped to his feet. "That's the baronet's carriage. Linden—perhaps it's best we be on our way. No need to overcrowd this place."

This time, he wouldn't be stopped. He headed for the door, offering a curt "Thank you for your hospitality" to my mother and a long, lingering look at Dinah before stepping out into the hall. Aylmer scrambled to catch up, setting his teacup down and offering his thanks as well.

"Oh, any time, Mr. Linden. Mr. Gillingham. Any time. We must have you both for dinner."

"That sounds like a capital idea," said Aylmer. "Doesn't it, Gillingham?" The rest of the conversation grew muffled.

I was still in my seat, even as Dinah stood and shuffled over to the hall.

I stared out the window, at the carriage that had halted. The driver got down and opened the door.

Sir Lawrence jumped out and my breath hitched.

He turned around, extending a hand, and out behind him stepped Arabella.

Chapter Twenty

I sprinted to the door, running my clammy palms over the front of my dress. Why was I nervous? I'd expected Sir Lawrence—perhaps not Arabella, but considering how I'd left things with her in the dark in that study, perhaps she feared if she did not come along, I'd use the opportunity to ruin her. As if her presence alone could hold my tongue.

I hadn't made a decision to ruin her for my benefit. I imagined Richard would not be happy with me if I did, either, even if I was sure he had no desire to follow through on his promise to wed *this* betrothed, either.

I'd only just reached the entryway, Mary having held the door open as Richard and Aylmer made their way out, when the two groups of visitors encountered each other just out front.

Sir Lawrence's jaw clenched visibly. "Gillingham." He nodded curtly.

"Sir Lawrence," said Aylmer, not a hint of guile on his politely smiling face. He gave him a bow, his eyes flicking to Arabella.

"Mr. Linden," said Sir Lawrence, directing his attention to the friendlier of the two. Richard had done no more than bow at Sir Lawrence, his eyes stuck on the ground. "Did I have the opportunity to introduce my cousin, Miss Hatfield?"

Arabella gave a small curtsy then looked up.

Aylmer's face softened, his mouth stuck slightly agape as her dark eyes batted up at him, but he quickly recovered.

I wasn't sure why, but my gut sunk slightly.

I'd never dared to think of Aylmer—or anyone—as anything more than an acquaintance or even friend, but his words to me before the Sacrament... His confession of his feelings.

I felt now as I felt then that those feelings could be easily swayed.

"Oh, do come in, Sir Lawrence. Miss... Hatfield?" Mother stepped outside, gesturing wildly.

"Thank you, Mrs. Sinclair," Sir Lawrence said. He turned to greet his hostess, Dinah frowning and stepping up as his gaze fell to me and the hardness in his face softened.

I tried to focus on Richard—saw what I hoped no other did as Arabella brushed a hand over his forearm, Aylmer's and Sir Lawrence's backs to the pair—and Richard yanked his arm away, adjusting his hat.

"Georgiana?" Mother said.

I snapped back to the moment, away from the sight of Aylmer and Richard climbing into their carriage, which had pulled up to take the place of the one that had brought our next guests. I felt as if I'd squandered the day's opportunity with Richard.

"Step aside, sister," said Dinah, her eyes fluttering. "Make room for our guests."

I looked down at my feet. I had walked right into the open doorframe in my haste to better observe everyone, blocking any entry.

"Yes, of course. My apologies." I curtsied just slightly, then stepped aside.

"Nora? Nora!" Mother called down toward the kitchen after she was the first one in. "Please refresh our tea and biscuits for our next guests."

"Miss Radcliff," said Sir Lawrence as he stepped inside, Mary taking his hat.

Our eyes locked.

My breath hitched.

"Sir Lawrence," Dinah said, elbowing me and curtseying herself. "I don't believe I've had the pleasure...?"

Sir Lawrence's trance broke. "Ah, yes. Miss Sinclair, this is my cousin and ward, Miss Arabella Hatfield. I would have introduced her to you last night, but she got away from me, and by the time I found her again, your party had left the ball."

Arabella winced at the line that "she'd gotten away from him" and, to my surprise, stepped forward and slipped her arm through mine, turning us toward him as if united as one. "Miss Radcliff found me. Last night. When you insisted I was missing."

"Did you?" Sir Lawrence's brow arched. "I would have thought that would have come up when I asked you where you'd been."

I looked at Arabella's profile, but she steadfastly refused to turn toward me.

She *wanted* her cousin to know I'd stumbled upon her?

I had to admit I was curious why. And perhaps aiding her could serve me somehow—if not, I could always admit the truth later.

"I did find Miss Hatfield at the party last night. For a moment," I said quickly. "I was about to join the Browns and leave early on my own, but I—" I swallowed. I couldn't even explain the part where I'd set out to avoid Mr. Smith. Not with Dinah listening.

Mother walked back toward us and gestured to the drawing room. "Please. Sit. It's so kind of you to stop by."

Arabella didn't drop my arm as we walked into the drawing room, and this time, it was she and I who sat together on the settee, the younger young woman only just letting go of me to fix her skirt as we settled down. Sir

Lawrence took the spot I'd had before, in a chair between Dinah and me.

Mother was a flurry with Nora's entry, a new tray of biscuits and two teacups on it, which my friend-turned-maidservant set down beside the other tray as she gathered the two cups left behind by our previous guests.

"You had a pleasant journey on your way here, I hope?" Mother asked as she stepped past Nora and started pouring the baronet and his ward tea.

"Yes, thank you. It's a beautiful morning, if a bit chilly." Sir Lawrence took the teacup offered after Arabella accepted hers.

"Miss Hatfield? Biscuit?" Mother held the tray out to her.

Arabella looked to her cousin as if asking for permission—or instructions—and he nodded.

"Thank you," she murmured.

After Sir Lawrence declined one and Mother sat down, the room grew quiet again. Dinah's gaze kept flicking to the window, and I knew she must have been waiting for the vicar to approach. He may even do so on foot.

"So, Sir Lawrence," said Mother, her teacup clinking against her saucer, "how are you enjoying your time in Hemlock?"

"Very well, thank you." Sir Lawrence took a careful sip of tea.

"I imagine your mother must miss you."

"She sends letters daily," said Sir Lawrence, clipped.

It was Arabella's reaction that I found of particular interest, though. Her teacup clattered against her saucer as she quickly moved to set it down, her biscuit missing only a single bite resting to the side of the cup. "Mrs. Sinclair, I was impressed by the view of the garden as we approached."

"Oh, thank you, dear. I'm afraid it's a rather poor imitation of its typical beauty just now, what with the end of summer and all."

Arabella ignored Mother's humble comment. "Might

Miss Radcliff give me a tour of it this morning?" As she went to gesture toward me, her fingers slapped against my upper arm.

It was the most words I'd heard her speak around anyone save Richard in that dark study.

"Excellent idea," said Sir Lawrence, setting down his teacup. "Perhaps we can all join you."

"Oh, no, please." Arabella jumped to her feet. "I hoped to get to know Miss Radcliff better."

"I'd prefer to stay in this morning, but thank you," added Dinah, her gaze flitting to the window once more.

Sir Lawrence smiled tightly, and Arabella stared down at me. I supposed she had need to speak to me about last night.

I stood.

"Don't forget your Spencer," Mother said. "And your bonnet. There's a bit of a chill this morning."

I promised Mother I wouldn't and spared one last glance at Sir Lawrence before exiting to the hallway to put on my pale-green coat, which came down only as far as the middle of my chest, and dark-green hat. Arabella waited patiently as I put on the rest of my outfit. Down the hallway a bit, the door to my stepfather's study opened and Mr. Sinclair poked his head out. "Stone? Mrs. Stone? I was wondering how close it is to lunch. Oh, ladies." He nodded at Arabella and me. "Headed outdoors? Best not take a chill."

"Mother's already warned us," I said as we headed past to exit through the kitchen. "We'll come in if we feel cold."

"Please do," he said, falling into line behind us as we headed for the back door. "Your mother will never let us hear the end of it if you catch a cold before you catch a husband." He chuckled to himself and moved toward Mrs. Stone, hard at work in the kitchen beside Nora.

Nora spared Arabella and me a curious glance, but Arabella threaded her arm through mine and practically dragged me outdoors before we stood a chance of lingering.

She didn't speak as we approached the back yard, and the small garden that no guest would likely request to see so eagerly, particularly as the weather got cooler and we headed into fall.

Arabella might not have even noticed it, as she kept guiding me farther and farther away from the house, putting the quaint garden far behind us.

Still, she didn't speak, even as the mounting waves of green and yellowing grass spread out before us.

"Miss Hatfield—Arabella?" I said, trying for more familiarity with her given name. "I think we've gone far enough."

Arabella shook her head. "It's just before us."

"'It'?" I didn't understand. I'd assumed she just wanted to talk about what I had witnessed. "I didn't plan on telling Sir Lawrence—"

But she cut me off. "You'd have nothing to lose if you did. Richard's threat to tell people you met my cousin improperly is nothing compared to our secret. Besides, Lawrence would be well aware of that himself."

"Well, yes, but..." I chewed my lip. "I don't want to cause you trouble." Tugging on her arm, I pulled her to a stop. It was true—but there were reasons I might have to ruin her if I couldn't separate her from Richard willingly. "I think you should release him," I told her. "From the engagement."

She sighed, her gaze flicking to the ground.

I tried another tactic. "He got himself engaged to a woman in Bathe. He admitted it. She broke it off after two weeks, but I'm sure he would have gone through with it instead of marrying you. She had a fortune, I hear." I lowered my voice. "And it was recently he asked for her hand in marriage. *After* he'd already promised himself to you."

I wanted to keep pressing the issue, tell her about Richard's clear interest in Dinah, but I gave her the chance to let that information sink in.

She looked up at me, and her dark eyes weren't devastated. Though they did shine, glistening with a hollow sort of sadness. "None of that matters to me. I *have to* marry him." She looked to her right, then. "Deep down, a part of you ought to understand. There's more at stake here than some silly girl's doe-eyed love story."

I turned to look where she was glancing so urgently, listening to Arabella's continued speech all the while.

"I tell my cousin I don't want to marry because I've already gotten engaged to the man I must. With things how they are, a secret relationship is my best chance of success."

Beyond the large apple tree, bedecked with fully ripe fruit—which I recognized as the tree I'd found myself leaning against when I'd arrived in this world—there was a flicker of dark-blue light. A circle that seemed to be shimmering.

I let go of Arabella and walked slowly toward it.

It was a portal, an opening in the very air itself. And beyond the portal, contrasting against the bright light of the day, were the gates of Bedlam Academy shrouded in night.

Chapter Twenty-One

A wave of anxiety, of *feeling* crashed against me like a gale of wind. Darkness emanated from that open portal leading to my old world, contrasting against the cozy, fall colors of the quaint countryside. I stared as long as I dared, checked over my shoulder to see what Arabella thought of this, but there were no indications she was the least bit surprised.

A jolt of pain shot through my head and I cradled my scalp through my bonnet

"I saw you there. The woman in the dress."

The words echoed in my mind.

The voice was familiar. *Professor Finch.* The name came to me all at once. Of course I remembered the professor, the latest one who'd Returned, who'd determined this year's goal had been to marry the viscount's son.

But how, until this moment, could I have forgotten her revelation that I hadn't died during the Sacrament? That I'd been there, at Richard Gillingham's wedding?

I'd dismissed her visions, then, known it to be impossible. I'd even felt sorry for the lady candidate bound to marry a gentleman Professor Finch had described as a "rake." She'd revealed he'd had relations with servants around town. I hadn't asked how she'd known. Perhaps she'd spent her time here in this other world in Bathe. Or Devynshore. Who knew how many towns there were where the man had left behind a trail of broken hearts?

So this wasn't some fluke, out of nowhere. Professor Finch had seen me here and here I was.

Straightening up, I stared at the portal. I didn't dare reach out for it, didn't approach those gates. There wasn't a single part of me that wanted to return there. There was no one I wished to see.

I didn't wish for the world's destruction, but I hoped never to return to it, either.

"Do you remember now?" Arabella spoke loudly and she took a few steps forward, fighting some unseen force as if walking against the wind.

"*Remember*?" I studied Arabella's face as she approached. "You're from—"

"Bedlam Academy." Arabella smiled wistfully. "I remember you a bit. The pawn for the year after me."

"Arabella..." My mind searched for the name. "Arabella Weston. The pawn for the year before mine." Now, close to the portal, it seemed clearer. Her face was familiar, though she looked so different in the proper clothes for this world. And she was... *younger*, surely.

"That was my name here initially. Raised in a school for young girls. When my cousin came and insisted on adopting me, he had me take a name his mother had picked from her late husband's family instead of the name I'd known. I couldn't say why, nor do I think it relevant to what I must do, so I haven't pried."

"But you're... you're younger than I am."

A slip of a smile crossed her lips. "So everyone here believes. But I've always looked young. Or in any case, I slid into this world's version of Arabella at a younger age than expected."

"And are you the late baronet's natural daughter?"

Arabella shrugged. "I have no idea who my parents were.

In this world, 'Weston' was likely my mother's surname, but I never sought her out. If she even lives."

"I..." I swallowed, my gaze unable to leave the portal for long. "How...? How is this open right now? Doesn't someone have to—"

"Die?" Arabella gestured at herself. At me. "And yet... we didn't die and we opened the way here."

Letting out a deep breath, Arabella waved her hand across the air in front of the portal. With a sudden flap of wings, a white bird shot through from the Academy, a glint of silver catching the bright sunlight on our side.

The portal grew smaller, smaller, and then it closed entirely. The bird, cooing and ruffling its feathers, landed somewhere up above us in the apple tree.

The wind died down, the leaves no longer rustling so hard.

"Did *you* open that?" I asked.

Arabella nodded. "I sent the bird ahead at my arrival, directed it to somewhere in your back yard, away from the observation of those in the house."

"You *sent* the bird?" I gazed up into the sky. I remembered white doves in the woods behind Bedlam Academy, how they'd seemed to flock to my—

"The jewelry," I said. "The pawn's jewelry."

Arabella nodded. "It ties us to them. These creatures who live between worlds." She held a hand up and stared intently, and sure enough, the dove perched on a long, pale finger she held aloft. It twitched its head again and again, cooing, a silver ring in its beak.

"But I thought the Board members usually took the jewelry after a pawn vanished," I said.

"And tuck it away in their drawers, their jewelry boxes. Where our little friends here will fly and snatch it back again, just as it's meant to be." Arabella chuckled darkly. "If any of the professors knew how important the jewelry continued to be, they wouldn't let anyone abscond with it in the first place."

She nodded at the bird and it took off, flying into the sky. I watched as it grew smaller and smaller until it reached the house and flew beyond, far out of my sight.

I breathed in the beautiful countryside air, my tense shoulders relaxing. It felt so much better here now, without the way to Bedlam Academy opened.

"Do the pawns *always* live, then?" I asked her.

Arabella bit her lip. "I don't know. You're the first one I've met, as far as I remember."

I smiled ruefully. "You must have been as surprised as I was, then. To find yourself here, in this world, with your memories, and those around you without a clue."

"You remembered from the start, then?" She had a sharp intake of breath. "I thought to expose you to the portal again, that it might jog your memory—"

"I remembered." I leaned against the trunk of the apple tree. "This is where I first woke up in this world. Though I will say exposure to that portal did bring a few important details back to the forefront of my mind."

"You remembered..." Arabella leaned against the tree beside me, briefly closing her eyes as she exhaled softly. "And what did the portal remind you of?"

"That I *will* marry the viscount's son," I said resolutely.

That made her open her eyes with a start.

The memory of Professor Finch's confession to me was fresh in my mind, as if delivered from the portal itself. "The professor who spoke of the year's goal said there was some irregularity—I assumed it to be my survival as pawn, that it had never happened before. Yet here you are."

"Here I am," said Arabella, pushing off the tree. "With the same goal as you. *That*'s the irregularity."

My stomach sunk as I looked down into her eyes, neither of us speaking for a moment that stretched on uncomfortably.

She wouldn't look away. She was *that* determined she was right.

"Last year's goal was..." I searched my memories. It had

never mattered much to me what another graduating class's goal was—what even my own class's goal was, considering I hadn't planned to be there for it. But I *had* known it at one time.

Though the specifics didn't matter, now that I thought about it. "You're betrothed to Mr. Gillingham, not married to him. If your class's goal was for you to marry him, then Professor Finch wouldn't have been sent back. We wouldn't have been sent here. Our world wouldn't still exist."

Arabella shook her head. "How little the Academy actually knows about anything."

I waited for her to explain.

She sighed. "I don't know everything, either, but I certainly figured out a few things." She watched the sky through the lattice of the boughs, as if searching for something. Another dove?

"You're right. That wasn't the goal my class expected to fulfill—and, as I'm quite aware by now, the chosen candidate fulfilled the task he was instructed to complete. But it happened far from Devynshore. I was alone there, not a single person from Bedlam Academy in the area, and it's a rare destitute, orphan girl who travels in this world. I had no opportunity to seek out others until my cousin became my guardian."

"Did you find anyone?"

"Not until the ball. And they were all underclassmen."

"The ones from my class. Dinah Sinclair, she's my stepsister here. Unity Dowding, a friend. Aylmer Linden, a friend of Mr. Gillingham. And Nora Fletcher, from the servant class. She's here. Did you recognize her when she came in with the tea?"

Arabella chewed her lip and shook her head. "I'm afraid I didn't even pinpoint that many. I'd never paid close enough attention to underclassmen before. Not when... I expected none of it to matter." She folded her hands together.

"When you expected to die."

She nodded. "But 'Professor Finch,' you said? There was a Beatrice Finch in the servant class in my year."

"She said she was a servant here. She said she didn't know you too well—but I'm sure she would have told someone if she'd seen you here."

"We don't know that," said Arabella. "We're not sure how memory works when crossing over at all. Perhaps she did see me and didn't remember. Perhaps since she never expected to find me here, she didn't think it noteworthy that she saw my face. *You* didn't seem to remember me. I assumed you had no memories of the other world."

I could feel my face flush. I felt a fool. "You look younger. And I didn't expect to encounter you here. I know that's foolish, since I obviously realize pawns can survive."

She took a few steps away from the tree, twirling into the sunlight. "And Beatrice never knew that. Even more likely, she never was where I was. She was somewhere else, helping last year's candidate with his goal."

"Which was?"

Arabella stopped her movement. "To kill a man, and make it seem natural."

My breath hitched and I stepped closer to Arabella, into the sun. "But I would have remembered *that*. A heinous goal like that..."

I'd been there last year, at the Sacrament, as the young woman before me had vanished into nothingness and the graduating class had stepped through the portal that had appeared in her place. Some had vanished through; some had just walked right to the other side of the room.

Arabella shook her head. "The professors found the goal... unpleasant. So they made up another one, about winning a fortune in a game of cards. But they made sure each member of my class knew the truth. And they swore us to secrecy, threatened us with the *suggestion* that the magic between worlds might grow unstable if we revealed the truth." She snorted. "They couldn't have known such a thing. But we were young, idealistic students—trapped in that school, taught everything we knew from people who'd been to this place. We thought they *knew*."

I clutched the front of my dress. "The Academy was... actually an escape for me. It may have never been a warm, welcoming place, but it was better than—"

"The Lower-Zone." Arabella shuddered suddenly, as if a burst of cold air had permeated this sunlight grove.

"My only real friend, though, was Nora. And I wanted her to be happy." Frowning, I stared across the field at the house. "She doesn't seem *unhappy*, but she's removed from me here. And she's always busy. These people here hardly ever give their servants time to themselves."

"That's a truth of the world the professors seemed to get right. I always felt bad for the servant candidates. But sometimes, we need Bedlam Academy students among their class. When gathering gossip—"

"Or having access to men to murder?" I guessed.

She sighed. "Perhaps. I have no idea how they did it in the end. Only that it was done."

I shuddered. "Professor Finch didn't mention that. But she did seem... affected. More so than any other professor I've known. I thought it was because she missed whoever became the sacrifice here to open a portal for her return home, but now you tell me—*show* me—it's the birds who open them. No death needed."

"Not for the pawns," Arabella confirmed. "Not for you and me, anyway. I can't say how it works for the professors' Return. Only the pawns have a connection with the birds, thanks to that jewelry."

"How do I summon a dove like you did?"

Arabella looked skyward, but there were no signs of a bird in flight. "I can't explain. I hope you find out. It's just a *feeling* when they're nearby. And you just *think* your wish to them. They won't communicate in words."

"At least there's that," I said, forcing a laugh. "If you told me one more shocking thing, I might have burst."

Arabella turned toward me, her features smooth and

almost expressionless. When she spoke, her voice was grave. "But Miss Radcliff—Georgiana. You didn't ask me whom the gentleman candidate of my graduating class was tasked with killing this past year."

I swallowed. I wasn't sure I *wanted* to know. Such darkness this talk of Bedlam Academy brought into this place of light and warmth.

"It was Sir Lawrence Fitzroy," she said plainly. "The baronet."

Chapter Twenty-Two

A sharp and sudden chill settled over my core.

"But-But you said the goal was accomplished, the man killed—"

"Senior," Arabella explained, reaching over to take my hand, which was shaking, in hers. "Sir Lawrence Fitzroy Senior. My guardian's father."

I put my free hand over my heart, willing the hammering inside to settle. The thought of the Sir Lawrence I knew to be the target of such an assassination... It had panicked me more than I'd believed possible, even if, taking just a moment to think about it, it didn't make sense. He was still alive, clearly.

"Does-Does he know?" I asked.

Arabella dropped my hand and shook her head. "Certainly not. He doesn't like to talk about his father much. His mother doesn't, either. I have a feeling the family was never close to begin with. I'm not even sure *how* the last baronet died. Or how they think he did, anyway."

I frowned. That someone from Bedlam Academy had been sent here to *kill* someone from this world was untenable. Even if one person had died so many more back home could live. I wondered how that person felt, saddled with guilt. If even a kernel of what the professors had taught us was true, despite evidence to the contrary, that candidate likely didn't even remember he was from Bedlam Academy. Which meant he wouldn't even have had the solace of saving so many lives to ease his conscience the slightest bit.

"Awful," I said after a minute. Whatever kind of man Sir Lawrence's father had been, it was still awful. I found myself staggering and Arabella threaded her arm through mine, directing us back toward the house, albeit incredibly slowly.

My throat was dry, my head woozy, but there was something else that we needed to discuss before we found ourselves in company again. "But none of that explains why you think you share my goal. Why you think *you* have a task at all."

"I've had visions," said Arabella quietly. "Ever since I got here. Almost every night. They're too consistent to be dismissed."

"Visions of you and Mr. Gillingham wed?"

We stopped, and Arabella turned to face me. "I know what kind of man he is. I'm doing my best to convince him I'm madly in love with him, but if I had a choice, I wouldn't marry. Certainly not *him*, even if I did."

I chuckled darkly. "So I suppose my warning you of his character did nothing to scare you away."

She shook her head. "I only managed to get him to agree to marry me *because* of his rumored rakish behavior. I ruined myself with him."

I swallowed and spoke softer, as if that would make the words untrue. "You had... relations with him?"

She nodded. "I made him think *he* was the one who wanted it, that I was hesitant. But it didn't matter." She put a hand over her stomach. "I even hoped I might come to be with child, make him feel more bound to marry me, but alas, the most I could do was secure his promise he'd run off with me to Bretna Brown."

"Something I imagine he hoped he'd never have to

follow through with once he'd gotten what he desired from you." I *tsked*.

"You're not wrong. Though by playing the innocent, naïve girl, I've at least stopped him from refusing to see me entirely. I think he feels a little guilt whenever our paths cross. He likely never expected to see me again after he left Devynshore." She cocked her head. "I have to wonder if my cousin coming to take me, to make me his ward, if that was this world's way of helping me along. *Now* I have a fortune, albeit a modest one, as Lady Fitzroy is quite stubborn that Sir Lawrence not make it too much. Before... my maiden-hood was all I had to offer him."

I shuddered. I hadn't even considered that myself. But it didn't take me long to figure out that wouldn't have been enough to secure his proposal. That it might have even spurred him to move on to another conquest faster.

Then again, as Arabella had said, he hadn't *entirely* turned her away.

"Do you think your newfound fortune has inspired him to consider keeping his promise with you now? He clearly would not have before, if he'd intended to marry that heiress in Bathe."

"Perhaps." She chewed her bottom lip. "But I'm still an orphan. Rumors are I'm a bastard, and I don't think his parents would approve. We'd still have to elope."

She was determined to see this through, that much was clear. But if she was mistaken—and I had to believe she was or I didn't know what *I* was doing here—there was more than just an unhappy marriage awaiting her. She'd be spelling the end of our world back home.

"These visions you say you have. Can you describe them to me?"

Arabella closed her eyes. "I see the wedding. Mr. Gillingham across from me in front of the vicar." She stopped.

"You see him clearly? His face?"

She frowned. "Well, no… It's him, I'm sure, and he's the right height. But the details are blurry."

"Then how can you be sure it's—"

"People are talking," she says. "In the pews. The viscount's son. Richard Gillingham. This title, this name passes their lips more than once."

Now that I remembered Professor Finch's discussion with me of her vision, this was shaping up to match it more and more.

"Am I there?" I ask, whispering.

She opens her eyes and looks at me.

"There's a woman… in a dress. A pawn's dress."

My stomach sinks. That was what Professor Finch had hinted at, wasn't it? That I'd be there, and not in the proper attire. In the dress I wore to denote I was a pawn. My gaze flicked to the house, still some distance away. That dress was there. In the trunk at the end of my bed.

I could, feasibly, wear it to a wedding, even if it turned heads.

"I don't know if the woman is you," Arabella says. "But I know she's not beside the viscount's son. *I* am. My point of view is from the front of the church, and the woman turning heads… She enters the church after the ceremony has begun."

"Arabella…" I took a few steps forward, swaying a bit as I tried to think it all through.

"You know something," Arabella says, coming up beside me.

"Your vision matches Professor Finch's. She told me I'd be alive in this world. I didn't believe it, and I didn't remember until you showed me the portal. But she described me there, at that wedding, in my pawn's dress."

"Positioned in front of the vicar?" Arabella asked. "As the bride?"

I shook my head. "She didn't say that… Though she didn't say that *wasn't* where I was. She was sure the one getting married was the lady candidate, the one to complete my class's goal for the year."

Arabella halted and smiled triumphantly. "So I was right."

I spun on her. "But you're not *from* our class! It was strange enough when I thought that I could be the lady candidate as the pawn, but for a pawn from a previous year to be the one? You must be joking. What would even be the point of any of my class coming here, a year after you did, if it was all up to you?"

"You were there. In my vision, in Beatrice Finch's..." She grabbed my hand and squeezed it, bouncing on her feet, her skirt rustling this way and that across her ankles. "I feel so vindicated! The reason why I couldn't succeed yet was because you weren't *here* yet. We couldn't make the vision come true."

"But I..." I swallowed. "But the others who came with me—they're clearly subconsciously trying to get me to marry Mr. Gillingham. If the magic that sent you this vision meant for *you* to be the lady candidate, wouldn't it have nudged them to find themselves in *your* orbit? To help *your* cause?"

"They don't know why they do *anything*," Arabella said, dropping my hand and fluffing off my concern with a gesture in the air. "If they have no memories of home."

"Yes, but that's what I mean. Their subconsciouses should guide them in the right direction. It's why I dared to imagine myself the lady candidate to begin with."

Arabella's joyful expression grew cold. "You mean to get in my way, then? To risk everything on your *hunch* that you're the lady candidate tasked with marrying the viscount's son?" She scoffed. "You ask why you would all be sent here, then, if I was to be your class's leading candidate all along. Well, why was I separated from my own class? Why did I remember it all? Why am I sent these visions? If not because I am right about this." Her head moved jerkily with each sentence, not at all the shy, humble girl I'd first imagined her to be last night. She turned to me, her brow narrowed. "Get in my way at your own risk. We shall see which one of us this world wants to marry that, that... rake." She laughed. "To be fighting over *him*." She looked me up and down. "You find no joy in the prospect of being saddled with him, admit it."

I wiped my palms down the front of my dress. "I don't. But neither do you."

"But that's the difference between us. I don't know you well, but it didn't take me long to gather this about you." She picked up the hem of her skirt and turned to retreat back to the house. "I don't *care*. I'll do what needs to be done. *You*, you'll be miserable—and you'll lose sight of your goal the moment you're tempted to reach for something you desire for yourself. That's why you're no leading candidate. You'll see." And with that, she headed on back without me.

I wasn't long behind Arabella, but I had to admit her words had shaken me.

She was right. She *didn't* know me.

But there was also at least an inkling of a feeling that she might have been right about her observation of me despite that.

I didn't want to marry Richard. And that gnawing feeling had thus far been enough to set my heart adrift.

It was the baronet. Every time I found myself around him, I imagined... that was what attraction, what love could feel like.

"Love" was a stretch, of course. Just as I'd felt Aylmer couldn't have been right when he'd said he loved me, I knew it was far too soon to fancy myself in love with the baronet.

Too soon. As if only a matter of time.

I sighed and filled my lungs with this fresh, country air. It didn't have the crisp, salty tang of the ocean air at the

Academy, but it was warmer, and that made it fresher somehow.

Then I followed after Arabella.

"Miss Georgiana," said Nora as I made my way through the kitchen. She and Mrs. Stone were hard at work on lunch.

"Nora, do you have those potatoes ready?" Mrs. Stone eyed her as she chopped into a plucked bird.

I winced, thinking of the dove that traversed the worlds, though this fowl was clearly larger.

"Yes, Mrs. Stone," said Nora, quickly gathering the diced potatoes in front of her. Her gaze met mine, as if to ask me to stay, but voices carried down the hall and it sounded like the door was open, the clop of horse hooves denoting a carriage pulling up in front of the house.

I nodded at Nora apologetically and headed down the hall.

"Oh, must you leave us so soon?" Mother asked. "Miss Hatfield and my Georgiana only just got back from their walk. Oh, where *is* that girl? Dinah. Dinah, come and say goodbye to our guests."

High-pitched laughter permeated the hall and I arrived at the end of it just as Dinah exited the drawing room, the two of us acting like pincers of sorts upon the group standing in the open doorway.

Dinah was smiling, her eyes shimmering in delight. I wondered what could have her so happy, but then Mr. Smith appeared from behind her. He'd come to pay his visit, then, when Arabella and I had had our "walk."

"Goodbye, Sir Lawrence. Miss Hatfield." Dinah offered quick, dutiful bows.

Mr. Smith stepped past her and extended his hand to the baronet, practically snatching the man's hand up. "Nice seeing you, Fitzroy. You're always welcome in the town."

Mother arched a brow at Mr. Smith's casual use of the baronet's surname, but Dinah's reaction was stranger. She burst into giggles as Sir Lawrence took over the handshake, not allowing Mr. Smith's eagerness to overdo it. If I remembered right, Mr. Smith shouldn't have been shaking Sir Lawrence's hand at all. That was something reserved for gentlemen of far closer acquaintance.

"Smith," he said back to him.

Arabella adjusted her Spencer coat and stared at the ground, busying herself with fixing imagined imperfections in the material.

"Oh, but *must* you go?" Mother reiterated.

"Mother," said Dinah. "I'm sure they have other calls to make."

I wondered at that. Had Sir Lawrence danced the rest of the night away with other women from the village?

"Well, Arabella isn't feeling her best," said Sir Lawrence. So that was the excuse she'd given him to make an early exit after our disagreement?

"Lightheaded," said Arabella, offering Mother a flittering smile.

"Oh! You're just hungry, dear. You're welcome to stay for lunch."

"You are far too generous." Sir Lawrence put an hand on Arabella's upper arm and guided her toward the open door. "Perhaps another time."

Mother wagged a finger at him. "I'll hold you to that, Sir Lawrence."

He smiled broadly, and my breath hitched at the sight. "You do that, Mrs. Sinclair. When you see Miss Radcliff, tell her—"

"Tell me what?" I stepped out from the hallway, surprised he hadn't noticed me earlier.

Dinah burst into giggles, and Mr. Smith joined her. She hushed him but couldn't seem to stop herself, so the two returned to the drawing room, arm in arm.

Mother sent a scathing look to their backs.

Sir Lawrence stared at me, his hat in his hand in front of his chest.

"I was sorry to have spent so little time with you this morning," he said softly.

I felt, somehow, as if a load had been lifted from me with just his words, just his eyes meeting mine.

"I'm sorry, too," I said—and I meant so much more than I could convey with that reply.

Arabella had been right. I was too easily distracted from my goal, and this was why she'd known that to be true.

She'd observed me with Sir Lawrence last night, even just for a fraction of the time we'd spent together.

And it was the baronet. The primary obstacle to me marrying the viscount's son, far more so than even somehow directing that rake's attention in my direction.

If I was failing at achieving this year's goal, it was the baronet who thwarted me.

Chapter Twenty-Three

"Well, at least that's multiple promises for gentlemen to come to a dinner." Mother tapped a finger to her lips as she stared over my head. "Did you and Miss Hatfield get on?"

I didn't realize she was speaking to me at first. "Oh? Um, yes." For a time, at least.

"Good, good. Make sure you start a correspondence with her. You can't write to any gentlemen, so best to get close to the ladies nearest them." Mother brushed past me, on her way to the kitchen. "And we'll send out invitations for our dinner soon. I just need to speak to Mrs. Stone about it."

"You want me to write to her?" I asked Mother, who stopped and turned around, looking at me as if I were parted from my wits. "But doesn't the baronet have a country estate a short carriage ride away?"

"You'll have to pay your visits when they come back. They're off to join Lady Fitzroy in Londyne tomorrow. I heard it from Sir Lawrence himself."

Leaving town? So soon?

I felt suddenly overheated. The baronet would no longer be an obstacle, a distraction.

And neither would Arabella. But what if *she* was right and she was the one who was supposed to be with Richard?

"But you just invited him for dinner."

"Oh, he'll be back. He promised. We'll invite him for dinner as soon as he does."

"But when will they—"

Mother hummed and went on her way, her song cutting short when Mr. Sinclair shouted, "Do those dulcet tunes mean that lunch is ready?" from his open study doorway.

"Oh, hush," said Mother, hardly stopping to speak to him. "Your daughters' social lives take precedence over one old man's hunger."

"I didn't realize they had anything to do with one another," my stepfather grumbled, but Mother was already in the kitchen.

I walked to the coat rack near the door and began removing my bonnet, followed by my Spencer. I intended to go upstairs and think about everything Arabella and I had discussed, eight years of study at Bedlam Academy continuously upended, but Dinah's giggles caught my attention.

I blinked. Had Mother just left Dinah and Mr. Smith unsupervised together?

I stared down the hallway in the direction of the kitchen.

I knew decorum meant I needed to be present for this guest's arrival, especially if he was paying a visit to those he'd danced with last night. And two unmarried people of different genders were not to be left alone, at least not out of sight of other people. I'd already been party to multiple instances of flaunting of such rules.

I threaded my hands together, took a deep breath, and walked into the drawing room.

"Mr. Smith." I smiled awkwardly. "Thank you for visiting."

The vicar, sitting beside the settee with Dinah, stood to his feet. He bowed, then practically dashed around the room to take my hand and kiss it. I hadn't offered him my hand, as was my right as a lady, I knew that much—and it was certainly presumptuous of him to put his lips to it. "Miss Radcliff. Always a pleasure. I would have greeted you sooner, but it was rather crowded there in the hallway." He kissed my hand again, and I felt like he meant so many witnesses in the hall wouldn't have allowed him such repeated intimacy. I shuddered.

Dinah's expression grew pinched, a visible flush to her cheeks as she leaped up beside him.

Only then did Mr. Smith drop my hand, and not for my lack of trying to get him to release it sooner.

Mr. Smith smiled broadly between Dinah and me. "Always a pleasure at the Sinclair-Radcliff house, yes, yes."

I forced a laugh and sat down on the chair beside the settee.

"Tea?" Dinah asked, gesturing for Mr. Smith to sit back down. There was already a rather full cup of tea in front of where he'd been sitting when I'd walked in.

He sat down and leaned an elbow on the arm of the settee nearest my chair, leaning over most ungentlemanly like. "So, Miss Radcliff, did you enjoy your walk?"

Dinah leaned over with a fresh cup of tea she'd poured for me, making a point, I thought, of draping her entire body between Mr. Smith and me. I thanked her and she shot me a bitter look.

"Yes, thank you." My whole world had become upended, but that wasn't discussion for polite Society. I sipped some of the tea. It had grown cold by now.

"Very fine weather today, indeed." Mr. Smith looked between Dinah and me. "I told Miss Sinclair as much when I got here and I asked after you. A fine day for a walk. Nothing I like so much as a fine day for a walk. No, I do believe God meant for us all to commune with nature to appreciate His splendor, not huddle together in pews."

Dinah settled back on the settee, her face alight as she captured Mr. Smith's attention. "I believe it was Sir Lawrence who observed that to be an odd thing for a vicar to say." Hiding her smile rather poorly behind one hand, she giggled.

Mr. Smith laughed, too, lifting his shoulders up and down as he leaned in toward Dinah.

Now that I knew their secret, I could see their attraction as plain as day. But I still wasn't convinced Mr. Smith felt as strong as Dinah did, letter or no letter.

I set my tea down. Mother still hadn't returned, and there was no sign of Mr. Sinclair, either.

So I'd be blunt about it. "Mr. Smith, what are your intentions with my stepsister?"

I didn't realize Dinah's jaw could drop quite so far open.

Mr. Smith, on the other hand, developed a pronounced facial tic as he clearly fought to keep a smile on his face. "Pardon?"

My gaze flicked to the hallway. Still no sign of anyone else. "You're waiting on my marriage to someone with enough money to make my dowry irrelevant, are you not? Then I can gift Dinah a sum grand enough to set you both up in comfort?"

"*Georgiana*," hissed Dinah, her teeth clenched as she spoke. "If Father or Mother hear—"

I kept my voice quiet. "If I'm to be so instrumental to these plans, I feel it best we speak openly."

Mr. Smith cleared his throat and looked from Dinah to me and back. Dinah slipped an arm through his.

"Mr. and Mrs. Sinclair wouldn't approve of the match, Miss Sinclair assures me." He patted Dinah's hand on his arm.

"And that's *all* that's stopping you?" I asked. At least he was acknowledging he'd discussed the topic with Dinah.

Mr. Smith tugged at his collar, his gaze flitting downward, then quickly jumped to his feet, Dinah's hand falling from his arm, as Mother's voice carried down the hall. "Excellent, excellent. Thank you, Mrs. Stone."

"Ah, Mrs. Sinclair," said Mr. Smith as Mother returned to the room. He made a great show of walking alongside her to the open chair in the room, then stood behind her, his hands on either side of the chair's back, as if it'd been necessary to pull the chair out for her, which it hadn't been.

Mother looked confused, tugging on one ear as she gazed up at the vicar. "Thank you, Mr. Smith. Will you be joining us for lunch? It's almost ready."

Mr. Smith steadfastly refused to look at either of us sisters, focusing only on Mother below him. "You'll have to excuse me, Mrs. Sinclair. So many parishioners to visit today, I'm afraid."

Dinah frowned. "But you always take Mother up on an invite for lunch."

Mr. Smith laughed, tossing his head back and his belly practically shaking. "Oh, bless you, you caught me. I simply can't do without the Sinclairs' fine cooking."

"Well, it's Mrs. Stone and the kitchen girl's cooking—" Mother started, but Mr. Smith was already headed toward the hallway.

Dinah shot me a look that would have sent many a student scurrying beneath a table back at the Academy and raced to her feet. "Mr. Smith. Surely, you can stay."

Mother arched an eyebrow at me, the corner of her mouth twisted up in a grimace, and rolled her eyes as she stood after just sitting down. I hadn't noticed before, but perhaps Mr. Smith's boisterous personality didn't strike Mother as particularly respectable. Perhaps, even if money were no object, she and Father would still frown upon a union between Dinah and the vicar.

I followed Mother out into the hall, where Mr. Smith was affixing his hat. "Always a pleasure, ladies. Always a pleasure. I'll see you this Sunday in church."

"Or in town before then?" Dinah offered, practically swaying up on her tiptoes.

He nodded at her, his jaw clenched tightly for a moment. "Or in town, of course. Such a small place. Always running into a friend."

And then he left, walking in the direction of town down the dirt lane.

Mother let out a deep breath. "How that man manages to find half his energy every morning, I'll never know. Come on, girls. Mrs. Stone is about to serve lunch."

She headed toward the study, calling out my stepfather's name.

Dinah narrowed her eyes at me, slamming the door behind her.

Mother let out a cry from down the hall, her hand on her chest. "*Dinah*! There will be no *slamming* of doors. Now get cleaned up for lunch."

"I'm not hungry," said Dinah, her voice growing hard as she refused to look away from me. "Don't send any food up to me."

She thundered up the stairs, every step louder than the next.

Mr. Sinclair stepped out of his study, looking up at the ceiling, where his eyes followed the harsh footfalls of his daughter's retreat to her room in the floor above.

"Oh, dear. Did Dinah experience a stomach cramp from all those biscuits you insisted Mrs. Stone make this morning?"

"Oh, hush." Mother whopped him across the chest. "Your lunch is ready, so you can stop your complaining."

She headed back in my direction. "What's wrong with your sister?"

My mouth opened. If I told on Dinah, logically, I'd lose her support in pursuing Richard. Though perhaps whatever magic was at work would still compel her to aid me. Or would it? Would this serve as a test, to see if this world wanted me to marry Richard or if it intended the bride to be Arabella?

I opened my mouth again and a sudden squeak down the hall got my attention. Nora was there on her way to the dining room, a large serving bowl in both hands.

"Nora?" I asked.

Nora fumbled with the serving bowl, almost dropping it. I ran forward and helped her catch it.

Mother let out a little cry. "My goodness! Be careful, you foolish girl."

"It's fine," I told her. "I'll help her."

I added my hands to Nora's and directed her into the dining room. We were alone there, if just for a moment.

I wanted to ask what had made the color drain from her face as she'd observed Mother asking me about Dinah, but before I could, we'd set the serving dish down and Nora stuck her hand down a pocket stitched into her apron, pulling out a letter.

"He left this for you," she said, her voice cracking, as quiet as could be, as she shoved a letter into my hand.

Before I could ask who, she'd scuttled back to the kitchen.

Chapter Twenty-Four

I glanced at the letter Nora had given me so discreetly. My name was written in slanted handwriting that seemed vaguely familiar. She'd said "he" had left it. No gentlemen were supposed to be writing to me without an accepted proposal first. No wonder Nora had been so nervous—though she'd acted as a messenger for Dinah in similar improper circumstances. Before I could open it, Mother's voice grew louder and I slipped it down the front of my dress.

I thought about excusing myself to my room like Dinah had, but I'd already missed breakfast. I was feeling light-headed from that, from all of the news.

It was a difficult lunch to get through, though. Mother and my stepfather kept up their banter, and I tried to follow along, but I kept thinking about everything: Arabella's reveal, Dinah and Mr. Smith, what I should do from now on, the letter...

Whom did I hope the letter was from?

Sir Lawrence.

But I couldn't see the man writing secret letters he slipped to the waiting staff.

Mother sniffed. "You're excused, Georgiana. If you're

going to stay lost in your thoughts like that, you may as well leave the table.”

I jumped up, satisfied to see at least half of my portions eaten. I didn't *remember* eating. I'd done it without thinking.

I forgot to say my goodbyes as I walked away from the table.

“My goodness,” said Mother, though I didn't stop to look at her. “You had better not act like that when we have company!”

My stepfather's voice was softer but still clear. “I would hope you wouldn't shout so when we have company, either, my dear.”

But I was already at the steps, pulling the letter out from my dress as I headed for my room.

Sunlight streamed in through my curtains, making it easy to hold the letter up to the light. I opened it, the wax seal snapping in half as I pulled the ends of the paper apart.

My heart sunk when I realized why I'd found the writing familiar.

Most beautiful Georgiana,

I must confess you have captured my heart. From the moment I first saw you, when I moved to this fine village, I wished to be yours. Please tell me you felt the sweet air between us last night during our dance at the viscount's ball. Please tell me you will be my bride.

Yours, E.

The letter fell from my hands.

"Sweet air"? "His *bride*"?

"E" for Edward Smith? I felt as if I might be sick. Still covering his tracks by not signing his actual name. But I'd seen some of his letters to Dinah. It was the same handwriting.

When had he moved here? Had there been *anything* between him and the Georgiana whose life I'd slipped into to give him such hope?

Did he really think Dinah wouldn't communicate with me about their own liaison? I presumed he'd written this before he'd come here, before I'd confronted him about his expectations regarding my stepsister. The idea that they'd wait for funds following my own marriage to a man of means hadn't seemed foreign to him, so they'd clearly discussed it. How could he think Dinah wouldn't have spoken of it with me before then?

When would he have given Nora this letter? Not after I'd confronted him—he wouldn't have had the chance. So while I'd been out walking with Arabella.

He'd either expected me to respond positively because of some interaction he'd had previously with the other me, or he'd just *hoped* I would. And then he'd known I'd get this letter after I'd confronted him, and perhaps now he realized that meant he had no chance with me.

Why in the two worlds did this man even *think* he had a chance with me? The confession of love in the letter made me hopeful he'd had no interaction with the other me in the past. Was it just the more immediate chance of gaining money through my larger dowry?

It had to have been. If I had the biggest dowry in the village, and Dinah's wasn't sufficient for him—because he could clearly have her, even if they had to run off to Bretna Brown—then he'd have to leave town to look for a wife if I wouldn't have him.

And I *wouldn't* have him.

No matter what Arabella might have said.

No matter if I was right and she was wrong and I was bound to marry Richard Gillingham, a thought that filled me with no joy.

The idea of marrying the local vicar—not because of his lack of fortune, but because of his clear lack of decorum— made me feel unclean.

Mary had left a basin of water in my room for washing up, and I used it to splash across my face, trampling over the letter on the wooden floor as I did so.

I stared out the window, at the lush countryside, and I had no more answers than I'd had before.

But for right now, there was only one thing I *could* do that made sense. Whatever the consequences might be.

I snatched the letter off the floor and headed to Dinah's bedroom.

The room was quiet. I knocked on the door.

There was a pause and then there were footfalls on the other side of it.

Dinah opened the door, glowering at me. "Have you come to apologize for what you did?"

I shoved the letter at her without a word.

The scowl disappeared as she took it and stepped aside, letting me into her room. But as I'd expected, her expression grew heavy as she shut the door and examined the outside of the missive. Her lover's handwriting. My name.

"Read it," I said simply.

She looked as likely to throttle me as speak to me. But she opened it up and read.

As her eyes darted from one side to the next and back again, her nostrils flared.

"No," she said, her voice shaky. "No, this is a lie."

She headed for her bed, tossing the letter to the floor much like I had.

She laughed then, though the sound had a sharp edge. "You copied his handwriting."

I gave her a double-take. "I'm not capable of such a thing. Nora gave it to me. Ask her. He gave it to her directly this time, it seems."

"You told her to lie." Dinah crossed her arms, and there were clear tears welling up in her eyes, even if she seemed determined not to shed them.

"Of course I didn't!" I tossed my hands up in the air. "Why would I make up such a thing?"

"You want Edward for yourself." Dinah swallowed.

"I most certainly do *not*." I sat down on the bed beside her. "Now that I know him better, I have to wonder why *you* even want him."

"That's it, then," snapped Dinah. "You seduced him in order to make me not like him. Well, it won't work. It won't work!" Her voice grew louder.

What was going on here? Dinah was throwing herself at this man whose heart had never fully been hers, it seemed, this man with no prospects and little decorum, and one who could be described as "mildly pleasant-looking" at best.

"I wouldn't do that. If all I wanted was to keep you away from him, I would have just told Mother and Father instead. But you're just admitting there's a possibility he wrote that letter himself."

"Of course there's a possibility." Her tone was vicious, as if *I* were the dumb one when it'd been she who'd been contradicting herself right from the start.

The deep breath I took was to steady myself, trying to remind myself of the generally genial stepsister she'd been in this world and not think of the bully who'd laughed as that poor underclassman had been threatened with certain death.

I put a hand on her shoulder as she stared the other way. "Why do you want to be with him?" I asked. "You're beautiful. And you're a lady, large dowry or no. You say I should marry rich so my husband would have no need of my dowry, but the same advice could apply to you."

Dinah's chin trembled somewhat. "But I love him. And

he promised. He promised he'd marry me. In so many words."

"Do you *want* a man coerced into keeping a promise he doesn't want to keep? Who'll throw himself at other options he thinks he has?" I thought suddenly of Arabella, only I knew now she didn't care if Richard's heart wasn't in her prospective marriage.

Since Dinah was being quiet, I decided to test the boundaries of her subconscious compulsion.

"I am quite serious that Mr. Gillingham is taken with you. If you act quickly"—*before his attention is diverted elsewhere*, I stopped myself from adding—"you might be able to secure yourself another match."

Dinah turned to me. She was crying, and she wiped away a tear silently. "You really think so?"

My back stiffened. What had happened to her demure refusal of believing in Richard's interest, her insistence that he and I were destined for one other?

"You could see yourself as the future Lady Gillingham?" I asked quietly.

"I could..." she said, chewing on her lip. She cocked her head, as if confused herself. "I really feel like he was the one I should have always been after, if only I'd met him before... Before Edward."

What had changed, other than learning of Mr. Smith's nature?

What had happened to the magic working at her subconscious?

Since last night... Arabella had opened that portal.

A portal that had brought more of my own self back to me, memories I'd realized I'd kept at bay.

What if she, too, was more her old self? If not entirely consciously, then closer to matching her old desires?

At Bedlam Academy, Dinah had been *certain* she'd be the lady candidate. All of that aside, she wouldn't have been satisfied with this cozy, somewhat impoverished gentry life. She *never* would have aimed to lower herself even further.

She would have wanted a title. Riches. Someone just like Richard for a husband. Half the time, I'd even thought her at least somewhat attracted to Aylmer.

But that had been because he'd been the best man available. He wasn't that anymore.

But then... if Arabella was right, or if Arabella's actions had changed things, shouldn't they have made Dinah and the others eager to help *her* cause, even if they were unaware of it?

Dinah shouldn't have wanted Richard for herself.

My stepsister laughed darkly and wiped another tear away. Then she took my hand. "Can I tell you Edward's and my story? Why I chose him? I know you've asked before. I didn't want to share it. But I will now."

It must have been the other Georgiana who'd asked her. But I was curious nonetheless and tired of thinking about the goal of those from Bedlam Academy.

The dark deeds of those from Bedlam Academy.

"I'll hear it," I told her, squeezing her hand.

"Edward—Mr. Smith..." Dinah seemed unsure of what name to use to refer to the man now. One denoted a closeness she must have struggled to keep feeling, and the other probably didn't fall as naturally from her tongue in certain company. "Perhaps I should go further back."

I nodded, releasing her hand.

"I've never felt... quite right," she said. "I know I've hid it well, and I'm not saying I don't adore Father, and Mother, and you, too—the fact is, I don't know *why* I've felt a little broken. I certainly haven't had a right to feel that way." She sighed.

The Dinah I'd known first had been broken, too. But she'd lashed out at everyone around her instead of retreating inside herself.

"Bedlam..." I started, watching her face for signs of recognition. Perhaps the portal being open so near had jogged something in her, too.

But all she did was tilt her head and study me curiously.

I cleared my throat. "You must have felt chaotic inside. I do, too, at times. I call that feeling, that sense of something being wrong, 'bedlam.'" It was as good a story as any.

Dinah quirked a careful smile. "I'm glad not to be the only one to feel it, though I'm sorry for you. I wonder if... Well, I always thought perhaps it was the loss of my mother, even if I was too young to remember much of her. Perhaps your *bedlam* comes from the loss of your father at a young age."

"Perhaps," I echoed, doing my best to smile. The baron in this world had not been my father in the old one, but that was the only face I could muster when she talked about him. And the only feeling I got from his *loss* from my life was one of satisfaction.

"Edward was the first person I spoke to about it." She looked at me with wide eyes. "And before you say I should have spoken to you, I was afraid to. You being a baron's daughter—having that enviable dowry. You couldn't understand. Or so I thought." She *tsked*, but it seemed directed more at herself than at me. She stared at the floor.

"Edward told me all about his own woes, being born a third son and his father forcing him into the church when he had no such ambition. How his oldest brother did nothing but amuse himself all day and not be chastised for it, how his other brother distinguished himself through military service. He felt simultaneously like the family's disappointment and like too much was expected of him. It didn't seem fair."

"What *does* he want to do with his life? If the choice were up to him?"

"Doing nothing like the heir to his family's estate would be ideal." Dinah scoffed. "But he promised me he'd find some vocation—or resign himself to the church. If we got married. If only he had enough of a fortune to feel secure in our situation."

"So he did ask you to marry him?"

"Not... Not outright, no." She whirled on me. "But how else could I interpret his talk about how he could be satisfied marrying me if there were only some way to find ourselves a fortune?" She started sobbing, leaning forward. "I thought he understood me, that gaping hole in my chest." She took a deep breath, her voice crackling. "But there was always this sense I got... He *knew* I was envious of your dowry and your connection to a title, and yet here he was, telling me he was fine without my title, but he couldn't overlook my lack of fortune." She wiped her eyes. "But foolish me, I thought, well, doesn't that just prove what you told yourself was lacking all along? And he *will* accept you, Dinah, if you can fix just one thing about yourself, the only thing remotely fixable."

Despite my misgivings, my distaste for the bully she'd once been, I gave her a hug from the side. "You shouldn't have to accept someone who only wants you if you move mountains to make yourself what he wants you to be."

"I know, but..." She started crying into my shoulder. "I didn't dwell on thoughts like that long. His letters kept me going—"

"He never should have sent you those letters if he was going to turn around and send me one." I refrained from talking about the thought that popped into my mind that perhaps I wasn't the only other recipient of such missives. Then again, if I weren't, there would be bound to be some gossip. "I don't understand. I was cordial to him during our dance, but I certainly never encouraged him."

She pulled back. "I talked to him about our idea that Mr. Gillingham might make the perfect husband for you," she said. "During our own dance. I wonder if... he was aiming for you all along, and he thought he had little choice but to try before it was too late."

"And he honestly thought I never knew about his promise to you?"

"Like I said, it wasn't an exact promise. And he said we should keep as quiet as we could. Perhaps he thought I never had spoken to you. He didn't ask if I had."

"He was the one who involved the servants." I sighed. "I

have *no* intentions of responding to him. Or of being anything more than the barest level of civil." I smiled at her. "And I suggest, perhaps after one more letter, you do the same."

She sniffled as she stared at me. "You really think I could do better?"

"I know it," I promised her.

She chuckled flatly. "I would have danced more last night if I'd come to this decision earlier."

"You might have never come to the decision if he hadn't shown his hand." I nudged her. "So perhaps everything happens for a reason."

I stopped myself at these words, the wheels of my mind turning.

Arabella's presence here, her visions, her retaining her memories... She was right. It had to have been for a reason.

And Dinah may have just demonstrated what that was.

Chapter Twenty-Five

I t wasn't until later that week that Unity was due to pay us a visit.

I'd written my letter to Arabella, and now, while waiting for Unity and Mrs. Dowding, I decided to ask Nora again what she thought of me pursuing Richard Gillingham. She was pounding dough, Mrs. Stone nowhere in sight. Mother had sent her off to the market.

"It's all none of my business, miss. But I wish you success whatever you may choose." She looked at me askance then, no doubt curious about the contents of Mr. Smith's letter. Then again, she was quite aware Dinah and he had been exchanging clandestine letters for longer. Perhaps she thought that one letter had been related to that, even if addressed to me.

More importantly, I detected less enthusiasm for my potential match with Richard than she's shown previously. Was Nora, too, affected by the portal opening nearby?

Nora pounded her palms together, sending a burst of flour into the air. She looked this way and that, then she lowered her voice, even if no one was to be found. "He sent another one this morning."

I clamped my lips together and held my hand out for it.

"This one's for Miss Dinah again," said Nora, reaching into her apron pocket and handing over the wax-sealed letter. "And Mrs. Bates keeps asking for a reply." She was referring to the servant whom Mr. Smith had sent.

"And you've told her there won't be one?" I reminded her.

"I have." Nora scrunched up her nose. "She did say her master won't like that."

"I imagine not." I cracked open the wax seal and gave the letter a cursory glance. I knew Dinah didn't mind and that she wouldn't read them herself. She'd sent her final letter, as I'd hoped she'd would, letting him know she'd seen the one he'd addressed to me and she was finished with him.

Only Mr. Smith didn't seem finished with her.

My love,

I wait in agony for your response. As I've written to you to explain previously, the other letter was but a bold move on my part, a hope to secure some finances from your sister before—

I folded the letter. Lies, all of it. I'd have no money of my own to give him before my marriage, even if I'd wanted to, which he'd been made well aware of. And to speak as if I *had* money and just withheld it from my stepsister yet would hand it over to him with a few unsolicited kisses forced onto my hand? Shuddering, I tucked the letter into the dress. I was sure Dinah would choose to burn it with the others, but I'd let her perform the task herself.

The front door to the house opened, and I knew Mrs.

Stone was bound to have returned, so I nodded at Nora and let her get back to it.

Mother wrapped her shawl tighter around her chest as she approached Mrs. Stone at the front door. "Any letters, Mrs. Stone?"

"Yes, ma'am." The head servant dug around in one of her baskets and pulled out a small stack of letters. "I stopped by and got those replies from the houses you asked me to pay special attention to as well. Mighty fancy place, that Wycliff Manor."

I jumped slightly on the way past them and to the drawing room. Wycliff Manor meant the viscount and viscountess. And Richard Gillingham.

Dinah was in front of the fireplace, practicing her embroidery. Checking over my shoulder to make sure Mother was still in the hallway, I pulled the letter out from my dress.

"*Another* one?" Dinah asked dryly.

I nodded.

"Anything I should know about in it?"

"I stopped reading halfway through. I couldn't stomach his accusations—"

"Into the fire." Dinah nodded, not even looking up from her needlework.

I tossed it straight in, picking up the poker to make sure every little bit was devoured by flames.

Once I turned back, it was to find Dinah with a pinched expression, her hand holding the needle and thread high up in the air.

"If he thinks he'll continue making a fool out of *me*..." She left the rest unsaid. There was a darkness in her voice, a stiffness in her back that reminded me of the Dinah I'd known even as she continued the innocuous task of embroidery.

Only that Dinah had been surrounded by hangers-on at all times, and so she'd been showy, boisterous. Now, I was her only audience, and I wasn't so carefully positioned under her thumb as those at Bedlam Academy had been.

Her wrath took on a different form without an audience.

"Oh, goodness me. Mrs. Stone, they have all accepted. Friday evening. Girls, girls!" Mother stepped into the drawing room from the hallway. "We are hosting a dinner Friday evening."

Dinah's head finally shot up. "Tell me you haven't invited the vicar."

"Mr. Smith?" Mother frowned. "The two of you get along *so well*, and even without that, it's only right that I should..." She flipped through the stack of letters in her hand and opened one. "Ah, yes. He's accepted."

Dinah's nostrils flared and I stepped behind the chair she was sitting in, resting my hand on her shoulder. "We can't ignore him forever. It would seem too strange."

"*I* can," she said, turning back to stab through the material in her hand with more force than necessary. "But there's no avoiding him at church regardless. So *fine*. Let him come here on Friday."

Mother, fortunately, was distracted, calling out my stepfather's name as she carried the stack down the hallway. "Now, dear, I won't hear anything about you preferring a quiet night in," she said clearly before their conversation devolved into faint murmurs.

A carriage approached and, as Dinah was clearly not going to turn around and confirm our visitors, I went to the window to look out of it. Generally, when the weather was agreeable, Unity and Mrs. Dowding were not above a walk. A chill had taken hold in the air, but it was still a fine enough day in the sunlight to justify a walk. I planned to go on one later this afternoon myself, after we'd parted from our visitors.

The carriage drew to a stop, and the first person to step out was Aylmer.

He turned around, helping first Mrs. Dowding and then

Unity out of the carriage. He must have come across them on his way and offered them a ride. Mother would no doubt extend her invitation for tea to Aylmer as soon as she saw him.

The driver shut the door to the carriage, and it seemed as if Richard, Aylmer's constant companion as of late, was not among the party.

All the better. I would test both Unity and Aylmer at once, without Richard here to observe what could only be odd behavior to a native of this place.

"Mr. Linden," said Mother, her voice warm as she approached the doorway and spotted the unexpected visitor, "so wonderful to see you."

The gentleman in question stepped aside as Unity and Mrs. Dowding made their way in.

"Good afternoon to you, Mrs. Sinclair." His eyes darted to me in the entryway to the drawing room and he tipped his hat toward me as well. "Miss Radcliff. I happened upon the Dowdings on my way into town and I offered them a lift."

"Oh, please stay," Mother said. "You can join us."

"Oh, I couldn't intrude on an afternoon you ladies had planned." Aylmer laughed as Unity and Mrs. Dowding removed their hats and coats, Mary appearing from the back of the house to hang them on the coat rack.

Unity scooted over to me and took my hand in hers, giving it a squeeze. There was something alight in her eyes as she shook her head slowly while smiling.

"Please stay," I said quickly to Aylmer. I wanted to discern whether or not he still hoped to see me with Richard.

"Well, perhaps I have a moment." Aylmer passed his hat off to Mary, who'd just been about to walk away, then removed his gloves.

"Oh, good." Mother clapped her hands together. "Mary, go alert Mr. Linden's driver he can pull around the back and take a break, then tell Mrs. Stone we have one more for tea."

Mary nodded without a word and Mother gestured for

her guests to head into the drawing room. Unity took my arm in hers and walked us slowly toward the fire.

"Miss Sinclair," she said to Dinah, who was still engaged in her embroidery.

"Miss Dowding," my stepsister replied, not looking up until she'd finished one more stitch. Then her face grew flush as Aylmer guided Mrs. Dowding into the room by the arm, Dinah's embroidery abandoned and slipped into the basket to the side of her chair. "Mr. Linden?"

"Miss Sinclair." He bowed at her as he helped Unity's mother to the settee. My own mother scrambled back and forth to the hall, as if watching Nora come over with the tea might help move things along faster.

Unity turned her back to the others and faced the fire, her voice quiet. "What happened to your sister's devotion to the vicar?" She snorted.

My breath hitched. "A rumor," I said quickly, glancing over my shoulder, but Dinah didn't seem to have noticed. She was up as Nora approached unsteadily with the tray full of tea and snacks. "Nothing but a rumor. And I've made her aware of the talk now, so she's going to be more guarded around the man."

"That's no fun." Unity snorted again. I wondered if a part of her reveled in seeing her former leader a bit under *her* thumb in this world. Dinah had a smaller dowry, and she seemed not to have a confidante as Unity did in me.

I guided Unity over to the corner of the room, a bench near the window that afforded us both space as Mother brought over a cup of tea for Unity first and then me.

"Miss Dowding," said Mother as she brought the second cup of tea over. "I've been so eager to see you since the ball. Your mother told me how well your playing went over with the people in town. And you accompanied my Georgiana, gave her a way to shine." Mother smiled, but then she frowned at me. "I wonder why your pianoforte skills have slipped. Perhaps we need to buy an instrument of our own?"

Of all the tasks I had to complete, spending my days

practicing to improve my musical talent was not one of them I, or Richard by my guess, cared about. "Consider the expense, Mother. Besides, I have Unity if such an occasion arises again."

"Yes, of course. And thank you, Mrs. Sinclair." Unity took a careful sip, arching her brow as Dinah sat kitty-corner to Aylmer, leaning just a touch on the armrest nearest the gentleman.

"Hmm, well, perhaps." Mother stared out over the room. "I appreciate your mother letting my girls practice at your house growing up. I suppose it's too late now to improve her talents. She's already made it clear to half the county she can only sing."

Unity nudged me with her elbow. "I don't know. I'd hardly say 'only' sing. Sir Lawrence seemed quite captivated with Georgiana's performance."

This made for a good segue. "And Mr. Gillingham did, too, didn't you say so, Unity?"

"Mr. Gillingham?" Unity took a sip of her tea. "I... I wouldn't say he noticed."

Mother bit her lip and nodded. "Oh, well... A baronet. Yes, a baronet will do fine."

"Over a future viscount?" I asked. I would not let either know my own personal preference for the baronet. Even if I hardly knew the man.

Unity laughed. "Well, aren't you setting your sights the highest they can go this far out in the country." She cocked her head. "Well, you do have an impressive dowry—and your late father's title—to recommend you. I should think even a viscount would be glad to have you as his wife." She frowned.

"But?" I asked.

Mother, too, was leaning in eagerly.

"It's nothing." Unity sipped her tea again.

"You're referring to the rumors of his betrothal to an heiress in Bathe," I said. "We asked him, and he explained it was all over between them."

Unity's eyebrows arched as she settled the teacup back onto its saucer. "You *asked* him?"

"My girl is not always one to mind her manners." Mother *tsked*. "But yes, he said it was quite over." Mother caught Mrs. Dowding's eye and made her way back to the fireplace and the rest of the group, taking a chair kitty-corner from Mrs. Dowding.

Unity set her teacup on a small table beside the window and I handed her my own to do the same.

"Well, it wasn't *that* betrothed to whom I was referring," Unity said, quieter. "Aylmer himself actually let slip the next juicy bit of gossip about the future viscount."

"Oh?" I asked, trying to read her features. I decided to try nudging at her subconscious goals once more. "And you think it should impede my goal in winning Mr. Gillingham's favor?"

She leaned closer, her voice hushing. "He has a reputation as a bit of a... rake." She practically whispered that last word. "Aylmer said he's sure the man is hiding *another* betrothed from everyone, though he can't get the man to admit it." She leaned back, patting my hand. "Rumor or no, you could do better, Georgiana. No, the viscount's son won't do for you."

And there was the truth of it. That was now three students from Bedlam Academy whose behavior had changed since Arabella had opened that portal.

So Arabella Weston—Hatfield—had retained her memories when brought to this world. The purpose of that, I guessed, was to free the Bedlam Academy students from whatever magic had guided them.

If I was to marry the viscount's son, I was now on my own.

Could Bedlam Academy students be happy here, unburdened by the goal of the graduating class? We certainly assumed all the previous candidates who'd made their way here had stayed after their class's goal had been completed, and I hoped they were happy.

Even freed from the goal of setting me up with Richard, though, Nora only seemed a shade of herself. She didn't seem *unhappy*, but could I allow myself to settle into domesticity while the friend I'd held dearest in another life spent her days working from dawn until dusk?

Could I go on with my life here, hoping Arabella was right and I wasn't dooming the world back home to destruction with my impassivity?

What would I do with myself?

It was clear my mother in this world expected me to be married. At the thought of that, Sir Lawrence's face popped into my head. Ridiculous. I hardly knew him. Yet I did know from years of study at Bedlam Academy, that fact was secondary to whether or not he would make a suitable partner in marriage.

"Georgiana? Where have your thoughts taken you?"

I realized with a start I was staring out the window, not responding to something Unity had said.

I looked up, just in time to see Aylmer approaching us both. "Ladies, I was just discussing with your mothers that it's a fine day for a walk. Miss Sinclair already accepted my invitation. Might you as well?"

Unity clasped her hands together demurely over her lap. "Yes, of course. What a wonderful idea, Mr. Linden."

Aylmer held his hand out to me.

Suddenly, I felt all eyes on the room on me. Unity pursed her lips, but her expression wasn't half as noticeable as Dinah's. She fidgeted in her seat and looked about to burst into tears as she stared at Aylmer's back.

She'd been set free of her obsession with Mr. Smith and now she wanted a better husband, that much was evident.

"Yes, thank you, Mr. Linden." I accepted his hand.

Aylmer disappeared into the back of the house to talk with his driver, and it was another bit of fussing as we all put on our hats and warmer things before we were finally on the road in front of the house. Only instead of heading toward the town, Aylmer suggested we head the other way.

"Wycliff Manor is in this direction," said Dinah, trotting to keep up with Aylmer, who seemed determined to match my pace. Unity walked just a few steps ahead of us.

"Yes. I did wonder if you ladies might want to pay him a visit."

My head cocked. Was I wrong? Did Aylmer still envision me marrying Richard?

"Oh, I don't know if we should drop in uninvited," said Unity.

"Oh, do let's," said Dinah, and the two women caught each other's eyes across Aylmer and me, their brows furrowing in reflection of one another.

Had Dinah moved on to Richard already, after monopolizing Aylmer for much of the morning?

"It's a bit of a long walk," I said, and at that, Aylmer slipped his arm through mine, his expression soft.

"I expected you ladies might be tired, so I instructed my driver to meet us there and offer us a ride back. Gillingham is expecting me. I only made the detour when I ran into Mrs. and Miss Dowding."

"Oh, good," said Dinah, and she ran a few steps in front of Unity, as if determined to be the first one there.

"Expecting a single gentleman isn't quite the same as expecting a full party," Unity said.

"He won't mind. I'm sure of it." Aylmer smiled at her.

Unity frowned but picked up her pace as Dinah moved even faster, perhaps unwilling to let her be the first one to arrive.

Aylmer chuckled. "I told Gillingham he'd be popular in the country. He's barely been here a week and he's already the most sought-after bachelor for miles."

I decided to take the opportunity to confirm his own level of interest in me marrying the man. "You put in a good word for me, though, I hope?"

Aylmer stopped and searched my face, his expression pinched. Then he smiled. "You tease me, I presume? And here I thought you to be one of the only women of good sense in the village who might not throw herself at the man's feet just because of a future title."

"'Just because'?" I let Aylmer guide us forward again, still arm-in-arm. "I think you underestimate the importance of such a thing for a lady."

Aylmer's pace slowed a little, the rest of our party getting smaller and smaller up ahead. "I most definitely do not. I'm well aware I have no such title to offer my bride."

So he was more concerned with finding his own wife than helping Richard find his? He had definitely been affected by the open portal as well.

I patted his arm. "You're a man of means. A gentleman. Any lady should count herself fortunate to attract your attention."

His eyes examined me through darting glances, a smile working its way onto his lips. "It heartens me to hear you say that."

My gut grew heavy. If Aylmer was freed from any concern about helping me wed Richard Gillingham, if more of his former self was now present in him, did that mean...

He still considered himself to be in love with me?

Chapter Twenty-Six

Aylmer had been a nice man at Bedlam Academy, and he was a gentleman now. If I had to marry, I would have preferred to be his wife over the wife of someone like Mr. Smith—even over becoming the bride of Richard Gillingham himself, if I never had to worry about the graduates' goal at all.

I certainly knew him—some form of him—better than I knew Sir Lawrence.

But I felt no desire to become his wife. Not if I had other options.

I'd guarded my heart against him and anyone for so long, it wasn't used to thinking of him as anything other than a friendly face in a sea of acquaintances.

I turned to him, removing my arm from his. "I was hoping you might pay my sister some special attention today."

"Your sister?" The lump in Aylmer's throat bobbed.

"Yes, she… She hasn't been feeling so confident as of late. And she holds you in such high esteem."

Dinah and Unity were practically out of our sight now, the two having forgotten to not leave us alone together.

Whether I or Arabella was right, I needed to make sure Dinah didn't turn her attentions to the viscount's son. Not that I wanted to saddle Aylmer with the bully from Bedlam Academy necessarily, but she *was* different here, even now.

Aylmer took my arm again, though his grip was looser this time, his back somewhat curved, his shoulders forward. "You were serious when you said you hoped I'd put in a good word about you with Gillingham, weren't you?"

"Well, I…" At the very least, whatever it took to keep him away from Dinah. I was sure I was at least right that she was not the leading lady candidate, as neither Unity nor Aylmer nor Nora seemed to particularly want Dinah and Richard together. "I should like to get to know him better."

Though truth be told, I knew more than enough about him to make a fair assessment of his character.

An unfavorable assessment.

Aylmer's jaw clenched as he started straight ahead. "I will do my best."

Even in this world, free to be himself, Aylmer's kindness prevailed.

The rest of the walk was uneventful, though I had to admit that my legs were growing sore by the end of it.

Dinah and Unity slowed as they approached the manor, though Dinah seemed strangely cheerful with having arrived a mere few seconds before Unity, the windburns on her cheeks giving her complexion a delightful blush.

"Shall we?" She bounced as Aylmer and I approached.

He nodded and led the way, and when Dinah took his other arm, I slipped out of his grip, smiling sweetly and making my way over to Unity.

"I swear that girl went faster every time I almost caught up with her," said Unity under her breath.

"She's awfully excited to be here."

"She wants that rake for herself," said Unity as quietly as could be. She laughed.

I forced out a chuckle along with her, unsure if I could find the humor in this situation.

We were greeted at the door by the thin-faced butler and a quiet, lanky footman, and after we'd removed all of our hats and coats and gloves, we were led down the vast, empty hallway toward a wing I'd never been in before. The place looked so different in the daylight, outside of a ball. Every footfall echoed louder, as if to emphasize the point that there were far fewer people inside this place this day.

We passed the study in which I'd come across Richard and Arabella together. How different the meaning of that scene seemed to me now.

The door was open. Like my stepfather, perhaps Lord Gillingham would not be involved in greeting guests stopping by merely for a short daytime visit.

"I understand."

The voice halted my steps. Ahead of us, Dinah and Aylmer still walked arm-in-arm behind the butler.

"Georgiana?" Unity asked, turning around. Her voice traveled down the echoing hall.

The man standing before the desk in the study, the one who had spoken, turned around.

It was Sir Lawrence Fitzroy, the baronet.

"You're supposed to be in Londyne at present," I said, dumbfounded.

Then I realized how foolish I was, speaking to the baronet, uninvited, from the hallway on my way to the drawing room.

"Evidently not," said Sir Lawrence, smirking, his own voice carrying as loudly as mine across Lord Gillingham's study.

Now we had the entire group's attention. Lord Gillingham himself, Richard's father, stood from behind his desk as the butler came back toward Unity and me, Dinah and Aylmer staying where they'd been but clearly confused.

"What's the meaning of this?" Lord Gillingham's voice boomed across the room.

Sir Lawrence turned over his shoulder to look at him, but it was the butler bowing and speaking quickly that drew everyone else's attention. As the older, silver-haired man had a bit of a hunch to his shoulders, his bow was particularly exaggerated.

"My most humble apologies, my lord. I'm taking this group of youth to meet with your son, and we seem to have caused a *disturbance*—"

"Very well, then. Carry on," said the viscount. "Perhaps make sure the *doors are closed* when traipsing through my hallways with strangers, Cooper?"

"Of course, my lord." The butler, Cooper, reached across me to shut the door, sneering at me all the while until Unity took hold of my elbow and pulled me backward a step.

My gaze was caught on Sir Lawrence's, though, almost until the last second before the door shut between us.

Cooper lingered a moment to stare at me then gestured back down the hallway. "Shall we?"

Dinah and Aylmer waited for Unity and me to step closer to them, Dinah speaking in a hush. "*Who* was supposed to be in Londyne?"

"The baronet," Unity answered for me. "Mother did say they left rather in a hurry earlier this week. He and his ward."

"Yes," I added, staring at our feet as we shuffled ahead. "They were eager to get back to his mother."

So why was he here mere days after his supposed departure? And in Lord Gillingham's study?

Did that mean Arabella was here, too?

"Your guests, sir." Cooper stopped at the doorway to a grand drawing room, complete with a wide window overlooking the sprawling garden in which I'd found myself hiding during the ball. Even though the flowers weren't fully in bloom any longer, the garden hedges looked more dazzling in the sunlight, and probably looked even grander still in the height of spring and summer.

Richard had been staring at a fire as we'd entered, one leg

crossed over the other thigh, bouncing like a thumping rabbit's foot as he chewed on a thumbnail.

Clearly startled, he shot to his feet at Cooper's voice and straightened his jacket. "Linden! You've... brought guests." His eyebrows lifted, a smile on his face as he spotted Dinah on Aylmer's arm. The smile vanished when he caught sight of me just off to the side of her.

"I didn't think you'd mind," said Aylmer. "We went for a walk and I told them you'd be expecting me."

"No, of course not. Have a seat, ladies. Cooper, refreshments for everyone. They must be parched after their long walk through these hills."

Richard stepped forward and held an arm out to Dinah, who accepted, moving from one gentleman to the next, and my gut grew heavy at the recurring thought that by freeing Dinah from Mr. Smith, I'd unleashed her into the path of the very man upon whom the fate of our world depended, in one way or the other.

I sighed. Even if my role proved to be diminished in this story, anxiety was bound to be my closest companion.

Richard guided Dinah to the chair nearest the fire, and before he could take the chair just beside her that he'd been occupying when we'd walked in, I brushed past him and took the seat.

Dinah and Richard both stared blankly at me at that.

"Thank you," I said to Richard, nodding as I fixed my skirt. Pretending I had anything to thank him for, as if he'd guided me to this chair himself.

Richard didn't say anything, instead taking a seat nearest Dinah on her other side, though still some distance apart, as Aylmer and Unity settled in together on a settee nearby.

"So..." Richard clapped his hands together as he leaned forward in his chair. "I hear we're to be your guests this Friday, Miss Sinclair. Miss *Radcliff*." He added my name as a rather harsh afterthought. "I do apologize that my parents can't make it."

"Oh, that's just fine," said Dinah, her teeth dazzling.

My back stiffened. "Mother invited Sir Lawrence, too, but she didn't expect him to come. Yet I see he's back in town already."

Richard turned to me, his face as white as a sheet. "You... know he's here?"

I cocked my head. "We just saw him speaking with your father in the study."

Richard jumped to his feet. "Excuse me."

And he left us, his guests, unattended in the drawing room, the fire crackling as the four of us all stared at one another, stunned, in silence.

"Well." Dinah laughed after a bit and crossed her arms over her knees. "It seems we've lost our host."

Aylmer rubbed a hand on his pants leg, staring after where Richard had retreated. Then he patted his knee and stood up as well. "Excuse me, ladies. I'll hunt him down."

And then he, too, was gone. Unity smirked as she slid down the settee closer to the two of us at the fire. "You don't think—"

But her words cut off as a servant arrived at the doorway, looking around with a furrowed brow, perhaps for her master's son, and settling the tray of tea and assorted small cakes on a table in front of us. "Should I poor it, misses?" The woman about my mother's age asked, her dress impeccably crisp, without a single stain like one might have found on Nora's or Mrs. Stone's apron back at my house.

Unity smiled at her. That was usually the lady of the house's purview, but perhaps Lady Fitzroy wasn't in. "We can handle it, thank you."

The servant offered a quick bow and exited the room as Unity picked up the teapot.

"Oh, just a little for me, thanks," said Dinah. "If not for that walk, I might not have had any. We just stuffed ourselves back home." Her eyes darted over the tray of cakes, far finer than anything Mrs. Stone could make for us. "Maybe just one of these." She picked up a serving tong and helped herself to two little cakes, covered in a sort of hardened. white cream.

"So," said Unity, handing Dinah a full cup, "as I was saying, do you think this could have something to do with Mr. Gillingham's betrothed?"

Dinah choked a bit on the cake. "What? The heiress in Bathe broke it off with him."

I frowned as Unity poured me a cup and handed it my way. *Was* that what this was about? But surely, Sir Lawrence wouldn't go directly over Richard's head, would he, if he insisted on Richard honoring his promise to marry Arabella? Wouldn't he confront the man himself?

But what if he had, and Richard had refused to act? Would he then approach the viscount himself, demanding honor be satisfied?

I remembered, from a brief Academy lesson, that there were rare occasions in which *duels*, albeit illegal in this place, arose when it came to a question of safeguarding a woman's honor.

Surely, Sir Lawrence and Richard weren't headed for such a fate?

"Oh, yes, I almost forgot," said Unity, leaning back in her seat and pausing to take a sip of tea. She locked eyes with me then, and I knew she wanted to discuss the other secret betrothed she'd told me Aylmer had guessed Richard was hiding. Whom I *knew* Richard was hiding. Unity did not elaborate in front of Dinah, I noticed, pretending she'd meant the woman in Bathe all along. "Well, that just means Mr. Gillingham is back on the market, so to speak, and probably more eager than ever to find a wife to help him forget his past mistakes. Sir Lawrence has no sister, but..." She frowned. Did she suspect Arabella's connection to Richard?

"Oh, no. Not Miss Hatfield." Dinah finished her cake. "She simply isn't an option for a viscount's son. You have to be mistaken."

I set my untouched tea down on the table in front of me.

Judging from Dinah's attitude toward the match, I was

sure I knew the answer already, but this was my chance to discover if either was compelled to help Arabella, which would prove, to me, the year's goal had definitively shifted.

"I think Mr. Gillingham would be lucky to have Miss Hatfield for a wife," I said. "She's quite accomplished. And she *is* the baronet's ward. I imagine she's not without a dowry."

Unity laughed once, just a touch unkindly. "My mother says she might have a dowry bigger than your own, Georgiana, if only Lady Fitzroy would give permission. It is of course at Sir Lawrence's discretion, but he's not keen to displease his mother, so they've arrived at a moderate sum. Perhaps their trip back to Londyne to see the lady secured that larger fortune that would make *certain* families overlook her... natural origins." She wrinkled her nose and set her teacup back down on its saucer. "But I doubt the viscount and his wife are the type for whom a dowry alone matters. What *I* want to know, Georgiana, is: does your recommendation of Miss Hatfield for Mr. Gillingham mean that you're done pursuing him?"

"*You* were pursuing him?" Dinah cocked her head as she set down her empty plate and wiped her hands on a fine cloth napkin. "Yes, I suppose you were at the ball. I'd almost forgotten..."

I wouldn't be distracted. "You don't think Miss Hatfield would make a better wife for Mr. Gillingham than I would?"

Both Unity and Dinah turned to look at me at that, shaking their heads. "You? The daughter of a baron?" Dinah said. "I don't care how *talented* Miss Hatfield is, no viscount would want a young woman of *unknown* origins for a future daughter."

"She's a relation of the late baronet," I said simply.

Unity smirked. "A *distant* relation, no doubt, so goes the rumor." She knew full well the rumor actually said Arabella was the daughter of the late baronet himself.

That *did* make Sir Lawrence her half-brother, and it did

make his concern for her welfare all the more understand-
able, I thought.

"Well, either way, I suppose that means there's little chance of my success." Dinah sniffled and looked at the fire. "Between that rumor and a *daughter of a baron* declaring her intent to pursue the man, I doubt I have any chance. Even if Georgiana insisted Mr. Gillingham seemed to regard me with a little favor." She shot me a dithering look.

She didn't seem hurt, though. She just clearly didn't want to compete with me for the man. But she didn't want Arabella to wind up with him, either.

"So you're not at all interested in Mr. Linden?" Unity hid behind another sip of her tea. "Or any... *other* gentlemen in town?"

Dinah whirled on her in her seat. "I like Mr. Linden very much, thank you." She didn't speak of any other man.

Unity's lips grew thin as she set her teacup down. "Mr. Linden's father and mine are old friends. Very old friends."

Oh. She was interested in having Aylmer for herself. Had that been true back at the Academy as well, and the feeling had flown through to this world? Before or after Arabella had opened the portal? I certainly hadn't been paying atten-tion to their romantic entanglements when I'd been throwing myself at the viscount's son myself. *They* hadn't even been as focused on their own interests as they'd been on mine.

"Yes, well, the Lindens are friendly with *everybody*," said Dinah. She turned to me, her nostrils flaring. "Oh, but if Mr. Linden is *particularly friendly* to the biggest catch of the town, how are *any* of the rest of us to compete?"

She *did* think Aylmer to be interested in me. Both of the lady tormentors of Bedlam Academy stared at me now, as if waiting for me to refute such a claim.

Aylmer's confession mere moments before the Sacra-ment flashed through my mind.

"You can rest assured, whatever you may think," I told them, "Mr. Linden and I are just friends. I hope to catch the eye of just one man." Only I wasn't sure if that man was Richard or in fact Sir Lawrence himself.

"Oh? And who might that one man be, if I may ask? Inquiring minds would love to know."

Unity, Dinah, and I turned as one to the sound of the male voice that had entered, unbidden, into our conversation.

Chapter Twenty-Seven

The baronet, unaccompanied by either gentleman who'd left us alone in the viscount's drawing room, stood in the entryway, a wide grin on his face.

"Sir Lawrence," said Unity, her back straightening.

The baronet stepped inside the room, waving a hand. "Oh, please don't mind me. I didn't mean to intrude. I only thought I should come say *good afternoon*—formally, that is —before I left, now that I know you're all here." He stepped inside and looked around, as if he might find more people hidden behind a chair or the curtains tied back on either side of the window overlooking the spacious garden. "Gillingham and Linden left you all alone?"

Dinah and Unity exchanged a glance, a little spark of their former comradery lit between them, though I was still certain Unity was more sure of herself in this place than she had been back home. Perhaps it had been the additional presence of that wretched William and Thomas that had kept her in the background. I did hope they hadn't been selected at all to come to this world. Now that I knew from Arabella that members of graduating classes could be separated here, I couldn't be sure.

"We thought they were off to meet you," said Dinah as

Sir Lawrence took the seat beside Unity that Aylmer had occupied briefly. "It was only mention of you that sent Mr. Gillingham out of the room, with Mr. Linden soon following after."

"Is that so?" Sir Lawrence looked to me, as if only my word would confirm it. I nodded once, curtly. "Most curious. I did not meet either on the way."

Dinah shot a look to Unity, her nose up in the air, as if the lack of the gentlemen meeting somehow proved Unity was entirely wrong about Sir Lawrence campaigning for Richard to marry Arabella. I wasn't so sure.

"You left town quite abruptly earlier this week," I said, drawing Sir Lawrence's attention back to me. "And how is Miss Hatfield doing?"

"Well, I think. Very well, thank you." Sir Lawrence threaded his fingers together, leaning over slightly on his thighs. "I did not expect to be back so soon, but business brought me to the viscount."

"'Business'?" Unity asked. Dinah rolled her eyes, the two clearly in some kind of battle to get him to admit his true purpose in coming here.

"Yes, nothing of interest to you ladies."

"I think you'd be surprised," I said, reaching over to grab one of the iced cakes. "Please do not confine our entire gender to drawing rooms and dances." I gestured around with the hand not holding the cake. "Current circumstances withstanding."

"I wouldn't imagine doing so." Sir Lawrence smiled as I helped myself to the cake. It was small—gone in as little as two bites—but just sweet and moist enough to prove a delight to my taste buds. "I do admit, though, I thought the running of an estate might be too dull to hold your interest, Miss Radcliff. It certainly seems to be dull for my mother, even if she holds dominion over our house in the country and our townhomes in Londyne and Bathe."

Dinah giggled. "*So* many residences for a bachelor."

Sir Lawrence blinked and leaned toward her. "Well, they

shall be for my wife, of course. My mother is doing her job to keep them all up and running until the lady in question makes an appearance."

His eyes darted pointedly to me.

I gulped down the last of the cake. I wasn't imagining this spark between us.

Unity and Dinah exchanged a look across the baronet, both clearly attempting to stifle a giggle.

"You'll have to enlighten us, Sir Lawrence," started Unity. "What qualifications are you looking for in the future Lady Fitzroy?"

"There's lineage from a respectable family, I presume," said Dinah before the man himself could do anything more than open his mouth to answer. "A respectable dowry, even if not wholly necessary to a man in your position, would lend more prestige."

"Accomplishments," added Unity. "Musical talent, for example—that is..." Her olive cheeks flushed a little. "A strong singing voice, at the very least."

It was my turn to blink in amazement. These two were highlighting my advantages, at least as far as they knew them to be, and according to the general view of those in this Society.

Was it *magic* compelling them to push us together? Reset by Arabella opening that portal? But why Sir Lawrence and not Richard?

Or was this just... the two of them being themselves, free of all of that in this place?

They clearly had no desire to see Arabella and Richard wed, so did that mean Bedlam Academy's grip on them was now lost entirely?

"Dance," said Sir Lawrence, leaning back in his chair. "I shouldn't forget a fine lady makes for an elegant partner on the dance floor. The year after a woman is married, she's the guest of honor at every ball she attends. My mother would say it wouldn't do to have the new Lady Fitzroy falling over her feet at every such occasion."

Dinah's and Unity's faces fell at one, Dinah turning to the fire and wincing a bit as Unity made a point of smoothing out a wrinkle in her dress over her knee.

My stomach hardened as I met Sir Lawrence's eyes.

If he wanted a competent dancer, it was clear I wasn't in the running.

"Of course, I speak only of the accomplishments those around me might prefer I seek out when searching for the future Lady Fitzroy." Sir Lawrence was quick to speak, having seen something in my face I hadn't meant to convey. "I personally find a sharp wit and a sense of adventure a far better advantage in a lady."

I wouldn't suspect those descriptors to be applicable to me. Certainly not in what little acquaintance he had of me.

"And would you call dancing despite forgetting the steps having a sense of adventure?" Unity supplied. She smirked at me over her cup of tea.

Oh. There was that.

"I would." The baronet stared at me.

I could feel my face flush and grabbed for my cup of tea, even though it had grown cold.

Dinah was the next to speak. "Sir Lawrence, you have not told us what Miss Hatfield is up to, so far from her guardian." Was this a sign this world wanted the Bedlam Academy graduates to push for Arabella's success?

"I imagine whatever the current Lady Fitzroy says she ought to be doing, as she is under the care of my mother," said the baronet.

"And is she out amongst Society there?" Unity asked. More interest in Arabella's affairs.

"My mother or Miss Hatfield?" He displayed a wide grin.

Unity and Dinah looked to one another with arched brows, clearly confused. Then they both laughed and I put my teacup back down on the table, not another sip taken.

"My mother is not fond of paying calls," Sir Lawrence

admitted, "but she can be relied upon to host occasional parties. My cousin is sure to get her share of Society there."

"So in other words, the world must come to her, rather than her going out into the world." Dinah grimaced. "To find that one's fate even in Londyne. I suppose there's no escaping it for *some* of us." Her eyes darted a touch tellingly to Unity. She was, I'd gathered, the lady our age in the village most likely to travel.

If anything, the comment only made Unity prouder, though, and she sat up straighter, giving the baronet her full attention. "I suppose there are many fine young gentlemen among your acquaintance for Miss Hatfield to meet there, at your Londyne home?"

I listened carefully to her tone, but I couldn't tell if she was merely being polite or had any subconscious interest in the matter.

"Yes, well..." It was Sir Lawrence's reaction that should have concerned me more from the start. Did he now know about Richard and Arabella's arrangement? Was that, perhaps, his reason for coming, as Richard himself may have suspected?

"Arabella is, I'm afraid, far too obstinate to put forth much effort in the matter, regardless of opportunities. She always has some excuse for why she must vanish into the woodwork at a gathering."

So he didn't know?

"Sir Lawrence," I found myself saying, "I thought you admired a fine wit and a sense of adventure in a woman. In this Society, I find it only the boldest woman who offers her excuses without hesitation, who refuses to join the game we all seem compelled to play."

"Oh?" Sir Lawrence tilted his head. "And may I ask what game, Miss Radcliff, is that?"

"The game of matrimony, of course." Threading my fingers together, I rested my hands over my knees. "It takes a bold woman content to not seek a husband."

Dinah and Unity exchanged a look at that. They seemed of the same mind once more.

"A woman with means of her own might have that option, but not all women are so fortunate," the baronet said, a grim smile on his face. "My cousin among those with little to provide for her should anything go amiss."

"You mean in the event of your untimely passing," I pointed out.

Dinah squeaked. Perhaps I was *too* bold.

But Sir Lawrence simply cocked his head at me, a grin on his face. "I suppose I do."

"Then you need only provide something for her in your will. My father did for me."

"Ah, but there, as I hear tell, you have been fortunate in having a cousin disposed to honoring those wishes." Sir Lawrence wagged a finger in my direction. "The new baron will release your dowry upon your marriage, so the story goes?"

"You *are* rather well-informed about Miss Radcliff," Unity said, smirking.

Sir Lawrence had the decency to stop and think over what he'd just said, his eyes fluttering. "But the point stands. As it is, with no sons of my own, a distant relation of mine is to inherit the title and the estate in the event of my *untimely passing*. I know little of the man, and there are no guarantees he would honor any wishes I had for my ward, who is completely unknown to him as well." He leaned back in his seat, staring downward. "It is one major impetus to me seeing her settled, and me as well for that matter. I know too well the chaos that can ensue with a baronet's untimely passing."

My breath hitched. How, for even a moment, could I have forgotten what Arabella had told me about Sir Lawrence's father? I wondered how *he* thought he had died, but I knew, even if I hadn't held my tongue before, that I had better hold my tongue now.

"Sir Lawrence." A male voice at the entryway drew all of our attention.

Sir Lawrence stood as Aylmer and Richard helped themselves back in, our host returned at last. Aylmer was all polite smiles, a nod toward the baronet, but Richard offered a cursory nod only, his hands behind his back as he stepped toward the window and stared outward, wringing his hands together.

As Sir Lawrence sat again, Aylmer took a seat kitty-corner to Unity, his attention on the tray with half its cakes missing, the dirty plates and half-filled teacups. "Gillingham. Perhaps the ladies are in need of more refreshments?"

"Oh, none for me," I said quickly. It felt like a lot of what the gentry did in this world was just sit around and enjoy endless refreshments.

"This is fine," Dinah concurred, helping herself to one more small cake.

Richard didn't respond to Aylmer's request at all. "It's a fine day. I thought to take a turn about the gardens."

"It's lovely," started Aylmer, "but the ladies walked all the way here, and I'm sure they've had their fill of exercise."

"Miss Radcliff," said Richard, holding a hand out in my direction as he stopped on his way to the door. "Care to join me?"

All eyes were now upon me.

"We just had a long walk," said Dinah after finishing her cake.

Richard didn't look at her, extending his forearm even lower toward me, his eyes locked with mine.

He had something to tell me.

"Yes, all right, thank you," I said. It was fortunate I'd had refreshment enough and was not tired.

Taking his arm, which remained stiff, I stood and let him escort me out of the room.

"Cooper," Richard shouted down the hallway. The butler appeared within moments. "Fetch Miss Radcliff her things, and my hat and gloves. We're to take a turn about the garden."

"Very good, sir." The butler bowed and left.

The rest of our party were not too far behind, though Dinah looked a little pale and Aylmer stepped up to offer her his arm.

A number of footmen returned with our things, Richard letting my arm slip from his as he grabbed his hat from one of them.

"Gillingham, Miss Sinclair isn't up for another walk," said Aylmer as Unity and I gathered our things and began to slip into our coats and bonnets.

"I'm all right," said Dinah, though she looked a bit green at the clear lie. "I needn't walk far."

"I'm getting my carriage for her," said Aylmer quickly. "It should have arrived by now."

Richard paused after putting on his second glove, staring at Dinah. He looked, for a moment, about to say something, one foot leaning forward as if about to offer my stepsister his arm himself. Then he looked over her head, down the hall, and nodded. "Very well. If Miss Dowding desires to return to her home as well—" He looked at her.

I made a pretense of tying my bonnet's ribbon and looking back over my shoulder to where Richard had been staring earlier. Lord Gillingham was at the foot of the stairs, speaking with his wife and occasionally looking back at our smaller group here.

Unity pursed her lips. "Well, if Georgiana isn't going to accompany her sister, perhaps I should—"

I turned back around to face Unity's discerning lips. Propriety or even an ounce of empathy would have me escort my stepsister home.

But there was more at stake here than either of those things.

"I trust you and Mr. Linden to take care of her," I said, sliding my arm back through Richard's. He'd clearly sought me out, and I couldn't leave this place without discovering why. "And Lady Gillingham is here, so she may act as my chaperone." The woman in question was clearly not about to join me on this walk, though. Richard wouldn't hear of it if she did. "I feel fine. I can walk home."

Richard arched a brow but said nothing, not waiting to call for his mother to join us, just guiding me toward the back of the house.

We didn't get far, though, before Sir Lawrence gathered his things from one of the footmen and spoke up. "Nonsense. I can give Miss Radcliff a lift home in my carriage."

And before anyone could object, Richard had taken me out of doors, Sir Lawrence still affixing his hat and gloves as he stood in the open doorway.

"I suppose I expected *someone* to join us," said Richard, a sneer on his face as he looked over his shoulder, "but I hoped to God it wouldn't be him. Least of all without someone else to distract him—ah, there we go."

I looked over my shoulder again to see what had caught his attention. Unity was joining arms with Sir Lawrence. She must have thought it more prudent to allow Aylmer to escort Dinah home and stay with me to make sure I found my way unencumbered. She did not believe me that the viscountess would suit as chaperone, then. So either way, she'd be leaving one woman alone with a man, but Aylmer had a longer acquaintance with her family, even in this world, if I understood it, to recommend him.

But wasn't Unity wary of leaving Dinah alone with him? I thought she sought his hand for herself.

The way she laughed as she and Sir Lawrence walked slowly after us made it clear to me that perhaps her eye had turned.

Sighing, I started forward. It shouldn't matter to me. Even if I'd thought Unity had been trying to help me back there with Sir Lawrence. He *did* make for a better catch as a husband, based on title and fortune, than Aylmer did. Unity would be wise to keep her options open.

"So are you infatuated with this baronet like all the rest

of them?" Richard asked snidely. "I thought you were so keen to throw yourself at *my* feet mere days ago."

I looked up at him. He dabbed at his brow with his free hand, clearly unamused.

"And you made it clear you had no interest in me," I told him. "And that you'd scandalize me if I so much as *thought* of making things difficult for you."

"Oh, yes." Richard started forward as we stepped between a towering pair of hedges. "A scandal involving the baronet himself, if I remember right. An improper introduction?" Had he really forgotten the details so soon? "Would that I *could* use that against him, but knowing his luck, the idea of Sir Lawrence Fitzroy doing something *scandalous* would just make him all the more irresistible to those around him."

"You clearly don't like the man."

"Tell me something I don't know." Richard plucked at a withering blossom along the hedge, crushing it between two fingers.

"He'll never give his blessing for you to wed his ward if you aren't more careful around him." My heart thudded. Was I really trying to help Arabella? Was that the right thing to do?

Richard's nose wrinkled. "Like I *care* about that man's permission. I wouldn't need it even if I sought such a match." He plucked at another petal as we passed. "There are other ways, and *some* women are up for that."

I turned over my shoulder. Sir Lawrence and Unity had not caught up to us—perhaps they had taken another branch of the garden.

"You promised Arabella—"

"On a first-name basis now, are we?" Richard stopped walking and turned to me, his lips slightly pinched. "You're the daughter of a baron," he said simply.

"I am." I was unsure where he was going with this.

"And you know, quite intimately, my true nature." He

tried to smile, but it didn't quite reach his eyes. It seemed like he was grinding this teeth.

"Perhaps *more so* than you realize," I told him. "Arabe—Miss Hatfield and I became quite the confidantes this past week."

He was undeterred. "Then I can skip all the pretense. The slow pace of courtship often bores me." Richard flung a hand in the air.

"'Courtship'?" My breath sucked out of my lungs.

"Or we can jump right to the end if you'd find that easier." Richard shuffled from foot to foot, his voice strained as he spoke the next few words. "Miss Radcliff, will you do me the honor of becoming my future viscountess?"

Chapter Twenty-Eight

I had to take a moment to be sure I'd heard him. "You're asking *me* to marry you?"

Richard clenched his jaw before speaking. "That was the implication, yes."

"But you—you've only known me a few days."

He nodded, his hands clasped behind his back.

"You don't even seem to like me," I added.

He pasted on a strained smile.

I spoke softer, leaning toward him. "And what of your promise to Miss Hat—"

"Ah!" said Sir Lawrence, appearing from around the corner of the hedges with Unity on his arm. "There you two are." He fluffed his hand in the air. "I'm surprised by how dizzying it is to find oneself walking amidst the hedges on a fine autumn day. I wouldn't have thought the flora abundant enough this time of year to impede the view, but I stand corrected."

Richard would not be distracted. "Yes or no, Miss Radcliff?" He spoke softly, but with a touch of desperation in his voice.

This was the moment I'd striven for, and so soon after my arrival, with little effort on my part—or less effort than

I'd expected, considering everything I'd tried since meeting him had ended in failure.

But all I could do was look beyond Richard to Sir Lawrence, who was focused entirely on me.

"Not until you explain yourself," I said under my breath to Richard, without even looking at him.

Unity dropped Sir Lawrence's arm and moved closer to a rose bush, gliding a gloved finger over a petal. It was only slightly withered by the fall weather. "You're right, Sir Lawrence. Look at the beauty of this bloom."

Sir Lawrence extended his elbow toward me as I stood there beside Richard, and the viscount's son's face reddened as he stared between us. I should have stayed with him, should have at least gotten myself engaged, as long as he was offering, and worked out the rest later, but there was something in his countenance that reminded me of my father—my real father, back in the Lower-Zone—and a gust of wind brought with it a fine, heady scent of pine from the direction of the baronet. I slipped my arm through the baronet's as Unity let out a little cry and clamped tightly to her bonnet. It was in a bit of danger of being sent flying in the wind, even with the ribbon she used to tie it.

"Unity," I said as Sir Lawrence and I passed her. "Are you all right?"

She laughed, smirking at the sight of our arms intertwined. "Yes, of course." The wind had died down.

"I trust you saw my sister off?" I asked her.

"I did." She frowned for a moment, and I wondered if she was thinking of Dinah and Aylmer alone in a carriage together. She shook her head and seized Richard's arm as he headed my way. "Mr. Gillingham," she said, sending me a sly look over her shoulder. "Perhaps you can give me a tour of these gardens yourself? I'm curious about the roses in particular."

Richard sputtered as he watched Sir Lawrence and me head for the next turn amidst the hedges, putting on a smile and turning to her with an "Of course, Miss Dowding," before Sir Lawrence and I were out of earshot.

"Forgive me for stealing you away like that," said Sir Lawrence under his breath. He didn't sound very sorry at all. "I was worried what he might ask if he had a moment alone with the two of you together."

"Oh?" I gazed up at the baronet's profile. He cut a dashing figure. "And what question might he have asked that so concerned you?"

Sir Lawrence pulled us around another hedge and stopped. "You're teasing me, Miss Radcliff." He pretended to look aghast. "I have the distinct feeling Mr. Gillingham didn't tarry long once he had you out here."

I bit back a smile. "I'm afraid I can neither confirm nor deny anything until I'm sure what it *is* I'm confirming or denying."

Sir Lawrence *tsked* and took us for another turn. Unity's voice carried over the hedges, but it was indistinct, and enough of a distance away that I didn't worry about encountering them. Despite my doubts that she was still under any compulsion to assist me, Unity was supportive. Perhaps she thought we both ought to try for any suitable husband we could, come what may.

"Let me propose this to you, then, Miss Radcliff." Sir Lawrence put the index finger on his free hand to his lips as we plodded along the dirt path. "If I deduce enough of what happened, you will supply me with the details."

"That sounds fair," I said, matching his slower gait. "Though I do have one condition."

"Oh?"

"That you allow me to guess *why* you're so curious about this matter in return."

"A lady always has the privilege to speak her mind in the company of a gentleman. Why do you even need to ask for my permission?"

I laughed, once—harsh. "We don't all act as one, Sir Lawrence."

He arched a brow at me. "Maybe not. But I have spent quite a lot of my time in the company of ladies, and I can assure you, the one quality they share is that they are eager to speak their minds."

He spoke, no doubt, of his mother and Arabella.

"I'll grant you that some may be, yes." I tilted my head slightly. "But I can assure you, there are a great many who safeguard their secrets. Even those ladies you least suspect capable of such a thing."

That got the baronet to stop and look at me. He seemed to be attempting to clamp down the smile broadening his lips, albeit unsuccessfully. "Well, that is another matter entirely. Ladies, from what I understand, must always keep a number of secrets. It lends a sense of intrigue to them."

"How you assign such strange qualities to a lady," I told him, shaking my head.

"And yet I feel there are many things you are keeping from me, Miss Georgiana Radcliff."

He wasn't wrong. But I was distracted by the sound of my given name on his tongue, the shiver that ran down my back.

He tapped his lips again. My breath hitched at the sight, imagining those soft lips bending down, pressing against my own...

I blinked hard and looked at the ground. Nowhere in this world would that have been appropriate, not between two unmarried people. Richard's behavior was the exception, not the rule.

"But I will let you keep most of your secrets—except that relating to Mr. Gillingham." Oh, if only he knew... But there could be no advantage to revealing Arabella's scheme. Not one that I could see yet. And I still didn't know what to make of Richard's proposal.

The baronet gestured to a wooden bench tucked against one of the hedges under a few branches of a small tree, in a spot that still attracted some sunshine this time of day, a boon in this slightly chilly weather.

I took a seat, fanning my skirt out below me.

Sir Lawrence remained standing. "You will forgive my boldness," he said, "and any occasion I give you to blush."

It was the way he said it, that slight smirk as he leaned over me, that made my cheeks pink already, and I was no longer sure I was ready to face his questions.

Sir Lawrence didn't comment on the blush he'd already brought to my complexion, instead leaning over me by taking hold of a low-dangling tree bough. "Gillingham abandoned his guests earlier, and I have to wonder if it was because he heard I was with his father."

"That was my assumption as well." I crossed my gloved hands rather properly atop one of my knees. "He got up immediately once he discovered your whereabouts, but I'm puzzled that he would have been unaware of your presence in the manor to begin with."

Sir Lawrence stood tall again, his shoulders thrust back. "He had to know *someone* was with his father. Lord Gillingham sent Cooper to tell everyone else he was not to be disturbed almost as soon as I was brought straight to the viscount's study."

I pursed my lips. "On that business you mentioned."

"Yes. That." He started pacing the length of the path in front of the bench. "We didn't pass in the hallway after I finished, as I paid my compliments to Lady Gillingham in the dining hall before I headed to the drawing room, where she told me her son had guests."

He stopped. "Not five minutes upon Mr. Gillingham's return to the drawing room, he suggested a walk. He asked you in particular." He nodded slightly toward me.

"That is no secret," I said. "You'll have to try harder if you want to know more than that."

His eyes were bright, wholly engaged on mine. "And though he scarcely had a moment alone with you here in the garden, I propose that he, well, proposed. To you. In this very place."

Considering my short acquaintance with Richard

Gillingham and his obvious disinterest in me, I *was* surprised Sir Lawrence had figured out that much. Too surprised, perhaps, to speak.

"The quick tension in your shoulders betrays you, even if that tight-lipped mouth does not," he pressed on.

"How could you possibly...?" I asked, unable to even finish my sentence.

"You see, a thought occurred to me when Gillingham took such a keen interest in you right away. He'd spoken to his father, and not mere moments before, the viscount had asked me to explain you to him."

"'*Explain*' me?" I asked, wholly confused.

"Yes, well, you'll remember how you called my name from the hallway." He sat down on the bench beside me at last, a lock of his dark hair waving over his forehead from beneath his hat. "A most welcome surprise, I must say. I wasn't sure I'd have time to call on you—or cause to, without my cousin present."

"You're always welcome at my house," I said before I even thought of it. My eyes widened. "That is, my mother wanted to invite you for dinner, anyway—we're having a dinner on Friday, you know. She just assumed you wouldn't be here for it."

"Oh, yes, well, I'd go gladly if I could, but I'm afraid I must head back to Londyne today—I only came to speak to the viscount."

So he hadn't been here to speak to the viscount of Arabella. At least, his playful demeanor betrayed no such heavy topic on his mind.

"Well, so I told the viscount you were the late Baron Radcliff's daughter, of your cousin's promise to uphold your father's wishes and award you a five-thousand-pound dowry."

"I feel as if I'm a piece of cargo being read about in a ship's manifest." I grimaced. "How flattering."

Sir Lawrence put his hand over mine at my knee. "Forgive me. I didn't mean to sound so detached. I did not find an opportune moment to bring up your wit and your warmth of character, but I'd spoken enough to the viscount."

I felt lightheaded as his hand squeezed mine, and we stared at one another for a long moment before he pulled his hand away and looked forward.

"The viscount had quite forgotten the matter of you being a baron's daughter. He remembered you only as Mr. Sinclair's daughter, a man of 'no consequence'—those were *his* words alone." Sir Lawrence leaned toward me, frowning, as if afraid I might rebuke him. I could tell he was sincere in not agreeing with the viscount, though.

And from what little I knew of the viscount, he considered himself a man of great consequence, though I could hardly attribute a single memorable characteristic to him myself.

"Regardless, he asked if I had a mind to take you as my wife."

My skin tingled in this chill, my heartbeat rapidly pumping blood.

My voice cracked. "I see now." I focused on Sir Lawrence's rather shiny shoe. "And so when you told him *no*, the viscount met with his son and he somehow convinced Mr. Gillingham that I was a fish to be snatched up immediately, before some other fishmonger got a hold of me."

I found I didn't care that Richard had been pressured to ask for my hand. Indeed, now it at least made sense, though I was surprised I was enough for the viscount himself to approve. All the more reason to think this world had, at least at one point, intended me—and not the poor relation of the baronet—for the viscount's son.

Sir Lawrence laughed, and the deep, throaty chuckle sent a shiver up my spine.

"I doubt the viscount *or* his son would appreciate being compared to a fishmonger, but I completely understand why you dislike being shopped for like the freshest fish of the sea." He sighed and looked upward, one knee bouncing. "But you mistake something, Miss Radcliff. The viscount wishes for only the best for his heir, that much is true. But more than that, he wishes to punish me." Sir Lawrence turned to me, his hand curling into a fist over his now-immobile knee. "I told him I *had* considered courting you."

Chapter Twenty-Nine

Despite my best efforts to remain composed, Sir Lawrence had caught me quite unawares.

He *had* considered courting me?

The thought warmed my heart, though I knew I was foolish for caring at all.

But he spoke in the past tense as well—a slip of the tongue or an admission that he'd only *considered* courting me and had come to a conclusion I might not like?

Finding I couldn't keep looking at him, I wrung my hands together and looked away.

"I wouldn't have been so bold as to propose so indecently early in our acquaintance," said Sir Lawrence. "To *anyone*. But the viscount has no such scruples for himself or his son. He views marriage as purely a duty. Perhaps you weren't so wrong to view him as a fishmonger at the market for the finest fish."

I chuckled lightly, but my heart wasn't in it.

"I knew almost as soon as I answered that he would put a plan into action for his son to have you for himself instead, so long as you impressed sufficiently with rank and dowry. But I wasn't sure a lie would have kept you safe at that point, either." He grimaced now, when I managed to look at him out of the corner of my eye.

I wanted to ask if this was his way of asking to court me, but I found the question stuck in my throat. An easier, if stranger, question first, then. "Why would the viscount wish to see you unhappy? If I were even more of a catch than I am, I could almost see a particularly driven man determined to snatch that fish before another man could, but that's not even what you mean, is it?"

He was staring forward, his mouth quirked in a smirk despite the forlorn look in his eyes. I couldn't help it. I put my hand on top of his, and he took my fingers in his grip, squeezing them gently without even looking at me.

"That isn't the question I agreed to answer."

"What?" I'd forgotten the playful deal we'd agreed to.

The baronet rubbed a thumb over my fingers, the two pairs of gloves between us not enough to stop my heart from thudding.

"I thought you wanted to guess *why* I was so determined to find out Gillingham's intentions with you this afternoon." He squeezed my hand one more time and let it fall, tapping his knee. "Well? Have you hint enough?"

My throat was dry as I pulled my hand back to my breast. "You intentionally thwarted him," I said. "You sought to stop him from asking me..." I couldn't voice it. Couldn't admit I'd been asked to marry the viscount's son.

"Yet he *has* asked." Sir Lawrence leaned slightly toward me, his warmth tangible in the crisp air. "You cannot deny that. You didn't seem sufficiently surprised that I thought he might ask you for your hand to deny that now." I chewed my lip. He had me there. A slight chuckle escaped from his mouth. "Oh, how irritated he must be with me right now."

I straightened my back. "Would it surprise you that I sought Mr. Gillingham's hand at the ball?"

The baronet took in a sharp breath. "So you act as quickly as he does."

I slouched a little. "Well, I didn't mean upon a first meeting—"

"No, no, it wouldn't surprise me. I very quickly took note of your interest in the man, and I did my utmost to *thwart* you, as you so aptly put it."

That got my attention. I turned to stare at him full-on, but he was determined to examine a cloud far off in the sky. He leaned back, his elbow on the back of the bench between us.

"You were kind to me," I said.

"I aimed to be." He nodded slightly, but he still wouldn't look at me.

"Because you didn't want me to wind up with Mr. Gillingham? You didn't know me then." He hardly knew me now, but I couldn't voice that point.

Though he still rested his elbow upon the bench, his body wholly relaxed, he turned his head then, and our eyes met.

"I said the viscount wishes to punish me, and I hold that to be true. But I'm quite capable of wishing unhappiness on him and his family as well—particularly the man's son. So yes. I had no intentions of letting you become an interest of Mr. Gillingham."

My blood grew cold. I had imagined the baronet too often this past week, both while I'd been certain I had to marry the viscount's son and since I'd become far less sure.

"You mistake me." Sir Lawrence sat straighter, rubbing both hands together. "I have no doubt Gillingham will wed eventually, and by all rights, I should be happier to see him wed to someone he has no particular attachment to. I can't stop every potential bride determined to stand in front of the altar with the man."

He couldn't have known about Arabella. I was certain he'd be even angrier if he did. But if not that, why this degree of dislike for the man?

"Though I admit to my pettiness, I long imagined finding Gillingham in love with a woman, only to snatch her for myself." He stared down at his hands as he bumped his palms together. "Only the cad is free with his affections, his flirtations, but never his heart. I half-wonder if the man has one." His lip curled.

"Mr. Gillingham only just met me," I said. "There was no need for your attentions to turn to me." I stared pointedly ahead of me, trying not to shiver when another gust of wind crossed over the hedges.

"Ah, but see, just the sight of his name on your dance card..." Sir Lawrence's eyes narrowed. "I didn't like the thought of the two of you together."

Unity's voice grew louder now, Richard's only occasional short sentences and grumbles echoing after. They were nearing us, wherever they were behind the hedges.

I stood, looking over my shoulder at the baronet. "You should be thankful for his sudden interest in me, then. If I marry him, he won't be happy."

"Neither will you," he said quietly.

I turned to him, where he sat on the bench.

He let out a little grunt. "I do not want *you* to be hurt. I meant what I said. I should not have told the viscount I thought of courting you. Not if I had any hope of keeping you out of their line of sight." He closed his eyes, as if something hurt him. "I only thought... If I told him *no*, you might not be free of them, either. If I offered myself as your suitor, you would have protection. You need protecting."

I opened my mouth and shut it. *This* was his aim, then? He had no interest in me, beyond whatever scheme he thought up against the viscount and his family, beyond some pity for me that compelled him to keep me out of the worst of it?

"No one's ever protected me," I said softly. It wouldn't make sense for this world's Georgiana to say—but then again, he didn't know my mother and stepfather. He wasn't overly familiar with the comfortable existence I had here. And in that moment, the way his eyes reached deep inside me, it was as if he touched that part of my soul, still hurt by being rejected, sacrificed, bound to be forgotten.

"You have not yet accepted him." He reached up toward my hand, then, just brushing the fingers. He smiled, staring at my hand as his fingers danced across my own. "I gathered as much. A happy bride-to-be—even a practical one—doesn't traipse off into the garden with a man other than her newfound betrothed." He met my gaze then, two of his fingers curling around two of mine. "I hoped to stop you. Before you talked yourself into something you might regret."

I blinked. "I know what kind of man he is."

He laughed once—harshly. "I doubt you do."

"I *know*. Men may have their secrets, but women do, too." I forced a smile on my face. "You were quite insistent on that point, if I recall correctly."

"Don't do it," he whispered as Unity's voice grew even louder. His chest hitched.

"Georgiana, Sir Lawrence." Unity's voice made me yank my fingers away from the baronet's, perhaps harsher than I'd intended.

Swallowing, I spun to face them. "Enjoying your walk?" I asked, smiling. It hurt to keep my lips in that position.

Richard's look was cold, Unity's words lost as I shirked under the glare. His gaze shifted to Sir Lawrence behind me as the man stood.

"The sun hits this spot just right," said the baronet as he offered his arm to me. I considered it a moment and stared back at Richard.

And then it occurred to me.

If Sir Lawrence—a man of far better disposition than his counterpart here—was clearly holding on to a grudge, Richard's malice must have run deeper. It didn't seem in his nature to hate by halves, even if polite Society kept such feelings restrained at a glance.

I turned to Sir Lawrence quickly, my back to Richard and Unity. "Look to your own house," I said, my voice as quietly as could be. "Protect Arabella. You owe no such allegiance to me."

The baronet's expression was blank, his eyebrows drawing together, but I gave him no time to ask questions.

I walked over to Richard's side opposite Unity and slid my arm through his, my grip on his arm shaky. Richard jerked his head back but didn't move to escape.

If Arabella was right and I helped her marry Richard... Sir Lawrence would be hurt. It was only a matter of time before Richard figured out that marriage to Arabella might have been the best way to punish Sir Lawrence for whatever transgressions had occurred between them.

And this despite Richard not knowing of her eventual importance to the baronet at the time of his dalliance with her.

"If you'll excuse us," I said to Unity, unable to meet Sir Lawrence's eyes. "My future husband and I have something to discuss."

Chapter Thirty

Unity dropped Richard's arm quite quickly, as if it has suddenly grew too hot to grip on to. "Georgiana?" she asked. "Are you serious?"

Richard let out a barking laugh and tossed his head back. "Marriage is no joking matter."

I nodded, focusing on Unity and maintaining the smile on my face. "Mr. Gillingham asked me just a short while ago. And this is my answer: I will be his wife."

I couldn't look at Sir Lawrence. I wouldn't. I couldn't waver, not until I knew more.

Unity's brows furrowed. "But you only just met. I could see establishing a proper courtship, but you—"

A gust of wind flew through the garden, rustling the hedges and trees to the point of covering up whatever else she had to say.

A bird took to the air from behind a nearby wall, its wings flapping against the current determined to force it down.

My free hand went to the top of my bonnet, my eyes closed. When I opened them, a glint of silver caught the sunlight. It was a dove that flew above me, a pawn's bracelet in its beak.

I can commune with this creature, I thought at once.

Guide me, I thought to it. *Let me know this is the right thing—not just to protect Sir Lawrence's heart from the devastation of his ward wed to Richard, but for the world back home.*

The bird flapped its wings harder, though the wind blew in equal measure, and I straightened up, finding myself the only one with her eyes open and a hand no longer on a hat to stop it from the wind carrying it away.

And the bird flew in a diagonal line upward, the shining, green emeralds woven into the silver chain tearing a hole across the sky.

For just a moment, had I been floating up there, I could have reached through and touched the bell tower of the Academy.

And then it was gone, the bird on the other side, the wind dying along with it.

Unity laughed as she straightened her bonnet. "What a windstorm. Perhaps it's best we get inside." She beamed and ran over to me, throwing her arms around her neck. "But congratulations, Georgiana!" She turned to Richard and grabbed his free hand. "Oh, what a wonderful bride and groom the two of you shall make! I couldn't be happier if I'd accepted a proposal myself!"

Richard laughed, awkwardly reaching across himself to offer my hand on his arm a quick pat. It was Sir Lawrence's eyes he sought next, though, a smug smile on the future viscount's face.

Sir Lawrence looked at me and swallowed visibly, a long, pained expression all the answer I needed to the question of how he felt about my actions. And then, without a word, he fixed his hat straighter on his head and headed through the hedges, back toward the house.

"Well, that's a fine fellow," said Richard, insincerity coloring his tone. "Walking off without offering Miss Dowding an escort."

A wave of nausea hit my stomach, a sense of my own

betrayal cutting me to the core. How it must have seemed to Sir Lawrence after everything we'd discussed.

But Unity's continued excitement, her sideways embrace, made me feel I'd done the right thing more than ever before.

I'd asked for the bird to guide me, and it had. It had reset Unity at least to subconsciously wishing for my marriage to Richard Gillingham.

"Oh, I'll catch up to him," said Unity. She winked at me. "I'll say you were right behind us if anyone asks. Best to give the two of you time to celebrate." She picked up her skirt with one hand and held her bonnet down tighter with the other, scurrying in the direction in which the baronet had vanished.

So this was it. The baronet was no longer stopping me. I'd succeeded in the first important task in my ultimate goal. I was sure Arabella was mistaken—or had somehow *removed* the compulsion for Bedlam Academy graduates to help with the pursuit of the year's goal with her manipulation of the portal. Either wittingly or subconsciously.

"So," said Richard, dropping my arm and turning to face me, "did you enjoy it?"

"Pardon?"

"Playing your little game?" Richard shook his head. "Running off with the baronet like that after I asked you such an important question. It was most infuriating." He leaned closer then, his lips nearly touching my ear. "But I see you can be as wicked as I often am. Well played, Miss Radcliff."

He straightened his back and smiled, and there was something unsettling in the way his eyes held mine.

This man thought of me as his equal in depravity.

At the memory of the baronet's pained expression, I felt, at that moment, Richard might have been right.

I took a step back. "I am *not* playing games," I told the viscount's son. The smile fell promptly from his lips. "I needed time to consider things. First and foremost, your engagement to Arabella Hatfield."

He rolled his eyes. "A folly of youth."

He hardly seemed old enough to lament about the "follies" of his youth.

"Nonetheless, you remain bound by your word. It is the lady's choice to end such an arrangement, as you made so clear when discussing your engagement with the heiress in Bathe."

"Oh, that was my father's doing." Richard waved a hand and settled down on the bench so recently vacated by the baronet. His nose turned up in the air as he offered me his profile. "He was awfully cross with me, I'll have you know. But I couldn't help myself." He sighed, almost dreamily. "She was beautiful. And I thought her fortune would make her a good enough option for my parents. I was wrong."

My knees felt wobbly, and I shuffled to the opposite end of the bench, putting as much space between us on the seat as I could. "What did your father do?"

"You needn't worry about it. He *told* me to court you, to make you my wife. You clearly have his approval, though I wonder if you've said more than two words to him." He chuckled darkly. "Though that wouldn't matter to a man like my father."

"I wasn't worried for myself." I gathered the material of my dress over my knee into one fist.

He sighed and crossed one ankle over the other knee, bouncing his foot. "It's nothing so nefarious. My father spoke to her father, and he pressed the need to have the woman in question release me from the engagement."

"And then her father found her a more tempting match?"

Richard glared at me. "I assume prudence won out in the end, not that she found the other man far superior."

I felt myself about to let out a single, sarcastic chuckle but managed to confine the laugh to a snort and a clearing of my throat, hiding the response behind a gloved hand.

It didn't go unnoticed by the viscount's son.

"She was besotted with me," he insisted.

Since the only clear example I had of a woman *besotted* with Richard was Arabella and I knew now that was an act, I wondered if Miss Heiress of Bathe, too, had just been interested in the status boost that came with marrying into a titled family.

Then again, he *was* handsome enough. There'd just been something about his air at first—and his total disinterest in me, clashing with my desperation to seek his hand—that had made him off-putting to me from the start.

And now, there was all the more reason for me to find him so.

But for a woman desperate for love or a chance of elevating her status, if he were to approach her with a smile and a kinder demeanor...

"Those aren't the only two you've promised yourself to, are they, Miss Hatfield and your lady in Bathe?"

Richard scoffed and uncrossed his feet. "I never meant any of the others seriously. Land sakes! An orphan at a school for girls. A maid. A butcher's daughter. For all the world, I can't understand why any of them actually believe me."

My stomach grew heavy, a pit growing deeper inside me. "You've promised yourself to two others, besides Miss Hatfield?" For I did hope there were no other orphans at a school for girls he'd seduced.

Richard fluffed a hand in the air. "At least. Though there have been many more who knew their stations and would not seek to force such a false promise out of me to begin with." He curled his lips in disgust.

He was clearly in need of self-reflection I couldn't hope to give him.

"Only one engagement was made public. Only one I would have gone through with." Richard shook his head. "The others have no chance of being believed."

"Except now that Miss Hatfield has been claimed as a

baronet's ward, she's risen above her original station," I said. "Hasn't she?"

The way he glared at me then caused my breath to hitch. "It will still come down to my word against hers. There were no witnesses to any exchange between us—I made sure of that."

"None until me, you mean."

His back stiffened. "But all the more reason for me to be happy with my *father*'s choice of bride for me. You, Miss Radcliff, are entirely more devious than you give yourself credit for. It will now decisively be to your advantage to claim you never saw a clandestine meeting."

If I was right—and the "resetting" of sorts of the other Bedlam Academy graduates was an indicator—then yes. If Arabella was right, well... Perhaps even she could see I could work this position to her advantage, if it must come to that.

I hoped it wouldn't. Strangely, the thought of causing the baronet pain with the news of Richard's debasing of his ward held almost equal weight to my fear of endangering those back home.

But there was a simple truth I knew, even if the baronet was not someone I knew well.

"He'll believe her," I said quietly. "He would believe her over you, I'm sure of it." I didn't need to say who.

Richard grunted. "Anyone who's ever met me might believe him if he starts talking about it—well, any of the gentlemen, at least. I don't think, the one present excepting, the ladies of the gentry are so intimately acquainted with my character." He straightened his jacket. "But it won't matter without proof. Not with a girl of *her* history." His nose wrinkled.

Did she have proof? She hadn't told me of it—she'd mostly dwelled only on her vision of the future.

Still, I wondered at Richard's show of bravado. Why else had he been so worried when he'd discovered Sir Lawrence had been meeting with his father without his knowledge?

"There's... bad blood between Sir Lawrence and your father."

Richard laughed. "I should think the real 'bad blood,' as you put it, ought to be between the baronet and me."

"*Ought* to be," I reiterated. I'd caught the words he might not have wanted to dwell on. He turned then, his jaw clenching. "But the matter is primarily between your father and the baronet, isn't it?"

"For all the attention my father pays to the man, I have no idea why *Sir* Lawrence should have any reason to dislike him." Richard *tsked*. "And the ol' viscount is always comparing me to him. He's better at *shooting*, he can control himself around cards, he doesn't make a fool of himself at parties." Richard spoke all of this to the air in front of him rather than at me, but he leaned closer now, though he still faced forward. "Well, I'll tell you why he's good at two of those things—he has *no* friends. No man our age can stand to be around him for more than half a minute before the silence drives one mad and one does all one can to get away." He leaned on the bench's armrest now, his chin resting on a gloved fist. "It never occurred to me he might be the one to find a suitable bride to please my father before I did, considering he hardly ever takes to the dance floor, and when he does, no woman can pry more than a word or two out of him."

That wasn't my experience with the baronet at all. Though I could see some of Richard's depiction in him.

"But I suppose he *is* a baronet. A viscount has greater standing, but I, unlike Fitzroy, have years or even decades to wait for that."

He seemed so bitter at that statement, I had to repeat his words in my head to make sure he was truly lamenting the fact that his father might live for decades yet.

"Sir Lawrence guessed Lord Gillingham would ask you to seek my hand, solely because he'd expressed interest in courting me," I said.

Richard laughed. "Yes. Clever man. Well, that and your

father's title and dowry were sufficient to qualify you in my father's estimations of a suitable bride for a viscount. Congratulations on that." He sounded anything but sincere and sighed. "Why couldn't your stepsister be the daughter of the baron in your family? She only just turned her attentions to me today." He seemed to spot a piece of lint on one glove and picked it off.

"She... She is interested in a good match," I said. "At first, she preferred not to stand in my way. But I thought, perhaps, my chances at marriage to you were at an end after that night. So I told her you seemed to favor her."

"She's just the type of beauty I favor." He sighed. "Fair and tall, willowy, and with a smile that draws you to her." The description at least somewhat applied to Arabella as well. He spared me a look. "You are not without your charms at a glance, but my mother was dark before she grayed, and I vowed never to find a wife who would remind me of her." I knew, from my studies at the Academy, that "dark" simply referred to the coloring of my hair. I was actually rather fair in complexion. "But you'll do. You are so different in comportment to my mother, I can hardly complain on that account."

"My, how you flatter me," I said. "And to think you boast so boldly of your success with women. But only those with a fairer shade of hair, I see."

Richard took my hand in his, and I recoiled even more than I had when Mr. Smith had done the same. But Richard gripped tighter. "My dear, you do not need flattery." With his free hand, he gestured at me. "Despite your obvious lack of social graces, you set a goal for yourself and you enlisted friends—do not think I have not noticed Linden's adamant endorsement of you—and you got what you wanted. I respect determination, even artifice, in ladies, so long as they realize they cannot pretend around me."

He pulled my hand closer, and my body slid along the bench toward him as he leaned closer to my ear. "Because Fitzroy thought of you for himself and my father approves of you as the future Lady Gillingham, there is no one now I'd rather wed. But I will not beg for you or flatter you or simper. You will never be the only woman to turn my head." He leaned back, inhaling the air between us, almost as if he could smell the rapid, thrashing beat of my heart. "Yes, I do believe you are made of stronger stuff than most of the women I encounter. Perhaps, then, I can enlighten you as to the truth of your ordinarily reclusive baronet."

He dropped my hand then, and a gust of wind nearly drowned out the words he next had to offer.

"Rumor has it he killed his father, the previous baronet."

Chapter Thirty-One

I jolted. Richard laughed as he leaned back on the bench, the first time I'd seen him genuinely amused all day.

But he didn't know what I did. That last year's Bedlam Academy graduate candidate was the one to kill the elder Sir Lawrence Fitzroy, if Arabella was to be believed. And I *knew* Sir Lawrence was not from my world. True, I had not been close to a single one of my upperclassmen, but there was no way I would have forgotten *his* face.

Besides, if there were any truth to the matter, this would not be the first I'd heard of it.

"You don't believe me." Richard held his hands up in surrender. "I have no proof, it's true. But the previous Sir Lawrence's demise was most suspicious. No one you ask would deny that."

I did my best to compose myself, tilting my chin slightly upward as I addressed the garden rather than the viscount's son beside me. "I will not ask such a thing in civilized company. But you, sir, have proven you are not civil when away from all of your peers. So you may explain yourself."

Richard paused. Then he let out a hearty, deep chuckle. "I must admit, I'd always dreaded being forced to marry the woman of my father's choosing. But you already entertain me." He stood, then, moving in front of me and extending a hand to help me up.

I lifted an eyebrow and took it cautiously, careful to put my hand over his entirely instead of letting him take hold of me once more.

He smirked but didn't comment as he threaded the hand around his other elbow. "The previous baronet died not yet six months past," he started, and I was relieved, at least, I'd convinced him to explain himself—whether I believed him to be correct or not. He was more than a little biased against the man he seemed to think his own father favored. "An accident while hunting, you see." His nose wrinkled. "I'd been invited to the baronet's estate that weekend, too. I wondered if I'd gone, if Fitzroy would not have dared."

"Dared to do what?" I asked. "You said yourself, there was an *accident*." I thought over where a student from Bedlam Academy might have interfered. Servants didn't shoot, at least outside of gamekeepers, who certainly didn't shoot alongside the lords of the estate.

"You imagine a stray shot," said Richard as he led me to a gap between the hedges at a languid pace. "You think I accuse the younger Fitzroy of shooting his father outright, pretending it to be a lapse of judgement. But you forget— our current baronet is a marvel at hunting, so my father keeps reminding me. Though I heard he's stopped the practice since that day when his father incurred his injuries."

"If not a stray shot, then what?" I asked. "A wild animal?" I wasn't sure how Bedlam Academy graduates might have arranged that. Then again, I knew Arabella to have some sort of control over those doves that crossed the portals...

Richard snorted. "No, their dogs are quite well-trained, and I've yet to see a rabid fox or crazed pheasant used as quarry for a gentleman's hunt."

I took a deep breath. I didn't like when this man teased me. When Sir Lawrence did so, I still felt he respected my intelligence.

So I'd have to prove myself to this rake again. "The gun, then. It discharged incorrectly."

Richard stopped us, Wycliff Manor now clearly visible straight ahead. "Yes. That is exactly it. I was not aware you had a knowledge of the instruments used in hunting. Your little house hardly seems an appropriate venue for a hunt, your stepfather hardly the man for it."

"I have not been hunting at home," I said, though it was possible the other me had. I still didn't think it likely. Mr. Sinclair didn't seem the type, as Richard had said, though I didn't like that Richard could so quickly get an assessment of my stepfather from such a fleeting acquaintance at a single ball. "But I am well aware of the mechanics of gunmanship." I thought of a name to supply that might suffice. "I've seen Mr. Dowding hunting, you know. They live in the village, but he's not above an invitation to hunt when offered, and Miss Dowding and I have long been close companions."

"Hmm," said Richard, starting us back up at our slow pace again. "I suppose I can't accuse you of lying there." He leaned toward me again. "This sort of lie is of no consequence to me, so I will not hold it against you if you just attempted to deceive me with it." He locked eyes with me, and I looked away—then cursed myself for making my falsehood all the more obvious.

"Just keep in mind that I won't appreciate lies of a greater nature," he said. "Not to me." He patted my arm. "You and I, we'll be deceitful quite often. To them. To others. But not to one another. I think I shall like a very honest, open marriage with you, my *darling*. At least in all things that matter."

The insincere drip of "darling" on his lips made me have to bite my tongue.

"So, dazzling detective," Richard continued, "can you deduce why the darkest corners of the gentlemen's clubs have been abuzz with the accusation that Sir Lawrence Fitzroy the elder was murdered by his own son?"

I still refused to believe it. "I imagine he handled the gun. In front of witnesses." But that meant nothing.

"He *loaded* it for his father, right before the very shot itself." Richard shook his head. "That's a servant's job. What kind of gentleman reaches over and insists on cleaning and loading his father's gun himself? One with a motive for doing so, I tell you."

I wondered. Who was that servant whose job it had been to load that gun? If I could find out, would I come across the face of a Bedlam Academy upperclassman?

I was more likely to believe that—I'd reconciled with the thought that such an awful task had been last year's goal—than believe Sir Lawrence himself had intentionally killed his father.

"The wound was not an instant kill," said Richard. "The man suffered for a few days after. Fitzroy played the part of a grieving son most admirably, I hear tell. Thus why so few people would suspect him."

This, despite Sir Lawrence and Arabella alike giving me the impression he actually hadn't liked his father. But did that preclude him from grieving for the man as he lay dying?

No, it didn't. I wouldn't be like Richard, searching for darkness in a man he perceived to be his enemy.

We were almost back at the house now, where Unity was sure to be waiting. I wondered if we'd find Sir Lawrence still inside, but my chest hurt at the thought that he'd left, no doubt, after I'd declared myself Richard's betrothed.

"And now Fitzroy is free," said Richard. "No longer having to answer to his father." Despite accusing the man of murder, Richard sounded almost... envious. He leaned closer. "Don't you wonder, then, why it was only with the previous baronet's death that Fitzroy produced this 'distant cousin'?"

"I'm aware of the rumors surrounding her," I said quickly, determined not to let him hold something over me. "That she may be the previous baronet's natural daughter."

"That's the story, isn't it?" Richard said. He held the

door for me and we stepped back inside the manor now, a chill lingering in the door as it shut behind us. "But I imagine the truth to be even more salacious."

I arched a brow at him as I turned to face him once more. Whatever he told me, I doubted it could surprise me more than him accusing the baronet of murder.

"Arabella may be the former baronet's daughter," said Richard, his voice hushed now that we were back inside his manor, "but when I first met her, she went by another surname."

"She told me," I said, removing my gloves, though I had no intention of staying long. "Her name was Weston."

"Ah," said Richard, tapping his nose, "but who else once went by the name of Weston?"

"I don't know, but you are certainly hoping to tell me, so you best get to it before we're interrupted." I slapped my gloves together in one hand.

Richard removed his hat and tossed it on a table nearby. "Lady Fitzroy, of course. The current baronet's mother."

I blinked, my mind trying to keep up with the revelation. But at first, my thoughts went to one thing. "You suspected she was related to Lady Fitzroy when you approached her?"

Richard lowered his head, his lips pressing slightly together. "I didn't. Weston is a common enough name. But you're missing the point—and I thought you to be a better deductress." He quickly removed his gloves and tossed them beside his hat.

I cocked my head. "You think Lady Fitzroy... is her mother? But then, why was she masqueraded as an orphan?" And how had Arabella never heard of Lady Fitzroy's maiden name? At least she hadn't seemed to suspect the woman of being her mother when I'd spoken to her about the name change.

"She only arrived at the baronet's house after the death of the former baronet. To me, that signals it was not *his* daughter, but his wife's."

"Impossible." My nose wrinkled. "She's younger than

Sir Lawrence. Lady Fitzroy giving birth to another man's child while still the baronet's wife would be quite hard to hide. Besides, Arabella seemed to think Lady Fitzroy didn't like her much."

Richard bounced on his heels, his hands behind his back. "Ashamed of her dark secret, perhaps."

I *tsked*. "Have you told Arabella of your suspicions?"

His brow furrowed. "I've hardly had time to chat with the girl since she showed up once again in my life. Thank goodness she quickly departed for Londyne. Even if I return there myself, it's a large enough city that there's no need for the two of us to find one another again."

"She won't give up on marrying you," I said softly. Only not for the reasons he thought.

Richard reached over and pulled gently on one end of the ribbon holding my bonnet to my head. "That's why you, my dear betrothed, will do everything in your power to help me avoid that fate." The ribbon came undone, and he reached for my bonnet, removing it from my head. A chunk of my hair, so tightly pinned at the back to give it something of an illusion of length, fell down, exposing how it went no farther than my shoulder.

"Interesting," Richard said, setting my bonnet down on the table beside his own and grasping for the hair. "I've never seen a lady in your position keep her hair at such short length."

I shivered as he twirled the lock around one finger. For a moment—the briefest—I could see how he could charm a woman out of her rightful mind.

I snatched the lock of hair back from him and pulled it behind my ear. It wouldn't stick until Mary had another go at it, but it would have to do. "My mother bade me to keep it hidden or no gentleman would have me as his wife." I straightened my shoulders. "But you're no gentleman, in a sense, I suppose."

Richard smirked at that, and his jaw opened, but before

he could respond, a deep voice called his name out from the end of the hallway.

"Richard, you're keeping your guest waiting. She seemed to think..." Lord Gillingham stopped as he neared, a footman appearing out of a room nearby and coming to take our things Richard had removed and set aside on the table. I held tightly to my gloves, watching with wide eyes as he took my hat away, dooming me to spend additional time here, I was sure of it.

"Miss Radcliff?"

Lord Gillingham's voice brought me back to the moment and I turned to him. His face was severe, deep lines down the middle of either cheek. "Am I to believe Miss Dowding? Am I to congratulate you and welcome you to our family?"

Richard chuckled once—darkly. "I've only just asked Miss Radcliff, Father. There's the matter of speaking with her stepfather yet." I could only imagine anyone needing my *real* father's permission to wed me back home. He'd laugh in their face unless, perhaps, they offered him something he wanted in exchange.

Lord Gillingham waved that aside. I could see why his son was so partial to the same gesture. "Mere formalities at this point."

"I'm sure you can speak to my father at the dinner this Friday," I said, a small part of me hoping against hope to delay the whole affair as much as possible. Surely, the magic at work here could not begrudge me that. "Are you and your wife coming, then, Lord Gillingham?"

He blanched, as if I'd just invited him to dine with us in a swamp. "Is there no way we can invite them here instead?" He stroked his chin. "It would be different if it were the home of the baron, of course. Do you suppose we should instead ask the current baron for permission for the lady's hand?"

"He's not my guardian," I said quickly. I frowned. "I

hardly know him." I didn't know him at all. "He's a distant cousin."

"A cousin who holds your dowry until the time comes, is that correct?" Lord Gillingham waved a hand in the air and turned to walk away. "That makes *him* the man to impress. I'll speak to my wife about it. Your mother and stepfather can dine here."

And he was gone down the hall, apparently not open to debate and having nothing more to say on the matter.

Richard scoffed at his father's back then grabbed my hand and kissed it, all charm. "*I* shall dine at your house on Friday. And I will ask for your stepfather's blessing then."

I opened my mouth, taking my hand back from him and about to ask why he was being so kind when I was seized from behind.

"Georgiana!" Unity squealed. "Congratulations!" she said again.

I shuffled to allow her to kiss both of my cheeks in turn, then she squeezed my hands together. "Oh, and for me to know before even Dinah. Before even your mother!"

"About that…" I said, checking over my shoulder to get Richard's confirmation. He shrugged. "Mr. Gillingham has yet to speak to my father, which he plans to do at Friday's dinner, so can we keep it a secret until then?"

Unity's eyes widened. "Surely, you can't expect me to keep quiet for two whole days?"

"Please," I said.

She chewed her lip and looked to Richard. He likely turned the charm on her because even with the otherworldly compulsion to see me married to the man back in effect, she caved. "Well, all right, if you're determined to prolong the agony of the wait. But I can't promise Sir Lawrence will keep quiet about it. He seemed *very* affected by the news." She nudged my arm with her elbow, a sly smile on her face.

As if I'd had two fabulous suitors and all that had remained was for me to pick the better of my choices.

If only things had been so simple.

"I doubt he'll talk about it." Richard chuckled darkly. "And if it does cross his mind to share the news, he simply won't have anyone to tell it to. Comes with the territory of being a recluse."

Maybe so, but he'd know *one* person very invested in the news at the very least. Surely, he would mention it to his ward. I opened my mouth to remind Richard of this, but he was already heading down the hall.

"Cooper? Cooper?" Richard shouted out his butler's name. "Where's my mother? I suppose I best tell her myself."

He turned around a corner.

I took Unity's hand. "Is he gone?"

"Mr. Gillingham?" Unity cocked an eyebrow. "He went to find his mother—"

"Sir Lawrence," I clarified.

"He left promptly." She nodded once. "I've been all alone in the drawing room, waiting for you to come. Lord Gillingham stopped by to ask what I was doing there, and a rather awkward exchange passed between us, but his demeanor improved upon my news." She smiled broadly. "Oh, I shan't be able to stop myself from telling Mr. Linden! I just shan't. He'll be as happy for you as I am." She kissed my cheek again.

I supposed it didn't really matter. I'd best tell Dinah sooner rather than later, though I was sure her renewed sense of trying to get me married to the viscount's son, if she did indeed also exhibit it, would override any hope I'd instilled in her of Richard courting her instead. "But you can't tell your mother," I said. "Not before I tell mine. I'd never hear the end of it."

"It's a deal." Unity offered me a hug again. "But why are you still wearing your jacket? I know we should be off soon enough, but you can't just leave the moment you agree to marry into the household. You haven't even seen Lady Gillingham today."

"I suppose you're right." With more than a little reluctance, I set my gloves down and began unbuttoning my Spencer. Carrying them in the crook of my elbow, I allowed Unity to thread her arm through mine on my other side and walked with her toward where Richard had disappeared to. My eyes darted briefly inside the drawing room and then Lord Gillingham's open study as we passed each room in turn. The viscount was in his study again, poring over a letter or some other document on his desk, this time alone.

It had been a mere hour or so before I'd seen Sir Lawrence in both these places, a warm expression on his face as his eyes had met mine.

Would I ever be greeted with such warmth from the baronet again?

Would he even still care, now that I'd committed myself to his enemy's son, to try to stop me?

He'd tried and tried before. And I had forged on ahead, despite it all.

Despite my own feelings. Despite my own heart.

How cruel this charming world was beneath the surface. To give me hope of something beautiful, only to tear it all away.

At least back home, hope had never been dangled before me.

A Spooky Games Club Mystery

CURSED WITCH, CUTE BROOMSTICK, SMALL TOWN MYSTERIES

Dahlia Poplar is a genuine witch, an unofficial gofer, and Luna Lane's only cursed resident.

With a werewolf best friend, a vampire ex-boyfriend, and a ghost for a hanger-on, Dahlia is far from the most unusual dweller of her sleepy small town, but she's the only one unable to leave. Dahlia has to perform at least one good deed per day—or she's one step closer to turning to stone.

Fortunately, the residents of Luna Lane have plenty of tasks for Dahlia to complete to avert the curse until Cable Woodward, fetching professor and nephew of her elderly neighbor, stops by for the semester on sabbatical. Attempting to help Cable's uncle work through the trauma of losing his wife, Dahlia uncovers the man's collection of board games, which leads to him reminiscing about the long-forgotten Luna Lane Games Club.

Dahlia reestablishes Games Club, only to find evidence of a number of horrible demises connected to the original group. While trying to uncover the truth about the deaths, Dahlia has to fight off her curse, protect her elderly neighbor from becoming the next victim, and most vexing of all, keep Cable from figuring out Luna Lane's supernatural secrets. Only with eerie board games like these, there may not be a loser — or even a winner—who survives.

Luna Lane's witches, werewolves, and vampires welcome you to the Spooky Games Club—in which even the winners could find themselves six feet under.

Witchy Expo Services. We host your convention, expo, or trade show—with a dash of magic!

Set up in a matter of days, our expos can host even the largest of crowds in our witch-run village of Cauldron Cove. We can offer what no other expo planners can: breathtaking illusions, instant teleportation from one end of the center to the other, floating item storage, and all the exceptional, magical touches that will make your event one-of-a-kind. Inquire about Cauldron Cove hosting your next event today by contacting Bernadette Toothaker, award-winning Head Witch General Manager of Witchy Expo Services for eleven decades.

Nimue Toothaker is ecstatic that her world-famous grandmother is about to retire and has chosen her as her successor in the family business. She's only been working on the expos for a few years, but she's confident she has what it takes to lead her fellow witches and warlocks in the business that defines their entire village. Unfortunately, her grandmother's sole condition for Nimue taking the job is that she share the position with her arch rival, an irritating warlock possessed of two minds—quite literally.

First up is Bookshop Con, where indie booksellers from across the nation host authors and sell books to passionate readers. Nimue's grand plans clash with her co-manager's persnickety demands, but their arguments cease to matter when a celebrated author drops dead in the convention center lobby. Nimue suspects murder, but she knows that if she ends the convention prematurely, the magic at work will destroy her beloved hometown. It's a race to catch the killer before they strike again—all while trying to prove she can handle the job she's so desperately always wanted.

The Never Veil Series

YA ROMANTASY

"The story is fun and engaging, featuring a female protagonist who will resonate with young teens." ~School Library Journal

"...A whirlwind of time-bending adventures that immerse readers in a maelstrom of plot twists and allusions to "Beauty and the Beast" and other fairy tale love stories, while Noll's understanding of gender-based social and cultural dynamics develops." ~Publishers Weekly

Nobody's Goddess (Book One in The Never Veil Series), winner of The Romance Reviews Summer 2016 Readers' Choice Award for Young Adult Romance:

> In a village of masked men, each man is compelled to love only one woman and to follow the commands of his "goddess" without question. A woman may reject the only man who will love her if she pleases, but she will be alone forever. A man must stay masked until his goddess returns his love—and if she can't or won't, he remains masked forever.
>
> Seventeen-year-old Noll's childhood friends have paired off and her closest companion, Jurij, found his goddess in Noll's own sister. Desperate to find a way to break this ancient spell, Noll instead discovers why no man has ever chosen her. She is in fact the goddess of the mysterious lord of the village, a man who refuses to let Noll have her right as a woman to spurn him.
>
> Thus begins a dangerous game between the choice of woman and the magic of man. The stakes are no less than freedom and happiness, life and death— and neither Noll nor the veiled lord is willing to lose.

Fangs & Fins (Blood, Bloom, & Water Series)

YA URBAN FANTASY AND PARANORMAL ROMANCE

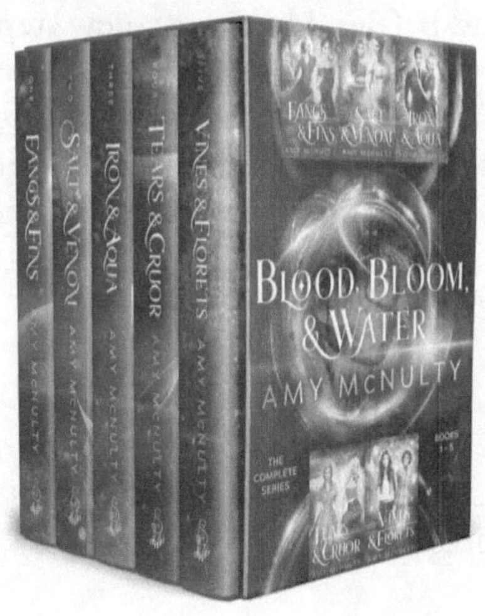

A dapper vampire. A sullen merman. Two heirs to a great conflict—and each needs to claim a beloved to become his kindred's champion.

High school senior Ember Goodwin never had a sister, but after her mom's remarriage, she now has two. The eldest is no stranger to her—Ivy is a witty girl in her grade who's almost never spoken to the shy bookworm before—but she's surprised to find the popular girl quite amiable. Their burgeoning friendship is tested, however, when Dean Horne, a pale, besuited charmer, shows interest in them both and plans to reveal his appetite for blood to the one who'll stand by his side.

Seventeen-year-old Ivy Sheppard is tired of splitting her time between her dad's and her mom's, particularly when her dad uproots their lives to move them in with his new wife and step-daughter. Used to rolling with her parents' whims, she tries to make the best of it and befriend her nerdy new step-sister. Her hectic life grows more unwieldy when she catches the eye of junior Calder Poole, whom she swears she sees swap well-toned legs for a pair of fins during a dip in a lake. Now she's fending off suitors left and right, all while trying to get to the bottom of the strange happenings in her town.

The first book in the Blood, Bloom, & Water series sets family against family and friend against friend as an epic, ancient war comes to a head in a supposedly sleepy suburb.

Ballad of the Beanstalk

YA FAIRYTALE FANTASY

A Library Journal Self-e Selection.

As her fingers move across the strings of her family's heirloom harp, sixteen-year-old Clarion can forget. She doesn't dwell on the recent passing of her beloved father or the fact that her mother has just sold everything they owned, including that very same instrument that gives Clarion life. She doesn't think about how her friends treat her like a feeble, brittle thing to be protected. She doesn't worry about how to tell the elegant Elena, her best friend and first love, that she doesn't want to be her sweetheart anymore. She becomes the melody and loses herself in the song.

When Mack, a lord's dashing young son, rides into town so his father and Elena's can arrange a marriage between the two youth, Clarion finds herself falling in love with a boy for the first time. Drawn to Clarion's music, Mack puts Clarion and Elena's relationship to the test, but he soon vanishes by climbing up a giant beanstalk that only Clarion has seen. When even the town witch won't help, Clarion is determined to rescue Mack herself and prove once and for all that she doesn't need protecting. But while she fancied herself a savior, she couldn't have imagined the enormous world of danger that awaits her in the kingdom of the clouds.

A prequel to the fairy tale *Jack and the Beanstalk* that reveals the true story behind the magical singing harp.

Terror. Callousness. Denial. Rebellion. How the four teenage children of leaders in the duchy and the neighboring empire of Hanaobi choose to adapt to their nefarious parents' whims is a matter of survival.

Rohesia, daughter of the duke, spends her days hunting "outsiders," fugitives who've snuck onto her father's island duchy. That she lives when even children who resemble her are subject to death hardens her heart to tackle the task.

Fastello is the son of the "king" of the raiders who steal from the rich and share with the poor. When aristocrats die in the raids, Fastello questions what his peoples' increasingly wicked methods of survival have cost them.

An orphan raised by a convent of mothers, Cateline can think of no higher aim in life than to serve her religion, even if it means turning a blind eye to the suffering of other orphans under the mothers' care.

Kojiro, new heir to the Hanaobi empire, must avenge his people against the "barbarians" who live in the duchy, terrified the empress, his own mother, might rather see him die than succeed.

When the paths of these four young adults cross, they must rely on one another for survival—but the love of even a malevolent guardian is hard to leave behind.

Read More Spectacular Romances from Crimson Fox Publishing

The Starlight Prince

A love story written in the stars.

Hunted for being a witch, Madelyne longs for somewhere to belong and performs a full moon spell to find her true love.

Across the galaxy, Kalas completes the aeons-old celestial ritual to show him the location of his fated mate.

Enchanted by Madelyne's beauty, Kalas flies to Earth to find her. And, with nothing left for her on Earth, Madelyne agrees to accompany Kalas to his home planet.

But as Madelyne adjusts to her new life, old doubts linger, and she just cannot understand why someone like her would be worthy of the crown prince.

Madelyne has spent her entire life being told she doesn't belong, and now Kalas must convince her it's more than just 'fate' that makes him want to claim her as his own.

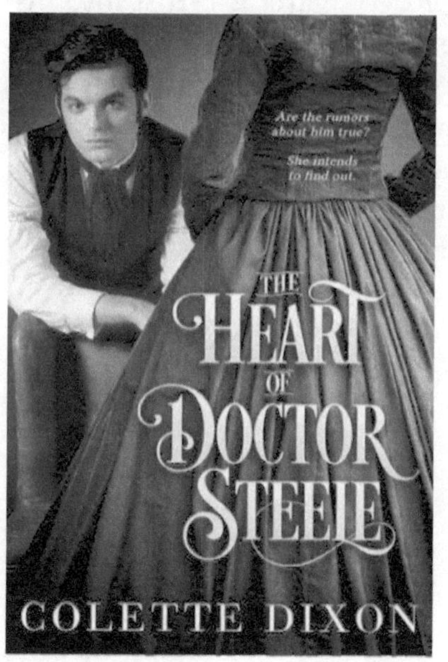

Are the rumors about him true? She intends to find out.

The mysterious Dr. Steele has taken up residence next door, and scandalous rumors about him are spreading through

Margaret Landeau's small Massachusetts town. Rumors of women he's ill-used and exploited for his experimental surgeries. Never one to believe gossip, Margaret arms herself with a basket of baked goods and ventures to discover the truth from the man himself.

John Steele has lost everything. His parents, his aunt, too many women he intended to save, and his good name. All he has left is his aunt's home in a far-flung village and a library he's stocked with whiskey. He has nothing to offer anyone. Especially not the bold woman next door whose passion for healing reminds him of the man he once was.

But when a dangerously ill girl arrives on his doorstep, pleading for help, Margaret is thrust into his world. She will learn who the real Dr. John Steele truly is, and soon, not even his dark past can stop her from fighting for the brilliant doctor she now loves. But he must deny his crushing desire for her—loving a man like him can only cast a shadow over her own bright future.